The King's Weaver

Novae Caelum

Robot Dinosaur Press

https://robotdinosaurpress.com

Robot Dinosaur Press is a trademark of Chipped Cup Collective.

The King's Weaver

Copyright © 2024 by Novae Caelum

All rights reserved.

No part of this publication may be reproduced, stored in a retrieval system, or transmitted, in any form or by any means, electronic, mechanical, magical, photocopying, or otherwise, without the prior written permission of the copyright holder.

This is a work of fiction. Names, characters, organizations, places, and events portrayed in this work are either products of the author's or authors' imagination or are used fictitiously. Any resemblance to actual persons, living or dead, business establishments, events, or locales is entirely coincidental.

Cover design: Novae Caelum

Formatting: Jackie Kranz and Novae Caelum

https://novaecaelum.com

For everyone who wanted to run away from themself and found themself instead.

Author's Note

I started writing *The King's Weaver* to convince myself that I could in fact write a cishet romance—if it had one of my favorite tropes (woman disguised as a man).

But, by chapter three it became abundantly clear this was going to be a book about queer love, queer discovery, and queer acceptance.

Which is fitting, I think. Since the story itself is about trying to be one thing and discovering who you were all along.

I have zero regrets. <3

This book, barring the occasional and inspired burst of strong language, is PG-13, with a note that it deals with grief, parental death, and mistreatment among family members. There are small amounts of gender dysphoria shown as well, though it's minor. There is no aggressive misgendering in this book.

Chapter 1

The Throne Room

Irava

It's spring, but the corridor outside the throne room is cold as a tomb. My breath mists as I pause with the other court mage candidates outside the broad oak doors, waiting for the guards to open them. I catch a reflection in a guard's polished shield, and for a moment, I don't remember that it's mine.

But it is. That young man with shoulder-length, light brown hair and dark brown eyes peering at me from behind wire-rimmed spectacles is...me. It's an illusion, but it's a damned good one. Because I'm not actually a man.

But no one here can know that.

Master Aldric, the court mage in charge of selecting the new court mages from among us candidates, bangs his staff on the stone floor.

"You will file in a straight line! You will not address the king directly, or any of the courtiers!"

I study him through my spectacles. He's mostly balding, his long gray hair neatly braided down his back. His clean-shaven face shows a nick on one cheek, and his right hand sparks with a ruby ring. Master Aldric has been the only weaver at court, the only court mage to use thread magic, since longer than I've been alive.

"You will bow to the king and perform exactly the magic you signed up to perform, no longer than two turns of the minute glass, and then you will bow again and cede your turn to the candidate to your left." He bangs his staff again. "Failure to follow these instructions will earn you an immediate dismissal. Failure will mean banishment from court. All who understand me, say aye!"

I shout "Aye!" along with the rest. My voice is an illusion, too, reality tuned a few tones down with my own weaving. I'm pretty proud of that—not that I can brag about it to anyone.

"All right," Master Aldric says, holding up his hands. "This is your chance to be a guest of the court and earn the king's— and my—favor. May you be men of honor and bring honor to your king and to all mages this day!"

I swallow hard. Yes, I'm a mage.

I'm also a woman.

I'm *also* a princess.

And those last two things would never get me in here on my own. Never let me get close to the king until it's our wedding day.

My name is Irava Anoran Varandre, Third Daughter of the Queen of Galenda. And my mother betrothed me to a murderous tyrant.

So I'd best see if the murderous rumors are true before I share my life with him. And my bed.

Gods help me.

The guards push open the doors to the throne room, a

slow creaking of enormous hinges. The earthy smell of stone gusts out, with cloying clouds of perfume.

The courtiers gathered inside, standing on either side of the wide center aisle, gawk at us. Frilled and serious and glittering, their faces deep umber, pale rose, rich ochre, and every tone between, their brocade and lace so rich it rivals the murals in any great hall.

But my eyes go straight to the man on the throne.

Torovan Braise, King of Barella. Young for a king, fit and with gray-green eyes that pierce the air around him. Black hair flows loose around his shoulders. A wide gold band set with emeralds is perched on his brow, adding to the intensity of his eyes. Smooth light brown skin. Heavy brow and strong chin. A hint of dark stubble. He's not smiling, but that doesn't lessen his visual appeal—gods, I hadn't expected him to be this handsome.

His knee bounces as he watches us candidates file inside, like he's only just barely bothering to be here. Like he doesn't actually care that this demonstration will show him who might be a mage at his court for the rest of his life.

This is my betrothed. This man. This is the man my mother decided I should marry.

For a moment, just a moment, his gaze locks on mine.

And it takes all I have to keep walking forward, walking toward him, knowing that I do have my illusion of thread magic woven around me, my distortion of reality. He can't see through it. No one can. I'm good at what I do.

I should lower my eyes, but I don't. I'm desperately searching for answers, and I know I won't find them here or now, but I can hope, can't I? I can hope that the eyes I'm looking into aren't the eyes of a killer.

But the rumors say otherwise. And there's nothing in that hard gaze that contradicts them.

I look down, taking my place in the lineup of candidates across the throne room.

Deep breath. Gather my will.

I'm one of only two weavers among the ten candidates. Everyone else possesses elemental magic. Which you're born with. But weaving—weaving, you teach yourself.

And Master Aldric, who takes up position on the sidelines, is the only court mage in fifty years who's been a weaver.

I have to become a court mage.

I have to get close to the king.

Because I'm not going to marry a man who killed his father to gain a throne.

Chapter 2

Threads

Irava

My mother promised me since childhood that I could marry whoever I wished. I am a third daughter, after all, with two sisters and three brothers ahead of me. I'll never carry the crown of my kingdom. And as I grew into a woman, I was never very *good* at being a court lady.

And then there was my weaving. My thread magic.

What man, who isn't absolutely desperate for a wife, would want a woman who's taught herself a magic based on willpower?

In the throne room, I stand still and try to look relaxed as the first mage candidate steps out from the rest of the line and begins his demonstration of magic to the king.

I shiver inside my coat, which isn't threadbare, but also isn't as well-made or extravagant as most of the other candidates'. A princess hardly has her own allowance, after all. That would let her have far too much power.

I made do with what I could find, and made do quickly. I

only had two weeks to rush from Galenda to Barella to sign up for the court mage trials in time.

I take a slow breath and do my best to concentrate on the demonstrations of magic, to learn what I can from them. These candidates are, after all, my competition.

The first candidate finishes a shimmery display of water droplets dancing through the air, and the next steps out to levitate daggers.

This causes some stir, but it's not unexpected. Candidates can only demonstrate today with what they can carry. The king doesn't seem concerned about daggers flying through the air—or maybe he's hiding it well. His eyes trace the daggers as they spin in a juggler's arc overtop of the candidate, other court mages ready at the sidelines in case anything goes wrong.

But nothing does.

"Next!" King Torovan booms, his voice resonating throughout the hall.

I startle. It's the first time he's spoken, and his voice has the weight of thunder behind it. Does he have elemental magic? I hadn't thought so, my mother hadn't said so when she'd told me what she'd done, and who I'd be marrying. And maybe it is only the acoustics of the cavernous room, the intensity in his eyes.

His knee is bobbing more furiously now. Like he only wants to be gone.

There are a few mages yet ahead of me—my own demonstration of magic will be second to last.

I didn't have much time to prepare for this demonstration. I didn't know there would even be a demonstration until I arrived at the palace and signed my name into the book for mages trying for a place at court. And minutes after that, I was ushered in here.

Truly useful weaving isn't always showy, not like elemental magic. At least, not what I can do while also bending reality around myself in my illusion as a man. But I think I can make a construct, a falcon, maybe—show something impressive and dangerous like the elementalist's daggers. Have it swoop a few times over my head, or land on my shoulder. It won't be a real bird, only the possibility of a bird, tied directly to my will.

Falcons can hunt, and falcons can kill. I can only hope the king sees use in that.

One by one, the mages down the line work their magic. Elementalists, all of them—sons of lesser nobles and rich merchants. I am neither of these things, and neither is my mage's persona.

I'm going to fail. I came all this way, a desperate hope to get out of a loveless marriage, to bring my mother proof that this marriage shouldn't happen, this treaty shouldn't happen. And I'll be turned away now—and what then? Should I try to rejoin the court as a lady? Try to get close to the king with another illusion? But I have less faith in my ability to carry that off than what I'm doing with my magic now.

The king calls, "Next!"

The mage candidate to my right steps out.

This is it. I'm up next.

I prepare for another flashy and disheartening show of elemental magic.

But no. *Oh.* I'd almost forgotten that this man had been loudly boasting in the courtyard when I arrived. He's sure that he'll be the next weaver at court.

He looks around my age, nineteen or twenty, and nobility

is etched into every line of his lean body. Sun-bleached brown hair, a golden hoop in each ear. Narrow, suntanned pale face. I remember this mage candidate's name, because he shouted it with his boast: Nikolai. And I remember how he looked at me in my plain coat, like I was of the earth, and he was of the sky.

He holds his hands up dramatically, and the hairs on my neck stand on end. He's going to do something dangerous, I can feel it, a sense of distorting reality all around me.

Weaving can be subtle. Weaving can be profound. But weaving can also be profoundly dangerous if the weaver doesn't have enough willpower to control the threads of reality he plucks into his own design. It's why few people even attempt to learn weaving. Why my mother was absolutely livid when she'd learned I'd taught myself.

No one wants to accidentally write a body part out of existence. Or explode the room around them as the pressures of reality try to right themselves.

Does Nikolai have that kind of willpower? This could be the demonstration to capture King Torovan's attention and put mine completely to shame.

Does the king see what's happening? Will he know this is far more dangerous than a mage juggling daggers?

Nikolai begins to weave threads of reality together with precise control, his face tight with concentration.

He braces against reality itself, creating a complex, swirling vortex of threads that only I can see—and Master Aldric, or any other weaver in the crowd.

King Torovan leans forward on the throne. The first time I've seen him actually interested in the demonstrations.

I bunch my fists at my sides but force my hands to open

again. To watch as my future goes up in ash in front of me, all of my chances draining away.

What is Nikolai building to? What reality is he trying to change?

Then Nikolai grunts. I feel the shift as his willpower starts slipping.

I hear one sharp, indrawn breath from the direction of the king, but my focus is wholly on Nikolai now, and the rapidly expanding threads of his woven reality.

I see the moment they start to explode.

Chapter 3

Approval

Irava

I once went out into a field outside my mother's castle and tried to weave reality to make people pay more attention to me. It was foolish, I know. Trying to weave other people's wills isn't just morally wrong, it's very dangerous. I was lucky to run away with only singed hair when my weaving inevitably exploded.

I was lucky to have gotten away at all.

Now, I watch Nikolai's threads pulse, go out of sync, and start to fragment. His eyes are wide, and I watch in horror as he frantically tries to pull his threads back in, to exert his willpower over them.

The king is on his feet now, and a nobleman beside him is trying to pull him back, as far from the out-of-control magic as possible.

We aren't very close to the king. But then, it's not likely to be a small explosion.

I have a moment, just a moment, to decide if I should run, or do...something.

Approval

Master Aldric, the court weaver, is moving toward us, while the other mage candidates turn to flee, but the master mage won't get here in time. Will he be able to hold the threads of reality where he is? To defuse the explosion?

I don't know. I don't know if I should, or if I even can and still maintain my illusion.

But I stay close to Nikolai and raise my own hands. I set the knot of my willpower that's holding my illusion in place firmly into the grasp of my subconscious.

Then Nikolai loses more control of his threads, and in a rush of acrid air, he's engulfed in a brilliant burst of magical fire. He's still fighting the main gathering explosion.

I steady myself as all else fades around me. I focus on my willpower, and on the threads of reality in front of me, fraying and unraveling, seeking to snap back into place no matter the chaos that will cause.

Reality doesn't care if it kills a few bystanders.

Reality doesn't care if it kills a king.

I reach out to the raging fire, deflecting the reality of heat from my arm and plucking at the shimmering, unraveling strands as though they were strings on a harp. One by one, I draw them away from Nikolai, pulling them into the only thing I can think of, the construct of a falcon I'd been planning before.

The bird takes rapid shape in front of me, still glowing with an inner fire. I build its beak and wings and feathers until it flaps its wings restlessly and takes off for the rafters, its glow cooling now.

Around Nikolai, there is only a thinning trail of smoke.

I exhale, blinking, and look around me.

The throne room is silent, so silent I hear the soft sounds of a crowd breathing. All eyes are fixed on me.

Master Aldric, on Nikolai's other side, is watching me with an expression I can't read. Nikolai, still stunned, turns to look at me, then his look hardens into a glare.

From the direction of the throne, I can feel King Torovan's gaze also bearing down on me. He's still standing in front of his throne, he didn't flee. And he's alight with tension, vibrating with it, even.

It doesn't feel like approval.

"You," the king booms. "What is your name?"

Oh, gods. I didn't expect him to speak to me directly, not yet.

I run my sleeve over my fogged spectacles. "I"—and I have to search my mind for the name I gave when I signed up—"I'm Caleb Ailin, Your Majesty. From Insa."

Insa is a town near the border to Galenda. My Galendan accent, even an aristocratic accent for a scholar mage, is plausible.

There are murmurs from the gathered courtiers, those who didn't flee. They will remember my name, and that the king singled me out. Is that a good thing? I knew I'd need to stand out to be allowed to train at court, to try for one of the places as court mage. But I hadn't wanted to draw this much attention.

But now the king, and everyone else, knows who I am.

King Torovan's jaw clenches. Did he hear my accent? Does he think I'm lying? Does he think I'm a spy? Will he even thank me for saving Nikolai's life?

The way a slightly singed Nikolai is still glaring at me, I don't think he will thank me, either.

I bow my head, hoping to appease the king's anger.

"Your Majesty. I only meant to help."

"My mages had it in hand." I hear the anger in his voice, and it burns in my core. Even saving a life, maybe saving many lives, and this tyrant isn't happy. "You will refrain from using magic in this court unless it's specifically allowed and supervised by *actual* court mages. Both of you weavers! Is that understood?"

His words sting, but I swallow my retort. I'm not in my own kingdom, and a mage candidate can't argue with a king.

Torovan waves a hand. "Enough for today. They are all adequate enough to continue training. Master Aldric—make sure your weavers don't cause any further trouble."

Beside me, Nikolai's glare fairly glows.

This isn't fair. I wasn't the one who started the explosion, I was the one who contained it. Can't the king see that? That I just saved Nikolai and who knows how many other people? Maybe even himself?

The king turns to one of his guards as the courtiers begin talking, but I have the uneasy feeling that his attention is still on me. I'd hoped to get close to him, but slowly, building trust over time. Not—not this. Saving a life is a better demonstration than conjuring an illusory falcon, but if it puts me in the king's disfavor, does that matter?

How many enemies have I made today, and why? Is the court of Barella so broken that saving a life is frowned upon?

Or are they all just afraid of weavers, and Nikolai inflamed those fears? And I inflamed them, too, by showing that I could contain the magic.

I don't have any friends to rely on here. In this palace, I'm on my own. Not even my mother knows I'm here. My only safety is that if I can find a convenient corner, I can drop my illusion, and no one will know I was the mage who just defused a reality explosion.

Should I run?

But I don't see everyone looking at me with fear. The nobleman beside the king catches my eye, gives a tight smile, and nods.

I recognize him from my mother's descriptions of the Barellan courtiers—tall and well-built, dark brown skin, with long dreadlocks clasped in gold tied back into a thick tail. He has a single diamond in one ear and is meticulously clean shaven. He must be Lord Valtair, the son of the former Minister of Finance and the king's oldest and closest friend.

As the candidates file back out of the throne room, I steal another glance at the king. He's still turned away, speaking with his guards, but I can't shake the feeling of his eyes on me. The disapproval in them I'd seen earlier. And maybe...something else. Had that been a flicker of fear? More probably, anger.

A shiver runs down my spine at the thought of being at the mercy of a man like him, a man who seems to breathe anger.

Is that my future?

Not if I have anything to say about it.

If the way to stop the treaty and marriage is to prove the king a murderer, then that is what I must do.

Chapter 4

Vigilance

Torovan

I hold my emotions tightly contained as I watch the mage candidate, Caleb Ailin, leave the chamber. His stride is upright, though he seems less sure, I think, than when he first walked in. All of the mage candidates are.

"Well, that was a spectacle."

I don't even turn. My best friend and advisor, Lord Valtair, saunters up beside me, his usual wry grin in place. But his eyes tell a different story.

They always do.

"So," he says, leaning closer, "do you think the first or the second weaver was meant to kill you?"

I snort. Though he isn't wrong that I'm thinking of that. All of these mages are dangerous in their own right, yes. And all of the seasoned court mages are here to help if anything goes wrong, to protect me if anyone tries anything. This demonstration would certainly be a good place to try.

I know how dangerous a weaver can be. Trained right, and with enough willpower, they can make or break kingdoms.

But even I, with my own sorry excuse for weaving, can't undo the death of my father. And I can't seem to bend any of the reality around me to finding out who killed him. Or who here at court might want to kill me and my sister.

"The first weaver overstretched," I say, finally turning away from the retreating mages. "The second...overstretched in a different way. I don't know if that's ambition or..." I give a tight shrug. I've long since lost hope that people did anything out of the goodness of their own hearts.

"I'll keep an eye on him," Valtair says. "But showing off or not, he saved lives. For that, he has my respect."

He grins, the smile not quite reaching his eyes.

"He's cute," he says, low and right by my ear, "but in a rogue scholar sort of way. It's the freckles, maybe. I like him."

I glare at him. Valtair's preferences in men are well known, but though I've had some dalliances with men, I usually prefer women. I've betrothed myself to a woman, which is a political marriage, yes, but I will need to have heirs.

Gods, I hope she is at least palatable, but I fear my luck ran sour a long time ago.

But Valtair isn't wrong that the weaver, Caleb Ailin, holds a certain appeal. The preciseness of his movements? The intensity in his eyes?

I haven't entangled myself with anyone since my father died. I've had no patience, no time, no appetite.

But Caleb Ailin met my eyes when so few in this room ever would. Not now that I'm king. Not with the rumors circulating about me.

Whether this mage candidate is attractive or not is irrelevant. I'm the king of Barella. I have no time to think about an affair that will never happen, with a mage candidate who might be gone tomorrow.

He might have tried to kill me if he hadn't decided to not let the other weaver candidate kill everyone else.

So had he instead been trying to impress me? To gain my confidence? That could be just as dangerous.

Only two of the candidates will ultimately remain at court, and the court mages seldom welcome weavers. They're just too dangerous and volatile—too willful, because they have to be. When Master Aldric retires, the other mages will welcome the chance to not replace him.

And I can't have a dalliance because there's my upcoming marriage—to a woman I've never met, from a kingdom that up until ten years ago tended to side with Barella's enemies.

The treaty was necessary, yes, with unrest around Barella's other borders. But if my future wife finds out I was with a mere court mage after our engagement—no, mage candidate, even... well, do I really need another enemy in my court?

Valtair claps me on the shoulder, and I stiffen. We're still public and visible, and that's not how you treat a king, even if he is your childhood friend.

Valtair catches the look and shrugs. "Off to the next meeting, then."

My scowl deepens. Valtair has been on me lately about treating the people around me with more respect, but he doesn't see that if I let the courtiers have an inch, they will take all of me and my soul along with it.

As I make my way through the crowd to the side exit, I can feel their eyes on me, assessing me, sizing me up. Parting around me. They don't see me as a person, but a king, a symbol of power to be used for their own gain.

How can I ever relax again? A king can never relate to his subjects, no matter how lonely he feels. There is only ever vigilance.

And this weaver who just saved a life by demonstrating that he does, in fact, have dangerous control over his magic? Over the very threads of reality around him?

He must definitely be watched.

Chapter 5

The Common Room

Irava

As I step into the mage's common room, the warmth of the blazing hearth is a balm to frayed nerves. The air crackles with the buzz of too much magic in too contained a space, and the candidates buzz with...well, with whispers and looks at me and at Nikolai.

Who is very definitely still glaring at me.

Master Aldric settles himself in a chair by the fire, hands folded over the gnarled wood of his staff, his face unreadable. Orange ghosts from the fire play over his pale face. It reminds me too much of the chaos around Nikolai, just before he lost control of his magic.

The other mage candidates form up in a circle around Master Aldric, and I take my place among them, ignoring the whispers and stares. Will this be the moment I'm dismissed? The king hasn't dismissed me yet, though I'm sure Master Aldric can do so just as easily.

I am, at least, used to whispers and stares, though I'd hoped to not have to deal with them here. I'd hoped, for a short time, to just be *other* than who I am.

Maybe the whispers will follow me, no matter who I am.

"Master Aldric," one of the other candidates says, the one, I realize, who'd been to my left. The one who hadn't had a chance to demonstrate his magic before the king.

I brace myself.

"Master Aldric, I wasn't given the opportunity to prove my magic to King Torovan. The weavers decided to cut the demonstration short with their lack of control."

I want to say that it wasn't my fault. That I might have saved this noble mage's *life*. But I don't. I've already called far too much attention to myself today. I have to survive at court long enough to actually get close enough to the king to find my answers—not that I'm sure at all that will happen now.

At least Lord Valtair, the king's friend, seemed to approve of what I'd done, if I could read approval in a nod.

"Yes," Master Aldric says slowly, "and you had no opportunity to make a fool of yourself, either, young Obrec. Count your blessings. Now—all of you, you've done well enough. And some of you were given grace—"

His gaze lands on Nikolai, and none too kindly. But Nikolai is still glaring at me.

"Master Aldric," Nikolai says, his voice deadly quiet. The other murmurs around us hush. "I petition you to dismiss this mage candidate, Caleb Ailin, as unfit to serve at this court. He sabotaged my—"

I flinch as Master Aldric bangs his staff down on the stone floor.

"I wasn't talking about the grace Caleb was given, Nikolai."

Nikolai swallows, but it isn't fear I see in his eyes, but rage. He finally, though, turns his gaze from me.

But now Master Aldric's attention lingers on me, and I'm not sure his smile is kind.

Sometimes, weavers can see other weavers' work as it's being woven. I usually can. But if I've set my willpower strongly enough, no one should be able to see that I have an illusion already in place. Not even, gods help me, the master weaver at the Barellan Court.

He turns to look around at the rest of the candidates, and I breathe a little easier.

"Today and these next weeks are as much a trial of your skills as of your discretion. To hold the position of court mage is to hold a position of power in this court. I will personally not recommend any mage who shows less than ideal discretion."

Nikolai opens his mouth again, and freezes as Master Aldric skewers him with a look that is *definitely* not kind.

"That includes any mage born of any station," the master says mildly. "This is a court in transition. There are many whispers about the death of the late king, most of which are not true. But just because something isn't true doesn't mean it isn't dangerous. You would all do well to guard your actions, to only and ever be as upright as you can be. Any indiscretion—any—will be counted against you."

His gaze lands back on me, and I know the other candidates note this.

I do my best to hide my own growing temper. Which has also never been ladylike.

I saved Nikolai, and possibly everyone in the whole throne room, if Nikolai's magic had been allowed to explode.

But I did something unexpected. And I showed—gods,

that's what this is about—I showed I have power. I showed that I not only could contain the explosion of another powerful weaver but defuse it entirely. Before Master Aldric had a chance to do it himself.

Or...

My arms and neck prickle with heat. What if Master Aldric couldn't have done it himself? I'd assumed, with his position at court, that Master Aldric would surely be more powerful than I am. But what if he's just a very good politician? There are elementalists in my mother's court who could hardly light a candle.

A single weaver, if powerful enough, can rewrite reality. Not usually in large or lasting ways, but...it is possible.

What if the king wasn't angry with me, what if that fear I saw was him marking me as a threat?

And what will happen, if I do decide I'll marry him, if he finds out that his wife is a powerful weaver?

I only barely listen as Master Aldric goes on to give us each the assignment of our quarters.

We will, blessedly, each be given our own room.

I'll be safe at night when my illusion drops. I can make an illusion linger after I'm asleep, but it's not as stable, and I've been worried about having to bunk with another—well, a man.

But my thoughts through this dry speech are on my magic. I've never really tested it against anyone else. At first, because I taught myself in secret, but then because my mother forbade it.

I know I'm a strong weaver. I know I'm good and solid in my willpower. Humility has never been one of my particular strengths.

But I never thought that I might step into the Barellan Court and be the strongest weaver here. Or maybe the strongest mage at all. No other mage had been able to diffuse Nikolai's magic.

I don't know whether to be excited about this or terrified.

My body, with my sweaty palms and racing heart, settles on terrified.

As the mage candidates file out to go find their quarters, Master Aldric calls me aside.

I glance over my shoulder at the other candidates—Nikolai is still hovering. He has, thankfully, turned toward the fire to brood. But I have the absolute sense that the back of his head is still glaring at me, too.

"I want to train you, Caleb," Master Aldric says as I approach.

I blink, because this isn't what I expect. I expect a reprimand at very least, or more likely, that overdue dismissal.

"You are one of the most promising weavers I've seen at this court, but with the willpower you displayed, you should have been disciplined enough to know that I would have diffused that situation if you'd only waited a moment more."

I bite my lip, then remember that's not what a man like Caleb would do, and so square my shoulders instead.

Nikolai hadn't had a moment. In another moment, he would have been dead.

But I nod. Because if I've made enemies today, I can certainly make allies, too.

"I would be honored, Master Aldric."

I bow my head, and he nods graciously. He expected no other response.

"Good. Then take this book—"

He produces a thick tome and hands it to me. I glance at the cover and feel my face heat. It's a guide to court etiquette.

I've read this book before—but Caleb Ailin likely wouldn't have, being the village mage that he is.

Is this a test? Does Master Aldric see something in me that he shouldn't?

But I take the book and bow again. "Thank you, Master Aldric. I will study this tonight."

His smile is grandfatherly now, and I don't like it. There's too much condescension there—and does he realize that I might be more powerful than he is?

Of course he does.

Have I just made a friend, or another enemy?

He dismisses me with a wave and calls over Nikolai.

Nikolai bumps hard into me as we pass, his shoulder checking mine. I might not be used to physical aggression, but I absolutely see the fight he wants to pick now. My shoulder stings from the blow, but I look down, ignore his provocation.

Nikolai doesn't look at me, either, as if he's decided I'm beneath his notice.

I'll need to be careful. Nikolai's mistakes, as a noble mage, won't count the same as Caleb's as a village mage.

I'm starting to regret saving his life.

Chapter 6

Investigation

Torovan

Every step is a battle as I stride through the palace corridors. I've been on this path and through these thoughts a thousand times before.

My father's death was ruled natural causes. No amount of investigation into his death has yielded any results, but I can't give up. I've spoken to almost everyone in the palace at this point, and no one has given me anything new—only condolences and promises of loyalty that feel emptier by the day.

Am I paranoid?

Am I going mad? My mother seems to think so. She was the one who found my father in his bed, unable to wake up.

A peaceful death, the court physicians said. No trace of magic, Master Aldric said. But my father was in his *prime*. No signs of ill-health whatsoever.

And he'd been a week away from signing a decree that would put limits on the power of the nobility and give some of that power back to the common people. It had been his dream.

I've had no time to think about that dream because I am absolutely sure that his death wasn't an accident. I have a sense of...not quite magic, but a *wrongness*. How can I explain it to anyone else, let alone prove it exists, without being able to put words to it myself?

But I can't have murderers loose at my court. I can't let my father's death go unavenged. And I can't bring a new wife here, or give my sister all the choices at court that she should have, without knowing my palace and kingdom are safe.

I pause outside a door to a kitchen servant's room, gathering my wits before knocking softly.

The servant answers, her eyes widening as she sees it's me standing there.

"Your Majesty. I will help however I can."

I frown, because of course my investigation has preceded me, and that line felt rehearsed. The last five servants have greeted me similarly. And they've had time to prepare their stories—if they have any stories at all. If there's any guilt to be found, and I'm not chasing after shadows.

Princess Irava Anoran Varandre will be marrying a husk, a shadow, with more shadows all around him. Yes, it's a strategic marriage. But I had hoped...of course I'd hoped for more.

The servant stares up at me, her eyes wide, lips pressed tight. She looks like a doe caught in a bowman's sights.

How much longer will I keep doing this? How much longer will I torment myself, and the palace staff, when I know I will find nothing this way?

Whoever killed my father wasn't the staff. Maybe there were staff involved in the plot, but they weren't the ones who'd thought of it.

Still, I ask, "Were you in the kitchens the night my father was…the night my father died?"

She shakes her head, but says, "Yes, Your Majesty. That is—that is where I work."

I stifle a growl. At myself, not at her. I should walk away now, but I press on. I have to. Every single corner must be searched, every person questioned. And I know by now they know all the lines of this game, but I can't stop.

I *can't* stop.

He was my father.

"And—and did you see anything suspicious that night? Anything at all? Anything out of place, or out of the ordinary—"

"No, Sire!"

She looks distressed, her hands up as if she must comfort me, and what sight do I give her if she's so distressed on my behalf?

She bites her lip and steps back, lowering her eyes. "Forgive me. Forgive me, Your Majesty." A deep curtsy doesn't cover her tremble.

Gods take it all.

I stalk away before I can do any more damage.

Valtair has lately taken to hounding me for haunting the palace when I should be ruling the kingdom. The missives and petitions I have to read have certainly been piling up.

It's been four months since my father died, but though my mission hasn't become less urgent to me, no one seems to care as much as I do. No one seems to want to.

And the rumors that I was behind my father's death and am running this investigation to cover for it are rampant these days. It's almost worse than the pity I saw in the eyes of the staff, like the kitchen worker today.

Almost.

I see it in the eyes of those I pass, that uncertainty, that fear.

Am I going mad, they wonder? Or am I a murderer?

Or both?

I glare back at them, daring them to accuse me to my face.

Chapter 7

Friends

Torovan

When I make it back to my study, I slump into the leather-backed chair behind the carved oak desk. Dryads frolic around the edges, too cheerful by far. There's a knock at the door.

"Enter," I say, without looking up. Only one person would dare to knock with that alacrity.

Lord Thaddeus Valtair steps inside, offering me his usual thin smile as he rights the feather on his hat.

That damned hat.

He sees my look and absolutely does not take it off. It's become a game of late—him trying to provoke me and my ignoring it until I inevitably explode.

"I heard you were haunting the kitchen maids again," he says.

I roll my eyes and sit up straight. "What do you want? I'm busy."

"Mm, looks like." He saunters to my desk and pointedly flicks at the dust gathering on a stack of papers. "Tor, the only thing you've truly managed in the last months was that betrothal."

"It's important for this kingdom to have an heir—"

He holds up his hands as he sits across from me, and finally does take off the hat.

Maybe sensing that I'm not in the mood today.

"Of course. Of course. But I've had no less than five—*five now, Torovan*—ministers approaching me, wondering when you will get to their proposals. The people would like to see their ruler actually rule, not brood his days away."

I lean forward, my chair creaking. "So what am I supposed to do? Whoever killed my father is still loose in the palace—or if it was an assassin, then whoever hired them. And they could do it again. To my sister, to my mother, to *me*."

Valtair waves a hand. "That's not the point. That is fact. But—whatever this is you're doing isn't working. And you do have your wife coming in a few months, do you want her to get a ghost of a man when she comes here at First Harvest? Tor, will you even have a kingdom by then if you don't actually do your duty as the king?"

He's sounding, in this moment, like his father, and if I tell him that he'll storm out of here.

So I shuffle the dusty piles on my desk.

So many papers stamped with seals in the red wax of "urgent."

"I went to the court mage demonstrations. As you suggested. And look how that turned out."

He takes a long, long breath, and I know I'm pushing him too far, an argument we've had so often it has its own road.

Valtair drums his fingers on the arms of his chair as he studies me. And I know I see worry in his eyes, but I can't acknowledge it. I can't look at what he sees in me that's concerning him.

I can't fall apart.

So I scowl, and he frowns back.

"Tor. I get that you need to do this. But you need to go about it in a different way. This is getting nowhere, and your latest obsession with interviewing—no, make that interrogating—all of the staff is making everyone jumpy."

I shrug. He's right that my investigation's not working.

And I've known it's not working, but it's the only thing left I can think of to do. I've exhausted every other trail, every other option. And giving up is not an option.

The doctors found nothing to explain my father's death, no marks, no obvious issues. No reactions when magically examined for poisons by an elementalist. His death was judged to be natural, but no one, especially not me, believed that. Not at first.

Now...now, after so many months of nothing...

Valtair sits back. We've known each other all of our lives—he's the brother I never had.

I know I've been unfair to him lately.

And still I growl, "I will continue my investigation. The ministers can wait."

He ignores me and makes an airy wave.

"I know you don't want to bring Master Aldric into this again—"

"He found nothing the first time."

"Yes," Valtair says, mostly patiently, "but we have two more weavers at hand now. They might be able to help us see—"

"I've tried," I say. "I've tried everything I know how to do. I can't see anything that would indicate magic, so it has to be something else."

"Yes, but, *very* respectfully, Tor, you're not as good a weaver as that mage candidate Caleb demonstrated himself to be last night. I'm not even sure Master Aldric could have done what he did--Aldric made no particular move to save that idiot showoff Nikolai, I've been thinking about that. And I really don't like it."

In my focus on my investigation, I hadn't thought much about Aldric's part in the demonstrations—or lack of participation—but yes, Valtair is right. I've known Master Aldric for years, and though many people do seem to trust him, grandfatherly as he is, I...haven't been as liberal with my trust.

I don't like the way he smiles at me, kindly and full of teeth. He knows I'm a weaver, though most do not. He trained me in what I know, and then very gently informed me and my father that unless I could find a way to strengthen my willpower to better hold my weavings in place, he couldn't continue to train me. He said training me would be dangerous.

I'm not sure I've ever quite believed that. Or did he feel threatened by my potential, could that possibly be why he pushed me away? Told me I didn't have enough willpower?

But what if it's true? What if I don't have the will? My inability to pull together more than the most basic illusions and constructs for moments at a time, all of them intangible, seems to support his assessment.

My inability to find my father's killer only strengthens that assessment.

So how am I supposed to have enough willpower to hold together a kingdom?

I'm ready to shove Valtair out and get back to not dealing

with the papers piling up on my desk, when he says, slowly, "Why not see if this Caleb is someone you can trust?"

I can't trust anyone. Except Valtair, but he's Valtair.

"Caleb did save a life," Valtair insists. "I know it's a stretch, and I know it's not ideal. I really do. But—Tor, you can't continue this quest with no answers. Either you'll have to admit that your father died of natural means and move on with your life, or get more unorthodox help. You can't keep haunting the palace like a wraith, venting your anger and your grief, while you put your life and everyone else's on hold."

My lips tighten.

"I will keep that in mind."

He knows when he's pushed too far, he knows I'm most angry when I'm still, but he's never cared. He only rises, gives me a criminally horrible bow, then saunters back to the door.

I narrow my eyes after him. I saw the way he looked at Caleb Ailin. And Caleb Ailin is...worthy of looking at. But Valtair has been in his own funk for most of this year, making a show of his various conquests at court.

"If you take up with Caleb," I say, then stop. I don't know what I was going to say—don't hurt him? Be discreet, because he's a commoner and you're the son of a count? That's never stopped Valtair before. And that's never bothered me before.

Caleb Ailin, for all his fierce determination in unraveling Nikolai Metrial's weaving, seems more genuine than most in this court.

He met my eyes in the throne room. And that is something that few people have dared these days.

Valtair stops at the door and rolls his shoulders. "He's not my type, Tor. He's adorable, but not my type."

I'm not sure that's true, but he's giving me space. For what

—for what, I don't know. If it would be scandalous for Valtair to take up with a common village mage, it would be impossible for a king.

I sigh, dropping my head in my hands as the door closes behind him.

Is he right about asking Caleb for help, though? Does this new weaver, who has enough willpower to both contain and unravel another weaver's ambitious weaving, hold the key to the answers I need?

I have to try. Gods help me, but I'm desperate, and I have to try.

Chapter 8

The Great Hall

Irava

As part of our learning how to fit in with the court as mage candidates—and the other mages learning if we can—we eat our meals with the court in the Great Hall.

I'm no stranger to palaces, and I've seen the Barellan throne room, but the Great Hall is something else entirely. It stretches out before me, a vast expanse of gray stone, marble accents, and gold that seems to drink in the sunlight streaming through the towering windows, taming it into shadows. Tapestries cling to the walls, and an entire wall of hearths roars, but they can barely keep the cavernous room warm. I only hope the weather will turn toward the spring mildness we should be having soon.

I push up my spectacles and step in with the rest of the candidates, careful to look impressed and intimidated by it all.

I glance up at the high table, where King Torovan is scowling at his food. Does the man ever smile? His strong jaw is set, and his brow furrows as he takes in each face around him. My pulse quickens as his gaze catches mine and...lingers.

Then passes on.

What was that look? Truly, what was that look?

I take a deep breath, and the scents of freshly baked bread and roasted meats makes my stomach rumble. Or maybe it's the nerves.

I'm not looking at the high table now as we wait for direction on where to sit, but I'd noticed a young woman beside Torovan. She has to be Princess Elsira, whose hair is just as dark and thick as his, her face a slightly darker brown, round and sweet. And her eyes are brown, not his lighter gray-green. She is his younger sister, I gather, by all of two hours.

I sneak another glance, just one. She seems lost in thought, her gaze distant and unfocused. She's not scowling like her brother, but she's not smiling, either.

I jump as a mage candidate near me laughs at something one of the others just said.

None of the other candidates have talked to me since the night before—and maybe that's as well. Friendships could complicate things for me. And Nikolai, at least, has taken to ignoring me entirely. So when servants show up to escort each of us mage candidates to different places around the room, I'm not overly worried.

I get worried, though, when I'm guided to a mid-tier table, where I find myself seated next to Lord Valtair. Gods, the king's best friend.

Shouldn't he be at the high table?

But he smiles at me, his charm turned all the way up, and I remember that he's well known to prefer men.

And at the moment, oh yes, I appear to be a man.

That...could be a problem.

He is handsome, of course. In that rakish sort of way that

all court rogues have. He's twirling a spoon in slim fingers that have *never* seen a day's hard work, I'd swear, and grinning at me. Very obviously not trying to hide his interest.

Gods, if I'd decided to try and disguise myself as another woman at court and someone in his position was showing me this kind of interest, I might try to take advantage of it. But here, being Caleb and *infinitely* discoverable if anyone actually did more than touch my hand, I wouldn't dare.

Lord Valtair wouldn't be flirting with me if I was a woman. And if I was a woman, I probably wouldn't have men flirting at me at all. If I was beautiful, and I wasn't sure at all that my servants at home could be trusted to be truthful there, then that was always overshadowed by my unwillingness to do all the things that ladies of the court should. Like never wear trousers. Or not teach themselves to be a weaver. Or swear.

I put on my best tentative smile to Lord Valtair. I'd play it as far as I could.

"Caleb Ailin, is it?" he asks.

He remembered? Gods, should I be flattered? I am, in an oddly warm way. The way he's *looking* at me. His dark, liquid eyes. I could almost hope, for a moment, that he didn't only prefer men.

"Yes, my lord—"

He waves the formality aside. "Everyone calls me Valtair. So, welcome to court, then. I can't imagine that was the welcome you were expecting."

I feel my face heat and duck my head into the bowl of steaming porridge that was placed in front of me, along with a platter of sausages.

I chance a look out of the corners of my eyes to see if the other mage candidates are watching this, and see one of them casting a jealous look my way, two more making moon eyes at Valtair.

I swallow, and keep my eyes down, my face heating.

"Thank you, my—Valtair."

"Village mage, huh? So, why the palace, then? Ambition? Do you have a sweetheart here? A woman or a man? Are you trying to kill the king?"

I choke on my porridge, spraying it back into my bowl.

Gods. *Gods!*

But I look up, and he's turned away from me, leering in King Torovan's direction. The king is—of course—scowling back.

What is this? Did the king ask his friend to eat with me? Because Caleb Ailin, village mage, certainly doesn't warrant this kind of attention from someone so close to the king. Not when there are other men around me more eligible, who actually want his attentions.

Valtair leans in. "Listen. I commend you for your display at the demonstration. I don't think you meant to upstage anyone, didn't want to make waves. Is that right?"

His tone is entirely condescending. Any glamor he'd held over me before is wearing thin.

I glance up because it'll be expected, then quickly look away again and nod.

"Caleb, Caleb. Be careful, love. Lord Nikolai Metrial isn't one to let go of a grudge." He's lowered his voice, moving closer, his breath hot on my ear. And I don't feel the sexual tension now, so much as…the warning. His hand on mine squeezes, but it's neither rough nor endearing.

"I would know," he says. He lets go of my hand.

Then he rises and, without looking back, makes his way toward the high table.

I swallow. *Was* that a warning? Or a threat?

Across the room, I see Nikolai sitting with another knot of courtiers, but he's not paying any attention to them. His eyes are on Lord Valtair, then darting back to me. And this time, it's not rage I see there so much as...calculation.

Which is far more terrifying.

Chapter 9

The Princess

Irava

I'm no longer even a little bit hungry as I scan the Great Hall, looking to see if the meal is close to finishing so I can make my escape without offending anyone. Is what I'm seeing in this court, all the animosity and games, because everyone thinks I'm a man? Do people never let the women see this ugliness?

But no, it was in my mother's court, too. It was in her signing a marriage contract and treaty with my life as the bargain. And it's here now in a court that might have lost one king by the current king's hand, and everyone knows it.

Before I can make an exit, though, I see someone else making her way toward me, attention following her as she goes: Princess Elsira. Why by all the gods would she wish to speak with Caleb Ailin, mage candidate?

There's a hungry gleam in her eyes. The carefully composed mask I saw earlier falters as she nears me, and color is blooming in her cheeks.

Please by all the gods do not let her be attracted to Caleb, too. I can't deal with any more of that today.

But she looks more flustered than anything as she takes Valtair's vacant place beside me. She smiles, a bit shyly, and it's weird to have another woman react to me this way, thinking I'm a man. Women usually are polite around me when I'm myself but whisper wickedly behind my back. The politeness, I'm sure, is only because of my title.

Up close, though, I can see the dark circles under the princess's eyes, the tired set to her mouth. She's the same age as the king at twenty-two. But just now, she looks older.

"Do you mind if I sit? Can we talk?"

How does she expect me to answer that? I can't very well say no to her. I'm well aware of the power any child of a monarch holds.

She's studying my face closely, enough that it makes me uncomfortable. I don't know what she wants from me. Is this a trap? Another test from the king or from Valtair?

"Of course, Your Highness," I say, making a seated bow. I really should get up, but she grips my arm, holding me in place. Like she's afraid I'll flee?

Elsira bites her lip. "Do you care to take a walk along the corridor?"

And now she seems younger than she should. Scared and hesitant.

And I *am* desperate for an exit, though this certainly isn't what I've been hoping for.

Did she come down here to rescue me, did I look that pathetic sitting alone after Valtair left?

I glance at the high table, where King Torovan is now frowning at us. Because of course he's frowning.

I decide in a moment. A private conversation with the princess could be a start toward understanding the king. And gods, if her brother did kill their father, maybe that's the strain I'm seeing in her, the weirdness in the princess's manner. She might be trapped in a palace with an evil brother and in need of rescuing herself.

"Of course, Your Highness," I say.

I smile at her, and watch some of her tension ease.

As we leave the bustling Great Hall behind, Elsira's steps quicken, her day gown swishing as she walks. I don't say anything, not wanting to speak first—but then, neither does she. Not until we're far enough from the Great Hall that the rumble of conversation has ebbed, and the loudest sounds are the staccato of her wooden heels on the stone floor and the more muted thumps of my leather boots. Well, and her guards' boots, too. Two of them are trailing a few paces behind us.

Elsira signals them back further, then touches my arm, turns to me. "Thank you. Thank you for saving Nikolai's life."

I stop with her, taking a deep breath. Nikolai? She's friends—or more than friends?—with Nikolai? Should I be worried?

Her guards have retreated down the corridor. And if she's a threat to me, they're here to protect her, not me.

I duck my head. "I was only trying to help."

"No," she says, "truly, thank you. I know he can be...difficult. Like my brother, I know, neither of them will thank you. So I will."

I look up, and her smile seems genuine. Though her eyes are still distant and shadowed.

If she cares about Nikolai, it's because she's a good person. She cares about the people around her. People like me, too.

That's such a rarity in a royal court that for a moment, I catch my breath.

And I want to ask her right now what happened to her father. I want to ask if her brother is treating her okay. I want to drop my illusion and show her she can trust me, if she needs to—this woman who might soon be my sister.

But we're still in the corridor, and I didn't go through all of this trouble to get to Barella and join the mage candidates only to have her expose me now. No, Elsira isn't someone I can trust. On the surface, she might be an ally.

But I can trust no one at this court.

"Also," she says, and resumes walking, "Valtair can be an ass, and you looked like someone he'd just been an ass to. It's not personal, that's just Valtair. But you do *not* want to go to bed with him, tempting as he may be, because he will break your heart."

I choke on a laugh, because that was *not* what I'd expected out of this serious and a little solemn princess. Elsira grins back, and I relax a little.

Maybe there is a friendly face here after all. Maybe I can't trust, but it wouldn't hurt to have an ally at court. Or even a friend.

"My brother didn't want me to attend the demonstration," Elsira goes on. "He has grown…more protective than I'd like." Which sounded like an understatement.

She narrows her eyes. "But Nikolai didn't mean to lose control of his magic. He's just so ambitious, he always has been. He will almost certainly replace Master Aldric when the master retires."

She blinks, and says quickly, "Though you have a lot of

skill, too! I'm not a weaver, of course, but I know how much skill is involved in what you did. You might have saved my brother's life as well."

"Thank you, Your Highness." And it does warm me. The first truly genuine words of thanks for what I'd risked and what I'd done. Though it might also have been a clumsy recovery for saying I wouldn't cut it as a court mage.

Her eyes shift again, turning more calculating. "I told my brother I wished to speak with you. I won that argument, with his condition that I assess your character for myself, and ask you to come to his study in an hour if I like you. And I've decided that yes, I do like you."

I almost stumble a step, but catch myself. So she hadn't just wanted to rescue me, or be rescued herself. She'd had her own mission and orders from her brother.

But she liked me? Elsira knows nothing about me. Nothing other than, when faced with an unraveling weaving, I'd done all I could to untangle it.

Or maybe Elsira is a better observer of people than I've ever been. A far better princess.

I think I like her, too.

I cough and make sure to make my voice a little deeper than my illusion normally does. Because under her piercing, expectant stare, and even with my illusions firmly around me, I feel far too seen.

I bow deeply. "Princess. I am honored, humbly, for your favor."

"Thank you. But—you may call me Elsira. Whatever anyone else thinks, I believe you've earned that favor. Now, I'll part with you here. Be at my brother's study in a turn of the glass."

Do I dare ask why the king wishes to see me? Or why he's tasked his sister with vetting me first?

No. I can't dare. I'm a mage candidate, and she's a princess. And he's a king.

I bow again. "Thank you, Elsira."

But she's already walking away.

Chapter 10

The King's Study

Irava

The guards nod to me as I approach King Torovan's study. I'm expected. I step between them and reach up to give a light knock on the walnut door—

Then catch myself, knocking more firmly instead as Caleb than I would have as myself.

I'm too nervous by far. I have to remind myself, and keep reminding myself, that he doesn't know who I really am. He can't. And he won't.

I still have no intention of marrying him, and no reason at all to think that he's not the murderer the rumors say he is.

But...Elsira thanked me for saving his life. Would that be the reaction of a sister toward a murderer? Toward someone she despised?

A muffled, "Enter," comes from the other side of the door.

I glance at the guards with their studded weapons and polished open helmets and ornate steel and leather armor, but they're completely ignoring me now. So I turn the knob and push open the heavy door.

The door slides across a thick wool carpet, a soft rustle on the floor.

The room smells of old parchment and ink, and sunlight filtering through the tall windows casts dappled shadows across the floor. King Torovan sits at his desk, his crown set to one side, wavy black hair a little mussed, shirt sleeves rolled up and showing well-toned forearms as he holds a pen over parchment like he wants to murder it.

He looks up, catching me in his gray-green eyes, and I freeze. His full glare is turned on me, but it ebbs a little as he sees me.

"Ah, Mage Candidate Ailin. Close the door."

I start, remember to breathe, and shut the door behind me. It latches with a definite thunk.

And then I'm alone in this room with a man who may or may not be a murderer. I've wanted to get close to him, yes, that's the entire reason I'm here in Barella. I want to know who he is. I want to see this man and his own truths laid bare, and know if they're truths that I can live with. Will I be able to face the future my mother laid out for me, or will I need to spend my life running from it?

But I hadn't expected to meet him face-to-face this quickly. I hadn't expected him to summon me on my second day in the palace.

I remember to bow.

"Your Majesty," I say, my voice trembling slightly. "You wished to see me?"

When I straighten, he's sitting back, studying me with an interest that makes my skin crawl. He doesn't bother to stand, but of course he doesn't—he's the king.

"How have you been finding your stay at the palace?"

I don't think he actually wants to know, but I say, "Thank you, Your Majesty. My stay has been pleasant."

"Good," he says, and no, I'm sure he doesn't care.

I don't know why he's called me here, and he doesn't seem overly upset with me now, but he tasked his sister with judging my character. He wants something from me.

Which might be a good thing. If I can stay close to the king, I can learn more, find out what I need to, and get out of this wretched court.

In the hearth, the fire cracks, and I jump.

Torovan leans forward suddenly. "Can I trust you, Caleb?"

What? I'm a stranger here. Loyalty is one thing, but trust?

I swallow and bow. "Of course, Your Majesty. I am at your service."

"Good." A flicker of something like relief passes over his face. "I have need of your...unique talents."

"Uh, talents?" I stammer. Gods, I hope he means my weaving. Lord Valtair was bad enough, and I saw another court rake making eyes at me, too, on the way out of the Great Hall. Because of course they would now that Valtair and the princess gave me their attentions. I'm no stranger to sexual politics at court.

I'm going red. I know I'm going red, even as the king says, "Your weaving."

I swallow, and can't help but catch his eye.

His eyes bore into mine. "You saw Nikolai's threads unraveling before anyone else. You saw how to fix it. I have a matter I'd like you to look into."

His knee is bobbing—I can't see it under the desk, but can hear the soft, fast rattle of his boot heel on the floor.

He's nervous. Gods, he's nervous about *me?* Or, what is he actually asking me to do?

Not, at least, give him sexual favors. There's that.

"I'll help how I can," I say cautiously. Because if he's going to ask me to cover up more of his crimes with illusions, I absolutely will not.

But there's a tension around him that speaks more of being hunted, rather than being the hunter.

Have I been wrong, have the rumors been wrong? He doesn't look angry just now, and it takes years off his face, edges off of his razored personality. This isn't the same man who watched the demonstrations yesterday with disdain, only calling out "Next!"

His mouth twitches, not a smile. "I want you to help me discover what really happened to my father."

I blink, and fight the urge to step back, step away from his intensity, which is rising again. Not anger this time, at least, not aimed at me. Of all the things I imagined King Torovan asking of me, this was not one of them.

He's asking for my help, though. Asking Caleb, who very obviously demonstrated his weaving abilities to the court yesterday.

Does that make sense? Does it make sense that the king would trust a complete stranger with a task this huge?

It makes sense if he's desperate.

And my world tilts. Because this is not what I'd expected at all.

"Of course," I say, my words coming out tight and hoarse. I clear my throat. "Yes, Your Majesty, of course I will help you. However I can."

Relief sags him back again, and I wonder what I've just agreed to. What is *he* so afraid of, and should I be afraid of it, too?

He rubs a hand across his cheek, smoother than the day before, and gives me a nod.

"Thank you." Abruptly, he stands. "Come with me."

Chapter 11

Absence

Irava

I follow Torovan through a door in his study that leads to dimly lit rooms. Heavy curtains shroud the windows, with little sunlight showing through. Some furniture is covered with linens, while others remain in the open. The air is heavy with the must of a house that's been vacant for months.

We walk through a sitting room, and then another sitting room. Shadows stretch across the walls like living things.

These were his father's rooms, I realize. They should be his now, but this space doesn't look lived in. The rooms are frozen, as if held apart from time.

I swallow as he removes a key from his pocket and unlocks an ornately carved set of double doors. We step into another musty room with an enormous four-poster bed, each corner a tapering spiral reaching toward the high ceiling.

This has to have been the old king's bedchamber.

Gods, has he brought me here to murder me, too?

I squeeze my eyes shut, trying to make my racing heart

calm. No, that isn't what's happening here. He's already asked me for help.

And why would Torovan want to kill a mage candidate? If he wanted me gone, he could have banished me at the demonstration. Not let me stay in the palace.

Or maybe that would have been too suspicious. Maybe he's afraid I'll see too much. He's as much as said it himself.

Oh gods, I should flee.

I turn to the doors, just as the king seizes the window curtains and yanks them open, flooding the room with too-bright light.

He stops when he sees me, frowning. A few wisps of black hair have escaped his tuck behind his ear and dance in the sunlight. For a moment, I can't look away. His beautiful smooth brow now furrowed, his lips drawn tight.

I can't look away, no matter if everything in me is telling me to flee.

Then, his expression closes. He has to know the rumors about him, has to know that of course I would be nervous coming here, for all kinds of reasons. Doubly so as Caleb Ailin, village mage, who's never talked to a king before, let alone been in a king's bedchamber.

It's not Torovan's bedchamber, though.

There is that.

I bow, which seems the safest thing to do, as my thoughts race.

Am I in danger here? I don't know. I truly don't know. Everything I thought I did know is unraveling, and I'm struggling to find the threads.

Is this man my enemy? Or is he a man who's recently lost his father and doesn't know why?

"Forgive me, Your Majesty—"

"There's nothing to forgive," the king says gruffly. "Stand up, please. We don't need to hold to ceremony here."

He's wrong. But I straighten slowly.

He's glaring at me, and somehow, that feels safer than the glimpses of that other man I've seen, the one who feels too much.

Torovan waves around us.

"I want to know what you see," he says. "Look with your weaving. See if there's—if there's anything to see."

I push my spectacles back up my nose—they'd slipped when I'd bowed. Then, I nod.

I'm not sure what exactly he wants me to do. Does he know that weaving is very hard to see after it's already been woven and set in the weaver's will? It becomes a part of a new reality then, with everything and everyone around it shifting to match. To see that it wasn't the original reality after all can be difficult or impossible. It's why I can hold my illusion around Master Aldric. Around everyone here in the palace.

And if there has been any weaving done in this room, if the king is trying to find ill intent, it would have been done four months ago. That's a long time for reality to settle and the weaving to fully become the new reality.

I'll look because he asked me to. But I don't think I'll find anything.

I glance at him, and he's still watching me, which tightens all my nerves. So I make sure my own illusion is firmly in place, then take a few breaths, trying to settle into the reality of the room. To see the threads all around me, ready to pluck and weave into new shapes at my will.

This slide into the deeper concentration of my magic steadies me.

Some threads will be easier to pull than others. The bed, the chairs—they're all inanimate, and though people can act upon them, can use them for their own purposes, they have no wills of their own. Their possibilities are finite, their histories settled.

It's much easier to weave illusions around living beings, or the possibilities they inhabit, as they are constantly in motion and not settled into any one reality.

Reality is hardly inanimate.

I spin in a slow circle, doing my best to ignore the king, who's hovering with his arms crossed. He's not an easy person to ignore, and this close, with my senses fully extended, I finally identify the scent of him—a bit of cedar, from his wardrobe, maybe. Some wood smoke, a hint of something sweet, like roses—which is a delicate scent I wouldn't have associated with this man. Did he have a bath recently?

And should I be thinking of baths at all here, in this bedroom? With this man?

I pull my focus back to scanning the room, looking for any reality that's out of place. Maybe less settled than it should be, or showing too many possibilities. Master Aldric has to have already scanned this room, so I'm doing nothing new, I suspect, and four months later it will be a lot less effective.

But as I spin, my own brow starts to furrow.

"What's wrong?" the king asks, unfolding his crossed arms as if readying to pounce on an answer. "What do you see?"

I keep turning, keep looking and feeling, and it's a moment before I can put into words what I'm feeling. Because it isn't what I'm seeing that's the problem. Everything I'm seeing looks as it should.

It's what I'm *not* seeing.

"This room is too...lifeless."

The king flinches, and I flush, regretting my choice of words.

"No, I mean—reality flows everywhere. It flows stronger around people and animals and plants, because these things change and grow and influence it more than things that don't have motion. So this room shouldn't have much motion if it's been empty for a few months. But, it should still have some. Possibilities of people coming in and out, or things being moved at some point, even if they're faint. But this room has... nothing. It's here, and it's reality, and everything's settled in that reality. But it has no flow."

I blink and turn back to him, lowering my eyes. "Forgive me, Your Majesty, I'm not making any sense. I don't know how to describe this."

He steps closer, and I tense.

He stops.

What was he intending to do? His arm had twitched but then stopped, as if he'd wanted to brace my shoulder, but then thought better of it.

I swallow.

"Please," he says, and there is desperation in his voice. His eyes are wide, his face earnest. And my gut twists to see this cold, lofty man so unraveled.

"Please, try to describe it. If you're seeing anything, anything at all, it's more than anyone else has seen here. Please, Caleb."

A shiver runs through me when he says my given name. He

said it before, in his study, but it's different here somehow. Closer, more intimate. And it's not actually my name, but I've held it as mine these last few days. I do have some claim over it.

I wipe my hair out of my eyes where it's fallen loose from its queue. And I carefully adjust my spectacles. They're the only part of who I am as Caleb that's actually a part of me—they're my own spectacles, which I've worn since late childhood. I rewove reality around my eyes several years ago so I wouldn't need them, but then wove it back again. The world doesn't always look so harsh when there's a barrier between my eyes and what's around me.

"Reality is like..." I feel foolish, giving an elementary lecture on weaving to the king, but he nods, so I forge on. "Well, it's like a tapestry, yes, and it can be woven, but it's also like clay. Clay, far from water, or fired in a kiln, is hard and unchangeable, but clay close to water and movement is malleable. This room...it's like it's forgotten that water exists."

I frown and move closer to the bed, where the feeling is strongest. I touch the thickly woven brocade covers and run my fingers across the raised pattern, feeling its firm reality. I feel its reality threads with my magic. But the reality still feels off. Like strings on a harp that's never been played and never will be. Like someone's encased it in glass.

"Why?" the king finally asks, stepping beside me and placing his own hands down on the bed. "Can someone hide magic this way? Hide elemental magic, or a weaving?"

I look up at him, a chill running through me. The feeling is strongest on the bed, and I want to step back, because I'm sure this is where the king his father died.

"I don't know how to do something like this," I say, "but there's a lot I don't know. This doesn't quite feel like a weaving, but I'm also not sure it isn't. But...yes. I think this could be an attempt to cover up something else."

His eyes bore into mine, and I don't look away.

"It's something," he breathes. "It's the first hint of an answer I've had in months. Thank you, Caleb."

My name again.

And would the hairs on my arms stand like this if he said my own name? If he called me Irava?

I look down, nod, dip into an acknowledging bow. It breaks whatever tension has been happening between us, but it doesn't break the oddness, the emptiness I feel in the room.

Now that I know what to feel for, I don't have to concentrate as hard to sense it, and maybe this was some of the feeling of abandonment, of being frozen, that I felt when I first came in.

He hasn't taken over his father's chambers, and I've wondered why, but I can't imagine trying to sleep in the same room, the same bed, that his father died in.

Likely, had been killed in.

Is it still possible that King Torovan has brought me here, shown me this, to try to throw me off his own trail if he killed the king? Maybe, but if he's this nervous, and desperate enough to bring a stranger here and into his confidence, is that likely?

He's clammed up again, arms crossed, glaring down at the bed now.

"Thank you," he says again, and his voice is harder now, back to being cold. A different sort of shiver runs through me, back to the fear of being near him.

Maybe he didn't kill his father—but is this still a man I could live with? A man I could share my bed with? Have children with? I'm not at all convinced he doesn't have secrets of his own.

"You may go now, Caleb. And not a word of this to anyone, or it will be your life."

When he says my name this time, I am unmoved. Mostly.

I square my shoulders, bow again. "Yes, Your Majesty."

But then he says, "Please, come back tomorrow. There's more I want you to examine."

And it's there again, the desperation beneath the turbulent storm.

I say quietly, "Yes, Your Majesty," and leave the rooms the way we came in.

King Torovan doesn't follow.

Chapter 12

The Dowager Queen
Torovan

Caleb's absence makes my father's bedchamber feel more still, more empty, more lifeless, as Caleb had said.

I look around me, trying to see what he saw, the lack of movement. But I never had full training as a weaver, and I can only see reality as it is: a room empty of my father's presence, of his life, robbed of any hope of happiness. Was that what Caleb sensed? A room where reality was traumatized by a person's absence?

The air is stagnant and too heavy with memories. I spent hours perched on the end of this bed as a child. My father waved his hands around, telling stories about Barella's long history, dreaming up his plans for the future.

I feel his absence so strongly I can't breathe.

But I have to. I have a kingdom that needs me, as Valtair reminded me again yesterday. And maybe it's time I start paying attention to those reminders.

As much as I might wish Caleb Ailin to stay and go over

every inch of the palace with me, that would draw the wrong sort of attention. Because if he's right that someone used magic to cover up what happened here, my father's killer could be watching for if it's been discovered. Better by far to take this slowly, as much as it kills me.

I touch the spot on the bed that Caleb touched, seeing his delicate fingers again tracing over the brocade patterns. And can I sense what he sensed here?

But I only smell his lingering scent, sweet and with a hint of cinnamon.

He was scared of me, when we first stepped into this room. Gods, I need to try to be less of an ogre, I really do.

I hear a soft click and snatch my hand away from the bed, looking up to see my mother emerging from the door to the corridor that runs between the king's chambers and the queen's.

My face heats, and I scowl, stepping away from the bed.

As the king, by rights, these rooms are mine. And by rights, as the dowager queen, she should have moved into the dowager's rooms farther down the hall. But she hasn't, and I haven't pushed. She was distraught for weeks after my father died, and I didn't have the heart to move her.

I'm feeling less of that concern now, however.

"Mother, you can't barge in here. These are the king's rooms—"

"You don't live in them," she says, looking around as she glides inside. "And I heard voices."

"I—just a servant. I want to have these rooms cleaned."

They haven't been touched since just after my father's death. There's an obvious layer of dust coating everything.

"It's past time," my mother says, running a finger across the ledge of a wardrobe and frowning at what she sees. Very pointedly doing so.

Dowager Queen Zinara is in her late forties and still strikingly beautiful, with her black hair oiled and pinned up in an elegant mass of waves and twists. I have her eyes, my father always said so. I have my father's nose and chin, though, signatures of the Barellan line.

"Mother, if I move in here, then I'll expect you to move to the dowager's chambers—"

"In good time," she says, continuing her inspection of the room, her green silk gown rustling softly as she moves.

"My wife will need your chambers—"

"You're not married yet." She gives me a pointed smile.

She doesn't exactly disapprove of my choice of a bride, more that I made the decision without her.

As it should be.

My chest tightens. When Princess Irava arrives, I will have to live in my father's chambers. And she will live in my mother's. That's also how it should be.

My hand that touched the place Caleb touched on the bed curls. Caleb met my eyes when he told me about the lack of life in this room. He met my eyes in the Great Hall. Will Irava? Will she thank me for making her a queen? Will she want to share my bed, or will she do so out of duty?

These thoughts, in this room where my father died, make my stomach turn. Maybe I'll renovate my own chambers into the new royal chambers. It's what they are now, as it is.

"You need to let it go," my mother says. She's watching me far too closely. "Elsira is moving on, so should you."

I'm not sure my sister is moving on, more that she just isn't showing anyone her own pain.

But I'm not going to argue with my mother, not here. Not when I'm feeling drained of life myself. And I'm not going to tell her about what Caleb saw, either. She already disapproves of my investigation and how long it's dragged on.

"Mother, I have much to do."

"And I have little," she says. "Torovan, let me handle some of the work. Your father always did."

"No—no, I'm fine."

Her opinions on how the kingdom should be run had always differed from my father's, and it was a source of tension between them. I'm sure they'll differ from mine, too. I know my mother.

Her gaze narrows, as if she can hear my thoughts, but she doesn't comment.

"I will leave you to your thoughts," she says, as if leaving was her idea. She pauses at the door, because she always must have the last word. Always.

"Torovan, take care that your personal feelings don't interfere with the duties you owe to our kingdom." She looks pointedly at my father's bed. "You must show a strong face for Barella, especially now. The people expect you to rule in strength."

I grit my teeth. This is what I am doing. I have so much strength that someone like Caleb looks at me with fear.

I don't want to rule with that kind of fear. My father didn't. My father was loved by his people, not feared, and would that be so bad?

To hear my mother, yes.

"Of course, Mother," I say, working to keep my voice level. "The people always come first."

Her gaze lingers on me for a moment more before she turns

again, her gown whispering against the stone floor. It's like the sigh of a ghost, and it sends a chill down my spine.

And now I'm alone again in this room, which doesn't feel empty anymore, but filled with memories I wish I didn't have.

My father lying on this bed, still and cold.

I swallow and stride out the way I came in, shutting and locking the bedroom door behind me. And out through my father's study and the rest of his rooms beyond, pausing only long enough in each room to yank the curtains shut in a puff of dust.

Maybe I shouldn't have brought Caleb here. I don't trust him, I can't trust anyone. He certainly doesn't trust me.

But I want him to. I want someone to look at me, like he looked at that room, and see my emptiness. And tell me how to fill it again, because I certainly don't know how.

I will meet with him again tomorrow, and that—that thought gets me through the mounds of correspondence that is my duty.

Chapter 13

The Illusion of a Flower
Irava

He didn't kill his father. It's the only thought I've been thinking all throughout the night, lying awake and staring up at my bare ceiling in the small room I call my own. It's the only thought I can think now, as I stand in the dew-soaked garden, my shoes damp on the wet morning grass.

I'm standing amidst a group of mage candidates. We're facing each other in two rows inside a courtyard of hedges, with Master Aldric slowly pacing between us. The sun is up, that bright squinting hour of the morning that's still cold but giving way to warmth.

I focus on my weaving under the watchful eye of Master Aldric. I haven't spoken to him one on one since he gave me the courtly manners book to read, but I've been trying to improve my show of manners to prove to him I'm reading it. Which isn't easy—I've never been very good at courtly manners. At least, the being quiet and not drawing overt attention to yourself part.

In the air in front of me, an illusion of a flower shimmers and blooms into pinks and greens. I practiced with flower illusions when I was just teaching myself to weave years ago, but I am far beyond flowers now. It's what Master Aldric asked of me, though, and it would draw less attention than something like a bird or rabbit, which are much more complex to weave into reality. And much more interesting.

"*Precision* and *control*," I murmur to myself, mimicking Master Adric's sing-song intonation. "*Precision* and *control*." It's been his mantra all morning, to both the elementalists and the weavers.

Just now, he's several candidates down from me, reprimanding an elementalist for trying to rush his magic and burning the tips of his fingers.

Nikolai is in the row across from me. He's decided I'm worth acknowledging again and has been shooting me glares all morning. Does he know I met with the king yesterday? But a few others have been giving me weird looks, too. Gossip spreads like wildfires in a palace.

Nikolai is also weaving a flower. But it is, I can't *help* but notice, much larger, and more colorful, and more detailed than mine.

Well, fine, then. I slowly enhance the reality of my own flower, making the colors more vibrant, the details sharp and intricate.

Nikolai notices, of course. The heat of his glares are becoming rivals to the sun.

He weaves several more flowers in the air in front of him, showing off his control.

And so do I, springing up a complex pattern of vines as well.

Nikolai sneers and adds several bees hovering above his own flowers.

So I make a flock of butterflies.

He sends his bees toward my flowers—or, no, toward me—

"Weavers," Master Aldric says, his voice cutting my attention.

Nikolai's bees waver, then unravel. I watch the rest of his weaving with alarm, looking for any signs he'll lose control of his magic again. But no, he has his hold on the threads of the flower yet, he's only let go of the threads he sent toward me.

I take a breath and bow to Master Aldric, who's approaching my weaving, inspecting it with a decided squint.

I'd forgotten. I'd forgotten, for a moment, and after all my thoughts of the king, after meeting with him and being squarely in his turbulent attention, that I'm no one here. I'm a mage no one has ever heard of, from a village far from the capital. I can't goad nobles. I'm not protected by my mother's position, or by my gender.

But Master Aldric says, "Good, Caleb, good. I would caution against taking on too many separate weavings at once, however. The greater the complexity of the weavings, the greater the demands on your concentration."

And the greater the danger to yourself and everyone else around you. He doesn't say that—but I'm thinking it. And more than one of the other candidates who can hear us are, too, as eyes go to Nikolai.

This was one of the first lessons I'd learned teaching myself to weave, and if Nikolai has any skill at all, it should have been one of his, too.

But Master Aldric doesn't know that about me. He doesn't know anything about me except my name as Caleb and what

I've demonstrated so far. He doesn't know I'm holding an illusion around myself while *also* maintaining a complex weaving of reality in front of me.

"Yes, Master Aldric. Thank you," I say, and bow again.

He smiles, a kindly smile, and turns to Nikolai, giving him much the same praise and admonishment. Which, I realize, hiding my own smug smile, Nikolai takes as an insult in itself. Nikolai wants the greater praise, and he isn't getting it.

I settle back into my weaving, only vaguely listening to what's happening around me as the practice drags on. King Torovan wants to see me again today, to see if I can tell more of what happened around his father's death, I'm sure. Our meeting yesterday wasn't a comfortable one, but I can't say that I'm not eager to finally have answers.

And maybe to hear him say my name again. Even if it's my name as Caleb.

Is that a dangerous thought?

I saw Torovan as a man yesterday and not just a king. I got a glimpse beneath his anger, and what I saw was...unexpected.

He *didn't* kill his father. And if I know that now, if I'm almost certain, shouldn't I leave the palace now that I have my answer? He isn't a murderer, just a tyrant.

Or is that an illusion, too? Is that what he wants everyone to see—or is that the conclusion people have drawn without him asking for it?

I certainly know about people drawing conclusions.

I do need to know more. I need to know if he's a man I can spend the rest of my life with.

And I *want* to know more. His piercing gray-green eyes have haunted me since yesterday. Since, if I'm honest, the moment I stepped into the throne room and he met my gaze.

I want to weigh the feeling of his closeness, the way he takes up space. The effect his scent has on my insides.

The way he says my name. Any name that happens, at the moment, to be mine.

Yes, these are definitely dangerous thoughts. I came to Barella to prove him a murderer. I was certain. So certain, after seeing his coldness in the throne room, that he must be.

I wanted him to be. I wanted to run from my mother, to run from her obligations, to prove her wrong.

Yes, my mother was wrong to betroth me without my knowledge or will.

But this man...

He isn't who I thought he was.

The sun is high when Master Aldric finally bangs his staff on the flagstone path—which he's been walking on all this time, making us candidates stand in the grass.

"We're done for this session! I will see you again in the common room this afternoon, one turn after the lunch hour. We will be assessing your solutions for various situations that may arise in court. This is a manners lesson, men! You will act accordingly!"

Will I be there? Will the king call me back to his study before then?

Master Aldric's eyes meet mine, just briefly, and he frowns. I don't know what that frown means. Is he still disapproving of my manners? Or does he know that I'm supposed to meet with the king? Should I tell him?

But Nikolai, as he moves past me on the way out of the garden courtyard, veers toward me. He doesn't check my shoulder this time, but leans close and hisses, "Watch yourself, villager."

How by all the gods does Princess Elsira have any kind of thoughts for this man?

But I've seen his type before. They don't go away when you back down from the fight, only keep pressing.

I shouldn't have goaded him, I really shouldn't have, but... that's done now. And I know that I'm the better weaver. I saw in the late king's bedchamber what no one else has seen. I unraveled and contained Nikolai's own weaving. If Nikolai wants to threaten me, he'll find I'm not an easy target.

And then I think about the weaving in the king's father's bedchamber. Hiding whatever really happened there. A type of weaving I've never heard of, or read about in any of my stolen books on weaving. That weaving suppressed reality in a way that makes my skin crawl. Someone, maybe someone still in the palace now, had to have made that weaving.

Maybe I'm not as skilled as I'd like to think. Maybe Nikolai's threats have teeth.

And even if the king has taken an interest in me, I still have no real allies in this court.

I shove my hands into my pockets and follow the rest of the candidates out of the garden.

Chapter 14

The Threat

Irava

Before I reach the edge of the garden and step into the courtyard of the palace, though, I veer off onto another path. My thoughts are spinning, with Nikolai's threat hot in my ear, and my meeting with the king ahead of me, whenever that will be. However that will turn out.

I need, just for a moment, to be by myself. Out in the sunlight and the spring air, where only the birds are chattering.

I want to drop my illusion. To breathe as myself, as Irava, to know what Irava should do.

But I can't, not here, not without the risk of being arrested as a spy—and then where would I be?

No, I've already decided I'm not going to run from Torovan. And maybe I should just tell the king everything. Who I am and why I'm here. Would he understand?

There was a haunted clarity in his eyes. He's certainly a person who knows what it means to be suspicious of those around him.

But that's part of the problem. Telling him I've lied my way into his court sounds like the surest way to break this marriage.

And do I want that still?

I tilt my chin up to the sun, my face warming.

Can I admit to myself that I also *like* being a mage candidate? I like people seeing my magic and not immediately discounting that I should even do it at all. People might not like me as Caleb, not everyone at least, but they're not telling me I shouldn't be who I am.

And Nikolai? It's not like I didn't know Nikolai had it out for me—but I really shouldn't have baited him. Gods, my stupid pride. Which is another thing princesses are not supposed to have, not in the same way that men do. Princesses are supposed to win their battles in the court of social opinions, striking from the shadows. A princess's victory is a takedown of an entire family without the family knowing what hit them.

But that has never been me. I can weave my illusions, yes, but I've never been socially subtle. I couldn't just come to court as a woman, I had to invent an entirely new persona for myself and then *be* Caleb.

So how, in all of my *immense* powers of subtlety, am I supposed to deal with the king?

He trusts me. And no matter the reasons for it, which are still good reasons, I am lying to him.

I find myself wandering down the garden paths, only vaguely keeping the palace in sight over the tall hedges. And each step brings me no closer to answers than the step before it. I know I must turn back soon, I must eat the midday meal and get ready for Master Aldric's etiquette lessons—gods—but I can't turn around. Not yet. Not and have to face *everything* back there.

I nearly jump out of my skin when a man's gruff voice says, "Caleb Ailin, come with me."

I whirl around. It's one of the palace guards, a tall, middle-aged man with curly brown hair and a weathered face I don't recognize. But he is wearing the armor, the insignia, the deep blue cloak of a palace guard. He's someone the king trusts.

My heart kicks into my throat. He doesn't look friendly. I'm deep in the garden, within a corridor of cypress trees. No one else is around.

But I'm not a woman here—is that better? Is that worse? Would the guards more easily do violence toward me as a man?

And why am I even thinking that—the palace guards are Torovan's. Torovan has no wish, that I know of, to see me harmed.

But what if he doesn't want me to have seen what I've seen?

I have no choice but to go with the guard. Running is only a course the guilty would take. And I'm still not done with this court in Barella. With this king.

My stomach knots as I nod, adjust my spectacles, and follow the guard down a different path. I debate asking whether King Torovan is in the gardens and sent him, but then decide against it. Torovan did say he wanted to see me again today, though he didn't say when. I should assume this is a summons, and that flutters my insides for a different reason.

We wind through several turns, the knot in my stomach starting to grow thorns, until we come out into a courtyard among the hedges. This courtyard is much smaller than where we were practicing as mages.

And this courtyard does not contain the king, but a stately woman in a green silk morning dress sitting on a stone bench at its center. Her glossy black hair is liberally streaked with gray, bound up in an elaborate style beset with jeweled pins. Diamonds, rubies, sapphires. They catch the light as she rises and turns, offering me a smile that's sugary sweet.

I've only seen her from a distance. I passed her in the corridor once among her own retinue of ladies and guards—of which the guard who brought me must be one of them. But she's unmistakably the Dowager Zinara, the former queen of Barella. Torovan's mother. I can see the resemblance in the particular tightness around her eyes, her sharp, calculating gaze.

Gods, and what does she want with me? With Caleb Ailin, the village mage?

"Young man," she says, tilting up her chin. Her voice is honed, like my mother's. This is a woman who has breathed power all of her life. "You have been causing quite a stir at court."

I kick myself out of my gawk and into a low bow. "Your Highness. It's a pleasure to see you."

"Yes, it is, I'm sure you didn't see many queens in your village."

"N-no, Your Highness." My stammer isn't entirely feigned.

She comes around the bench she was sitting on like a bobcat emerging from its den. Eyes all bright and shining as the gems in her hair.

"There are things one can reach for, given one's birth. A noble may seek to make a royal marriage if their family is rich enough. Or a farmer may seek to marry the barrister's daughter. But a court mage—a court mage exists in a place all his own. Titled or untitled, he can't add to any royal line, lest he pass his magic to another generation. Magic is useful, Caleb, but not to those of us who rule kingdoms and empires. Our minds must be clear of such primitive things such as elements or illusions."

My heart jumps into my throat. Does she know I met with the king? Or is she talking about when I walked out of the Great Hall with Princess Elsira? Does she think I've been trying to court her daughter? It's not a trivial thing in this court for a nobody to talk to royalty. I'm far, far too used to being royalty myself.

But can I claim I'm nobody here if all three of the royal family have sought be out?

And should I point out the second thought that's rising up, that I'm a weaver and that sort of magic isn't hereditary?

Gods, I can't correct the Dowager Queen, as much as I want to.

The Dowager steps closer, puts a hand under my chin, and tilts it up. We're nearly the same height—she's taller than average for a woman, and Caleb would be short for a man.

"My son," she says, "is ruling a kingdom. He might not yet understand the full responsibility of that, but he certainly does *not* need the scandal of romancing a court village mage. Am I understood?"

I flush hot, before the blood drains again from my face. So this is about Torovan. She knows I met with Torovan. Does she know I'm meeting with him again? And she assumes that I'm —that he—

I choke, because her grip is tightening, and my nerves are jangling.

I'm not romancing the king. I'm the farthest thing from

romancing the king—and does he even like men, like Valtair? The Dowager seems to think so. If I marry Torovan, will he even want to be with me? Would he find me attractive as myself?

I might marry him and be consigned to life without a husband ever to share my bed, only left to have affairs of my own—if I can manage the subtlety of being discreet. Or would that, in fact, be ideal? I don't want to be married at all. Not yet. Not to someone I haven't chosen.

And why by the gods am I worried about that when his mother is bent on choking me to death?

"Yes, Your Highness," I finally manage, and she lets go. I have the wits not to rub at my jaw, at what will surely be bruises on my cheeks—not that my illusion won't cover them.

This is his mother? Is it a wonder that he has the temper that he does?

I understand him better already.

"Good," the Dowager says, straightening her puffed sleeves. "Then you will not meet with the king again."

I stand up straight. "But—"

She looks up at me, and I snap my mouth shut.

"You will not," she says more slowly, "meet with the king again."

Then she sways past me, motioning to her guard on the way out. Not looking back, not acknowledging me in any way.

I stand among the hedges, my heart pounding, the sun warm on my loose, mussed hair, the birds still chirruping in the trees.

I want to cry.

And I want to run.

But instead, I straighten my own clothes out, wait a few unsteady breaths, and then follow the Dowager out of the gardens.

Chapter 15

Sensing

Torovan

I decide, this time, not to summon Caleb, but to find him myself. I've been buried in my backlog of reports and missives and pleas and sycophantry all day, and a walk through the palace will clear my head.

And is it a little strange that my steps are lighter today, the corridor walls less dark, the heavy weight of the wood carvings showing Barella's long history throughout the halls less oppressive?

I have a direction. I have some answers, finally some answers—my father's death was not an accident. My intuition was right. Something happened, something was covered up, and I have someone who will help me find what, and who.

I find Caleb coming into the hallway that leads to the mage candidate's quarters. There are a few other candidates lingering in the hall and I ignore their startled bows as I pass, though Caleb, when he sees me, looks like he wants to run.

His face is flushed, and it occurs to me too late that it might not have been the best idea to show favoritism to him here, in this place where he's staying. Or to come get him myself—but it's my palace. Gods know I spent my sweat this morning trying to keep this palace running smoothly.

So I straighten my shoulders and scowl. Which comes much easier than it should.

"Ailin. With me."

He bows. Says in a small voice, "Yes, Your Majesty."

And it clenches my chest that he looks scared—scared of me? I thought we'd at least gotten past the worst of that yesterday. He agreed to help me.

I set my jaw and lead the way back up to the royal suites.

Caleb doesn't say a word.

As Caleb and I step into my father's chambers again, a subtle shiver runs down my spine. As it did the day before. The air is still thick with my father's presence, and with memories. But today—today I wonder if it's not also thick with that lack, that absence that Caleb felt before. Can I feel it, too? My weaving is nothing compared to Caleb's skill, and it may never be. But surely I should be able to sense if someone tried to muffle the very air my father breathed.

Caleb looks around my father's chambers. Not the bedroom this time, but the second, inner sitting room, where my father kept his desk. Not quite a study, as I have—my father liked to do his work in the open. He'd let Elsira and me play around his desk when we were children, never tiring of questions. Always keeping toys in a large wooden chest in the corner.

I glance over—the toys were long ago put into storage, but the chest is still there. I think it holds blankets now.

I take a breath. "We'll start with the desk." I move toward

the large slate and walnut desk. "Anything you can see here—this was where he spent most of his time."

I haven't been back to my father's desk since he died. I'd asked Valtair to pull out anything immediate and important to the kingdom while I stood in another room. He left my father's trinkets: the small lacquered map coaster that was a gift from a traveling artisan. The folded, hand-woven apron Elsira made for him when she was ten, because he occasionally slipped down to the kitchens to bake his favorite flat cakes. Both halves of the broken arrow that I used to fell a stag when I was twelve.

I touch the cool surface of the polished slate desk top. Not marble, because my father said he wanted a reminder that not everyone in his kingdom was born to the privilege he had.

Anger and bile rise in me, and I stand very still, not saying a word, as Caleb comes around the desk and leans over it.

I wait. I wait, while I slowly burn inside, all the rage that someone would wish to kill my father, a man who only ever loved his kingdom, scouring me from the inside out.

Caleb abruptly straightens. "I don't see anything unusual here. I don't even feel in this room what I felt in the—"

He waves in the direction of the bedroom. Then looks up at me.

He's close. And this close, I can see the light freckles on his pale face, the flecks of gray in his brown eyes.

He adjusts his spectacles and looks down.

"Fine," I say. "Thank you. Check the rest of the room."

He nods, not looking up at me again, and I hate that he can't look at me. I hate that whatever rage I'm feeling inside has made its way out to him—this isn't the person I'm supposed to be.

Or maybe it is. Maybe it's best that no one sees past the

ogre they think I am. I'm going to be married soon—and it's not safe in this palace, in this kingdom, to be near me. I knew it before, but doubly know it now, after Caleb found what he did in my father's bedchamber.

Caleb takes a step back, turns around to survey the room again, his lips pulled into a tight line of concentration. I can, just barely, feel that he is weaving something, though I don't know what. And I can't see the threads, like I know other weavers sometimes can.

My chest tightens with frustration. I would rather be checking all of this alone, not bringing anyone else into this mayhem, but I've tried. I've tried and strained every weaver's sense I have and still found nothing. Caleb did instead.

Caleb makes a full circle, turning back around toward me, and I wonder if he's going to stop before he faces me again.

But he freezes, his gaze not on me, but on my father's chair, just beside me. Caleb's delicate brows draw down and he steps closer.

And he's close again now, his cinnamon scent rich around him. His hair isn't as neat as it could be, his clothes—decent enough for a merchant, but too plain for the palace—crinkled around the edges.

His lips part in surprise. He leans down and points at the chair.

"There's a concentration of reality here. More than there should be." He frowns and straightens again, biting his lower lip as he glares down at the chair. "If there's less reality than there should be in the bedchamber, there's more of it here. But just here, not throughout the rest of the room."

I shift, tearing my attention from his lips—which I definitely should *not* be looking at.

Can I see what he sees? But I don't, not with my natural eyes. I take another step back, glance at him to make sure he's still frowning at the chair, and then carefully look with more concentrated weaver's senses at the chair. I can maybe—maybe—see something, a ripple in the feel of reality, but I don't know what I'm looking at. It doesn't look like anything more than... something.

And damn that Master Aldric never taught me what I needed to know. Damn my failing willpower.

Caleb's crouched and looking around the front of the chair now, so I reach out with my weaving and nudge some of the surface threads of reality around the chair. They still have the lingering touch of my father's presence, and I pull back again, because oh gods.

Caleb jerks up, nearly banging his head on the desk top as he stares up at me, his eyes going wide.

Oh, no. I hadn't thought—I hadn't wanted him to see—

I step back, another step away.

Chapter 16

The Weaver
Torovan

Caleb stands, drawing himself up, a fire coming into his eyes that I haven't seen before. His brows pinching, cheeks a little flushed.

"You're a weaver," he says. It's an accusation.

He looks back at the chair. "You—I felt you try to touch the threads around it."

He looks back at me, fire continuing to build. His nostrils flare.

Is he going to tell me how incompetent my touch on reality was? Did I disturb his careful perusal? Will he dare to mock me to my face?

But he's just looking at me, expectant.

When I don't say anything, when I can't think of what I should say, he asks, "Why did you ask me to look at this if you can already see it? Or—"

He shuts his mouth. And I can only watch as his anger turns to something else. Suspicion. And it's not hard to see where he's going with this. Because the deadened reality in my father's chamber was from a weaving, and here I am, already accused by the public rumors as the man who killed my father to take his throne.

But I certainly wouldn't bring in another weaver to show him this if I was guilty. I wouldn't ask another's help.

I square my shoulders and glare back at this mage candidate, who dares to presume so much. I wonder if I should simply dismiss him now—bar him from the palace, even—

And what good would that do but strengthen my appearance of guilt?

I deflate, crossing my arms, not knowing what to do with my hands. I glance to the side. Anywhere but at Caleb's accusing eyes. "I can't see the weaving here. If it is a weaving—"

"It is. This one definitely is, and so is the one in the bedchamber."

I shrug, a tight acknowledgement. "I can't see them. I didn't see them before, and I didn't know they were there—and not for lack of trying." I meet his eyes again, and it's hard, but I'm the king. He's only a court mage—not even that, a mage candidate. "I don't have to defend myself to you."

He blinks, some of the fire leaving. But not all of it. He holds up his hands. "But you are a weaver. I didn't know—"

"I'm not," I say. "Not in any way that matters." I push past him around the desk. "Check the rest of the room. I want to know if there's any other places that are...off. Suspicious. Anything you can see."

He doesn't press again, not right away. But I can see the questions building in the glances he casts me while he looks around the rest of the room.

And this was a mistake. All of this was a mistake, that he now knows about one of my greatest shames. That I was foolish enough to hope that I could use my weaver's senses, when they've hardly ever worked before.

I make myself busy nudging trinkets around shelves and tables.

"So," he finally says, "it's not a kingly thing to be a weaver?"

What the hells kind of question is that? There's something loaded there, something I'm not sure how to pry open.

He reaches to touch books on a shelf—weaver's texts. My father kept a few, none of the forbidden works of course, just a few basic books. He never learned to weave himself, though.

But Caleb isn't wrong, and though my father never actively discouraged my desire to learn weaving, he never encouraged it, either. My mother hated it, wanted me to have nothing to do with the magic of willpower.

I think it has less to do with the danger involved than the appearance of a king having magic at all. Elementalists are born to their magic, and that magic has never yet touched the Barellan royal line, which is a point of pride. Weavers, however, are craftsmen, and though it is tolerable for the nobility to take up such a craft, it will never be suitable for a prince, or for a king.

I open my hands. "I never had the willpower, if you must know." And there—if he hasn't guessed it already—it's in the open. My great shame.

He would have figured it out anyway. This Caleb Ailin is far from a fool.

I expect...I'm not sure what I expect. Contempt, maybe, from a weaver who can unravel another's threads mid-explosion. Or maybe revulsion. Or maybe just...apathy.

But he stops his perusal of the room and gives me an

incredulous look. "You? *You* never had the willpower? Gods, I—"

He snaps his mouth shut.

"You what?" I ask, circling around toward him.

He gives a shrug. "I really don't think you lack the willpower to weave. But—I'm just a village mage. I wouldn't know—"

"You are, more than likely, more powerful than Master Aldric, if you can see what he cannot."

Or, and it isn't like this idea hasn't been growing, Master Aldric might not have seen the weavings in the bedchamber and on my father's chair because he put them there himself. Because he doesn't want anyone else to see them.

It isn't impossible. Maybe it isn't even improbable.

Caleb's cheeks redden, and it is—gods. I shouldn't be attracted to this man. I shouldn't be thinking about anything other than what we were here for, definitely not thinking about how his blush makes the freckles on his face stand out like sparks in a fire.

Am I trying to distract myself from my shame? Am I trying to distract myself from everything else I'm feeling being in these chambers?

I can't help moving closer again. And there, right there, is my lack of willpower. That is why I can't be a weaver.

I turn away again in disgust.

But Caleb steps around me, says, "Do you think you don't have enough willpower? Did someone tell you that?"

I haven't given him permission to be this forward with me. He is a mage candidate at my court. I asked him for help using his weaving skills, not for advice.

But I pick up a small figurine of a cavalry horse from an

end table, say, "Master Aldric determined that to teach me further would be dangerous. Now please, let the matter drop." I set the horse back down on the tabletop with a sharp click.

"Willpower isn't inherent," Caleb insists, following me as I move toward a bookcase. "Willpower can be trained and honed. It's not easy, but that's the point."

His words stir something within me, a traitorous something that had stopped hoping a long time ago. I've been impotent in this search for my father's killer, and yet Caleb sees what I cannot. Can he be right about this? Was Master Aldric truly wrong? I could hope, I've always hoped, but—

But can I take the word of a village mage, who certainly has an interest in getting on my good side if he'd like a place at court, over the word of a trusted advisor who's been in the Barellan court for years?

If Master Aldric had anything to do with my father's death, then yes, I can.

"I can teach you," Caleb says, and the words shoot through me like lightning.

Failing at becoming a weaver has haunted me for years. It's a weakness and a shame I've always tried to hide away, even from those I trust the most. That it didn't matter to me. That it doesn't matter now, and it's for the best that I never became a weaver, because no king has ever been a weaver. No king of Barella, at least.

But now, standing here with Caleb, I feel—I feel like he can see through that lie.

And it does matter. That Caleb came here and saw what I could not matters—it matters, because if I had been trained, if I was truly a weaver, I might have seen it months ago myself. I might have already found who killed my father, punished them, and rid the kingdom of that danger. Protected my sister and my mother. Made the kingdom a safer place for everyone.

Is there a trap in his offer? Is this only to gain favor?

But his face is so earnest.

And can I afford to say no?

"Yes," I say. "Yes. I would like that."

Chapter 17

The Disguise

Irava

I couldn't tell him. I couldn't tell him about the dowager's threat, and I should have told him, I shouldn't even have been there, but now...now I've agreed to teach him. I *offered* it. Oh gods, what was I thinking?

Nikolai has threatened me, and he'll only get angrier the more time I spend with the king. I'm sure Torovan's coming for me in the mage's quarters is already the talk of the palace.

And the Dowager Zinara threatened me about meeting with Torovan, and now I have again.

And with Torovan, I've seen the evidence that someone, a weaver, tried to cover up what happened with the king. If the weaver didn't kill the king themself, then they were an accomplice.

I came to this palace looking to prove the king a murderer, but I've found myself instead chasing a conspiracy, and I have no idea who the enemies are. Everyone. Everyone could be my enemy.

Except, maybe, Torovan. And that...is an unsettling thought.

The next day, Torovan and his men go on a hunt. I learn this at breakfast, when it's the chatter of the day. I shouldn't feel disappointed, or that he should have informed me—I have no claim over him. Not as Caleb, anyway, and if I want to continue to be here and be in his trust and use my magic, I must be Caleb.

I should feel grateful. Our meeting is delayed. Might be delayed indefinitely, even.

I really should leave the palace before my life is truly in danger, if it isn't already.

But the Dowager Zinara, who's taken her place at the high table for the first time since I arrived at the palace, has announced that she will hold a garden party this morning, and the court is welcome to attend.

And...and I've been thinking ever since the day before that maybe, just maybe, her threats weren't about me romancing the king, but that she knows I'm helping him find his father's murderer, and she doesn't want me to find out what happened.

As I eat, only half listening to the nobles chattering away around me, I wonder if the king being away, and the dowager having her party, is an opportunity.

Maybe his mother's threat is just a mother's threat.

My own mother has her opinions on who her children should marry. Not that they are good ones.

If I might marry into this family, I should at very least find out more about what I'm getting into.

I glance up occasionally at the high table, but the dowager hasn't seen fit to acknowledge my existence. She has to know

I've seen Torovan again. He came to find me, publicly, at my quarters. And I try not to burn at that memory.

Or quietly tuck it away.

So will the dowager exact her revenge by trying to destroy my life from a distance? That would be the acceptable feminine way to go about bringing someone down.

Princess Elsira catches my eye when I'm looking and gives me a wan smile. Then she looks away again. Her smile seems more forced than when she was with her brother at the high table before. She turns back toward her mother, the very picture of the polite princess.

She isn't happy. I know that. I *know* that. I know what it's like to have a mother who dictates your every move and criticizes when you step off a very fine line.

And with all of these things, and all of these thoughts, I decide on my plan.

After breakfast, before the mage candidates are called to the first practice session of the day with Master Aldric, I find a quiet corner in a little-used corridor and drop my illusion, quickly weaving another illusion around myself of one of Dowager Zinara's ladies-in-waiting.

I watched Lady Denala flirt heavily with Nikolai two places down from me at dinner the night before. I'd been distracted by my second meeting with the king, and what the dowager might do about it, but I'm ever-attuned to Nikolai's moods. It's only survival.

Lady Denala had the most obnoxious laugh, and there's no way I can forget the simper of her voice or the way she fanned her bosom every time Nikolai said anything even remotely complimentary. And then a few more times for good measure.

Not that I can replicate that masterpiece of a performance

for any length of time, or with any real skill, but I'm going to do my best. I'm not the best actor, but I am *excellent* at my illusions. And it only needs to hold up for a little while. I'm hoping I won't have an active audience anyway.

And now, I stand outside the entrance to Dowager Zinara's chambers, my heart pounding. It can't be uncommon for Lady Denala to be here, because the guards only nodded to me on the way up.

I've worked up what I might say if I'm challenged—that the dowager had left a favored bracelet in her rooms and asked me, Lady Denala, to retrieve it for her garden party.

No one yet has challenged me.

If I'm discovered, it could mean my life.

But if I don't find out what's happening in this palace, and don't find some clue why the dowager had such a strong reaction to me meeting with Torovan, it might also mean my life.

I take a deep breath and push open the door.

The apartment is empty, thank the gods. The dowager's own guards are all down in the Great Hall.

Now, inside the apartment, I exhale in relief, wiping slick palms against the real fabric of my pants beneath the illusory dress.

I close the door behind me and survey the sitting room, gathering my willpower to focus, looking for anything out of place—any sort of clue at all—but I don't even know what I'm looking for. All I really have is a hunch, that maybe the dowager knew about my visit with Torovan to his father's chambers and that she tried to intimidate me for it.

I've learned to trust my hunches. Weavers thrive on hunches to navigate the threads of reality, pulling them into different alignments. I'm not going to stop trusting my gut now.

But I was wrong about Torovan. I was so wrong about Torovan.

But was I? Or had I been running scared on what I'd been told, running because this marriage hadn't been my choice when I was promised a choice?

I peer at the underside of couches and squint at closed and locked drawers. My fingers trace the spines of books on the shelves, searching for any titles that stand out to me, but they're mostly dull political volumes, not even the few weaver's volumes that were on the late king's shelves. I recognize a few of these from my grandmother's library.

I don't see any weirdness of reality, like I'd seen in the late king's chambers. No lesser reality, no heightened reality.

I press on into the study, where I'm met with more of the same. Papers stacked neatly on the desk, their contents disappointingly mundane.

The dowager has to have secrets. She's just that kind of woman.

Well, there's the bedchamber.

I hesitate at the door, steeling myself before pushing it open. It's one thing to enter a chamber with Torovan there to give me permission, but I have no illusions at all that I have permission to be here now.

But the moment I enter, I feel it—that same offness that shrouded the late king's bedchamber. It's that absence of reality, a void where life should be more present. And here, especially, knowing that the dowager lives in this chamber, there should be vibrant strings of life and possibilities. But it's as if the essence of the room was drained away, leaving only emptiness behind.

This is something. This is a big something. Does this mean I was wrong about the dowager after all, and she's also been marked for death by this unknown assassin?

I cautiously step further into the bedchamber, looking for anything out of place. The opulent bed with its rich fabrics, the ornate dressers and vanity...everything seems normal, but that feeling of emptiness clings to the air like fog.

I quickly survey the room, knowing that time isn't on my side. But as desperately as I search, I still find no answers beyond the shroud of lesser reality itself.

And then I hear them—voices outside the main door to the dowager's chambers.

I freeze, head cocked, listening for the sounds from the other room.

The door latch rattles.

I catch my breath.

I need to go. *Now.*

I do a quick spin—did I leave anything out of place? I don't think so, but no time to fix it now.

With my illusion of Lady Denala still wrapped around me like a cloak, I slip out through the back servants' entrance.

And run straight into Lord Valtair.

Chapter 18

Caught

Irava

Valtair throws up his hands to catch my shoulders before I barrel into him.

"Lady—Lady Denala, you're in a hurry, is everything well?" He squints. "I thought I just saw you coming up the stairs—did you run?"

Oh shit. I thought Lord Valtair would have gone with the king on his hunt. And Lady Denala had been at breakfast at the high table, so I'd just assumed she'd stay with the Dowager. But then, she hadn't stayed at the Dowager's side last night, but with Nikolai.

And now my heart kicks into a pound at the thought that I might have to deal with the real Lady Denala, and soon.

Lord Valtair's eyes narrow. His sharp eyes scan me up and down.

I knew before not to underestimate him, but I don't like how he's studying me now.

I manage a smile and try to pull back from his grip—which, he lets me. But then he lays a hand on my arm.

"Wait. I haven't been to see Rosson lately. Is the leg any better?"

What? Rosson? Leg? I have no idea what he's talking about.

And it must show, because he gives me a closer, harder look. And I try to resist the urge to squirm, because I know my illusion won't hold up under the closest scrutiny.

I hold my breath and *will* reality to show that I am, in fact, Lady Denala, not myself. I pull that reality to myself like a tide to the shore.

"Your brother," Valtair says more slowly, like I'm clearly out of my mind today. "Is he well?"

Brother. Oh, and oh gods, has Valtair had an affair with Lady Denala's brother? Does he know her well?

"Yes, my brother," I say, "Rosson. He's well enough. Yes, he'd like you to visit."

Valtair stiffens, and I don't know what I've said wrong.

His grip on my arm tightens.

"Really? Because last I saw him, he told me absolutely never to come back. Which he does every single time I see him. I've never yet heard him say he wanted me there."

Well, and double shit.

Something shifts in Valtair's eyes, and his fingers dig into my arm.

"Come with me," he says, and then gives me no choice as he drags me down the hall.

"What—I'll scream—"

"Everyone knows I only prefer men. You're hardly in danger."

Though his voice says otherwise. Maybe not that kind of danger, but I absolutely know I'm in trouble.

I frantically try to think through if I should scream, if that would be a good idea, but I don't know him well enough to know how he'd react to that. He doesn't have a reputation for violence, not from everything I've heard so far, but that doesn't mean he doesn't have those tendencies. So many men do.

Lord Valtair opens a door to the right—a linen closet with stained glass set into the door—and drags me inside.

The scent of freshly laundered sheets and towels fills my nostrils, but it's quickly replaced with the musk of his cologne as he shoves me up against the wall.

"Who the hell are you?" His voice is low and menacing, and I can feel his breath hot against my neck. "Torovan said he thinks a weaver's responsible for his father's death, and you're sure as hell not Lady Denala."

I draw breath, but he shoves me back again.

"And if you are the one responsible for this, I'm dragging you to the dungeon myself. Torovan can rip the truth out of you when he comes back. What a terrible time to go on a hunt. We'll get our weavers to—"

I throw up my hands. "I didn't kill the king, gods, I'm *helping* Torovan—"

"By sneaking into his mother's chambers?"

But his grip loosens, a little. He's peering down at me with confusion written all over his face.

Then the confusion clears, and his eyes widen.

"Caleb?" he asks incredulously. "But—but you—he wouldn't have asked you to go into the dowager's bedchamber—"

He shoves me back again. Rougher this time, man to man. "Did you have something to do with the king's death? Is that why you're here, and gods, we're all fools, you're so powerful—"

"No! Valtair, no, I swear—"

"Not that your word means anything at all right now."

He lets go of me, hands clenching and unclenching. His brow is furrowed, eyes hot coals. It's not the same fire that the king gets in his eyes, not that heavy inferno. This looks like how my brothers would look if any of our family was threatened.

"You care for him?" I ask. But I already know the answer. Valtair and the king have been by each other's sides since they were children. That's well known. "Why aren't you with him on the hunt?"

He shifts. "I don't like hunts, but that's hardly your concern. And you don't have the right to ask the questions here. I'm trying to decide if I should throw you in the dungeon anyway, or lock you up in Torovan's chambers until he returns. Or, if you're as powerful a weaver as you seem, if you'll even let me. Or if you'll just escape."

I take a deep breath.

He hasn't shouted for the guards or tried to arrest me, no. He's still tense, though, and he's seeming confused again. Well, and he has a right to be, doesn't he? I've made a mess of everything here.

"I really am trying to help," I say. "The dowager—she told me to stay away from the king."

His brows rise. "So you thought it would be a good idea to break into her bedchamber? Are you an assassin, Caleb?"

"Gods, no! No." I hold up my hands. "And if I was, I'd be a lot better at it than this."

He shifts. "Can you drop the illusion, it is utterly unsettling speaking to Lady Denala knowing that it's you instead. I don't like that you impersonated her—she might act the fool to suit her needs, but she's not. She does everything to have enough money to treat her brother's injury."

I bite my lip. Of course no one is ever what they seem. I should know that.

And neither is he. Right now, he isn't acting like the man who sat down beside me at breakfast that first day and tried to intimidate me with his flirting.

I swallow. I've hardly thought of him outside the context of Torovan, and maybe he prefers it that way. Or maybe he doesn't.

This man grew up beside a king, but he's a lord in his own right. He's the son of the former Minister of Finance, an heir to a powerful family. Valtair has power of his own outside his influence with the king.

He's staring at me, all of his focused intensity aimed at me, and just now, he's hardly less intimidating than Torovan.

But I can't drop my illusion like he asks. Not without showing him who I really am first. I have to become Irava again, myself, even if just for the moments it takes to reweave the illusion of Caleb around me.

What will Valtair think about my lying to the king? Will it make him more or less suspicious of my being in the dowager's chambers?

And why does it also feel profane, here with this man who obviously cares for the king, to show him who I am? I'm not Valtair's enemy, I'm not even Torovan's. I just wanted to get out of a marriage I didn't want, just wanted, for a time, to not have to be a princess my mother could command, without any real will of my own. No matter how strong my willpower.

I watch the suspicion growing in his eyes again as I hesitate.

"Caleb—if you really are Caleb, and that wasn't just a stupid guess, what were you doing in the dowager's chambers?"

"Looking for clues. And I found one—her chambers have the same muted reality as the late king's. I didn't have time to figure out more."

Valtair unbends. "Her chambers have been magically altered too? You can prove that?"

"I could show it to you, if you were a weaver."

He opens his mouth, and I can almost hear him saying that the king is, Torovan could look at it.

But he snaps his mouth shut again.

"I know he's a weaver," I say.

I watch the war on his face. Not wanting to trust me, but not wanting to let me go, either. And knowing I'm a powerful enough weaver he might not be able to do anything about that.

If he hadn't already guessed who I was, I might have thrown a bird construct at him and fled. But he did. And that makes everything complicated. Because he'll absolutely tell Torovan.

And I don't want to leave the palace now, not now, when the king is starting to get the answers he's needed. When I promised to teach him. When the dowager might be in danger —or in on this herself.

I don't want to leave for reasons I'm not yet willing to face. Willpower be damned.

I need Valtair to trust me. Absolutely need that.

"Valtair. I'm just trying to find the truth."

"And what the hell does that mean?"

I bite my lip, then drop my illusion.

Chapter 19

Tell Him

Irava

Valtair jumps. "What are you—wait—you're *not* Caleb—"

I ignore his crisis as best I can and rapidly reweave the now-familiar reality of Caleb around me.

"I'm Caleb," I say. "I *am* Caleb. But—"

I let go of the threads of my illusion again, more reluctantly this time. I feel utterly naked in Caleb's clothes, but my own appearance as myself, before him.

It is as profane as I'd thought it would be. My hair is loose, cut on the road to the same length as Caleb's would be. I'm not wearing any cosmetics. And I am wearing trousers and Caleb's barely-passable-for-court coat. Which is a little big on me without the illusion to fill it out.

"I'm Irava Anoran Varandre. Um, betrothed to the king."

Valtair blinks for several long seconds. The dusting of gold on his eyelids flutters, some pieces flaking off.

"What the actual fuck?" he finally says.

I hunch further in on myself. I want to put my illusion up

again, but I know that isn't the best move right now. Not when he's currently trying to pick me apart like a puzzle with his eyes.

Valtair shakes himself. "Okay. *Okay.* Tell me, please, how that makes any kind of sense."

"I didn't want to marry him," I say in a rush. I brace against the wall behind me. "My mother arranged it, and then told me. And there are a lot of rumors that he killed his father—"

"Not true."

"I know that *now,* but I didn't before. Would you marry a man who was supposed to be a murderer? I had to know, and to find that out, I had to get close enough to see for myself."

He lets out a long sigh. "Gods of the earth. Irava, is it? Why, by all the gods, did you decide to—" He waves at me. "To —I can't believe that you're—I *flirted* with—I *never* flirt with women—"

I shrug, at a loss for what else to do. "I'm not a good court lady, if that makes a difference. And I needed a disguise."

"You could have just asked him—no, no, I see the point there, no decent murderer would just confess to the crime."

He spins around, glaring at the linen closet around us, then sighs and sinks down on his heels, leaning back against a stack of towels.

Slowly, I sink down too, crouching near the door.

He tugs on one of his dreadlocks, rolling the end through his fingers. I've never seen him so uncomposed.

"So what am I supposed to do with you now?" he asks.

"Trust me. I wasn't lying—the dowager threatened me, and I found...something...in her chambers."

"And you should tell Torovan about that. You should tell Tor about all of this, gods. Gods! You shouldn't be telling this to me. What the fuck am I supposed to tell Torovan?"

"No! No, don't tell him, I can't tell him, he's only just starting to trust me."

He aims a finger at me. "Which trust, I might point out, is misplaced."

"It's not," I snap back. "He needs me. I can see the weavings the other weaver left behind, and I'm going to teach him how to see it, too. And—"

I look down at my bare hands, up at him. "Women can't be court mages. Or even weavers at all, can they? Would he even let me help him, could I be any help at all, if he knew I was a woman?"

Valtair groans and thunks his head back against the stack of towels behind him.

"It is a very stupid rule, I know," he says. "I've known women who would make excellent mages. And a whole lot of men who don't."

He looks up at me, frowns. "I am glad you saved his life. Whatever you did at the demonstrations. And I think I'm a good enough judge of character to know that you're sincere when you say you're trying to help. But gods—*gods*. What is your end to all of this? Will you tell him who you are? Will you marry him? Will you tell him *before* you marry him? Because I can tell you right now, the way he talks about you, about Caleb—it's not casual, Irava. I've been fearing I may have to pry him out of Caleb's arms to put him in, well, yours." He puts a hand over his eyes. "Gods this is so ridiculous. He can't cheat on you if you're already there, can he?"

I swallow, too loud in the close quarters, the stuffy, cloying air.

Valtair's cologne is truly horrible.

"I don't know what I'm going to do," I say.

And after a moment's consideration, he says, "Well, at least you're honest about that. I don't like, not at all, keeping anything from Torovan. But I also know when something might be good for him. And you—" He shuts his mouth again, once again swallowing what he was going to say. This time, though, I don't know the answer to that.

He shakes his head and stands up, then reaches a hand down to pull me up.

"You'd better do your illusion again. And if anyone sees us coming out—well, you are a *very* cute man. I can work with that."

His lips quirk up, but it's not quite a smile. He watches me, tense, as I reweave my illusion.

"You won't tell him?" I ask, in Caleb's deeper voice again.

And I settle, my nerves calming, as I'm back in this now-familiar role. Here, in this court, it's something I know.

He shakes his head, still watching me. "No. No, I—I think this one is between you and him. But you aren't wrong to think he's unlikely to trust you after you've already lied to him."

He's quiet a moment. And I find myself holding my breath.

Valtair might be a court rake—hardly the only one, but as the king's friend and advisor, the most visible.

But he knows his power and place in the court. It's written in every casual line of his body.

With the king as distraught as he is, as consumed with his investigation as he is, how much of the kingdom's direction lately is Torovan's idea, and how much Valtair's?

For a moment, just a moment, I wonder if Torovan *should* trust his longtime friend.

"I want justice, too," he says. "Torovan's father was my king, too."

Heat washes over me at my suspicion, because Valtair and Torovan grew up together. Valtair had to have known the late king well. And the rage, the grief that flickers across his face, is plain.

"Find who did this," he says. "I want to know, and I want to keep Tor and Elsira safe. But don't you dare hurt Torovan. Don't you *dare*."

I swallow. And nod.

But I don't know how to keep that promise. And with Valtair's look turning back to exasperation, he knows that, too.

"Okay, do what you must," he says, "but please—by all the gods of all the seasons, tell him who you are. It has to come from you, and tell him soon. He's going to have to get over this, but he will, I think. If he really—yes. Yes, I think he will. Gods help me for conspiring behind his back. You do know this is minor treason? Lying to a king?"

"Like you've never lied to him?" I throw back, more a deflection than a challenge.

"Of course I have. But not *this* kind of lie."

The look he gives me is...dyspeptic. Scrutinizing. It makes me want to squirm, as if he's measuring me up for suitability for...for what?

Before I can ask, or tell him that no, I don't have any wish at all to hurt Torovan, not anymore—Valtair gives a sharp, decisive nod and slips out the closet door.

Chapter 20

After the Hunt

Torovan

When I ride home at sunset with my guards and the handful of nobles I brought with me, the pack horses laden with game, the sight of the palace tightens my throat.

We hadn't gone far on the hunt. And, truly, I know the gamekeepers stock the forest around the palace, because otherwise it would be hunted out. It isn't, in any way, a real challenge to hunt anywhere near the palace—for that, I'd need to go leagues in any direction.

But on a hunt, I can lean into the rhythm of my horse, I can draw my bow and focus the entirety of myself on my goal. I don't have to think about how the court views me, or how—or how Caleb views me—or how I'm going to turn a kingdom still in turmoil from the loss of a good and steady ruler into something that I, cold stone king that I am, can rule.

Even Caleb is afraid of me. He still offered to teach me, though. And am I a fool for riding away from that today? For needing a day not to think, but to run? To not have to think about how him teaching me could be a very, very bad idea, even though I wish to be a weaver, to right my greatest failure, with everything I am.

I keep telling myself, in the moments that I allow myself to think about it, that learning to be a weaver is for the kingdom's benefit. It's a skill that can be used in battle if I hone it well enough. Caleb could ride with me into battle. Not just a court mage, but a mage knight. Barella has had so few of those in the last hundred years. But then, Barella has managed to keep out of the worst of the wars that surrounded us.

And to stay out of those wars, I must, absolutely must, ally myself with Galenda by marrying the Princess Irava.

I bare my teeth and spur my horse to a gallop down the long tree-lined lane that leads to the front palace yard. Leaning, once again, into the feel of my horse and not thinking. Not thinking at all.

Valtair is there in the courtyard to seize my reigns when I slow, and I can tell by the set of his jaw that something is wrong. But he bares his teeth in a smile as he tries to calm my panting stallion.

I dismount, because staying on my mount will only keep him restless when he needs the attention of the grooms.

Valtair hands my mount off, and then follows me silently into the palace. Which is also not a good sign. Valtair without words is a storm waiting to happen.

And it does happen, two steps into the corridor of the royal suites. He's followed me all the way up, his steps heavier than usual, but he's waited until we are out of range of the most eager ears.

"Tor," he hisses in my ear. "You went out on a hunt? When you have a kingdom that desperately needs your attention? What by all the summer gods were you thinking?"

I shoot him a dark look. He's not mad that I went out on a hunt, though he himself can't stomach them. His small talent in elemental healing sets his empathy far too high. His talent that he conceals, because elemental magic might be tolerated in lesser noble bloodlines, but his is one of the highest.

I flex my hand in my glove—there's a bad scratch on the back of it, hastily bandaged. I'd removed my glove to better feel the balance of my bow, but a passing branch jagged the back of my hand. If Valtair knew I had that cut, he would try to fix it, because that's the person he is.

Not the uncaring player he tries to make himself out to be at court.

Well, he is a bit of that, too.

But I will fix it on my own, or find one of the palace healers. Valtair's not the only one with elemental healing, though he is the only one I actually trust.

"Let's get to your suite," Valtair says under his breath, "so I can yell at you properly. Like I should."

We exchange a look. And I resign myself, because he will certainly run through all of my flaws, going into details I don't want to think about.

I'm the king, but Thaddeus Valtair is the brother I never had.

I sigh. I'm tired, and I'm grimy, and I'm hungry now that I smell the faint hearty aroma wafting from the kitchens. I pick up my pace toward my suite, because it's better to get this over with than draw it out.

When we get to my sitting room, the candles already lit by the servants in anticipation of my return, I listen with half an ear as Valtair paces, berating me for all the reasons why I shouldn't have left the palace today. They range from the mountain of correspondence that I have been slowly dwindling down, to the palace being too unsteady right now, the mood too unsettled, for the king to be away for an entire day. He goes on, too, about my mother throwing a garden party today—something I haven't done so far in the entirety of my rule. He says she's won that little bit more social favor of the court over to her. Away from me.

And none of this, I sense, is what's truly upset him.

I carefully tug off my hunting jacket as he talks, loosen the straps of my leather armor—only light armor for a hunt. I loosen the throat lace of my under-tunic and finally turn to Valtair. Because I think I've worked it out.

"You're mad about Caleb."

He splutters to a halt. And for a moment, he just stands there, the orange flow from the hearth flickering across his face.

"Yes," he finally says.

"You're jealous. Because I've—" And I've done what? I haven't made any moves toward the mage candidate—not actual moves, anyway—I've asked him for help. Which was Valtair's suggestion, even.

I rub at my face and sink into the nearest chair, suddenly exhausted. No, I haven't eaten since when we breaked from the hunt with a lavish midday picnic in the woods. Which I hurried through, picking at my food, because in the moments when I stop I think about the woman I have to marry, the stranger, and my stomach turns to stone.

I finished quickly to get back on the hunt, not having to think.

Valtair, who hadn't been wearing his feathered hat when he met me in the courtyard, and that should be sign enough that he was distressed, grabs a hold of his hair, his face a grimace of pure frustration.

"No, I'm *not* jealous," he says, letting go. "Tor—you're going to get hurt. I know the way you look at him, just, maybe—I'm not even saying don't. Maybe he's good for you—"

"But he's not the person I'm going to marry," I say, sitting heavily back in my chair.

Valtair just stares at me, hands open, at a loss.

"I know, Valtair. I know. I can't get attached, and I'm not. He's only helping me with my investigation."

"He's teaching you how to weave," Valtair says.

I sit up sharply. "What? Did you speak to him? Is that why you're upset? I'd trust Caleb to teach me far more than Master Aldric. I already know Caleb can unravel threads if they get unstable, so there's far less danger—"

"I'm not worried about your safety!" Valtair nearly shouts. "Not in this, anyway!"

And I draw up short again. There's more he's not saying. More I don't think he will say.

"What happened today, Valtair?" I ask. "What happened with Caleb?"

"I—just—"

He looks stricken.

"I can't tell you, Tor. It's private."

"Since when have you kept anything from me—"

"Gods, Tor, a lot. I keep a lot from you. I help you with

everything, but do you even see that I'm bending everything around you right now—"

I sit up, my stomach sinking, my anger rising.

"I'm the king. My subjects should—"

He cuts at the air with his hand.

"Gah. Just—Tor. It's not mine to tell. But, just—ask him, all right? Ask him to tell you what he told me. It's nothing... uh...bad, but just...just ask. And that's all I'm going to say. King or not."

My stomach knots. Because gods, I shouldn't have said what I said, calling him my subject, not my friend. I know that. I know.

But what thing that he learned from Caleb could make him this upset? It takes a lot to rattle Valtair.

"Okay," I say. "I will."

But I'm not sure that I will. Because I don't want to ruin the one possibly bright point of hope in my life just now.

"Do I need to send him from the palace?" I ask, hardly wanting the answer.

I'm not sure I'd do it if he says yes.

But Valtair shakes his head, and I crumple back in more relief than I'd ever admit to.

"No, not that kind of thing. Like I said, it's not bad. But— and the rest is not really my business."

And now my insides are re-knotting themselves.

"I'll see Caleb tomorrow," I say.

He nods. "Right. Now—you had a long day, you haven't had anything to eat." He takes a breath, and I watch him try to calm down, to change the subject.

And why can't I not be an ogre to my friends, too?

"Do you want to raid the kitchen?" Valtair asks. And puts on his best mischievous grin, waggling his eyebrows at me.

I take it like the peace offering it is.

I'm not sure I have the energy or will for that after this conversation, but I nod, and push myself up. Because Valtair's good will means a lot to me.

And because being alone gives me time to think.

Chapter 21

Valuable

Irava

I don't sleep well the night after my confession to Lord Valtair. I'm afraid he'll tell Torovan, and the thought of Torovan finding out from anyone but me that the man he's trusting to help him catch his father's killer is lying to him, too, sits sourly in my throat.

Sits sourly in my soul.

But can I tell him? *Can* I tell him that the man who offered to teach him, and all the trust that will need, is a lie?

In the Great Hall the next morning, the chatter and clatter fades to background noise as I push soggy oats around my bowl. I'm not hungry, and I've only managed to eat a few spoonfuls. Princess Elsira decided to sit with me, and that's making some waves in the nobility around us, and I know I should be paying attention. Everything in me knows that. But it's just buzzing in my ears. All I can think about is him.

Torovan.

He's at the high table, and I've been doing my best not to look at him. Because I know there's speculation now. There's always speculation in a court. He sought me out yesterday, at my own quarters. At Caleb's quarters. No, he didn't go into my room, but that's hardly the point.

I feel the weight of his gaze before I see it. That prickle on the back of my neck, the tightness in my chest. I look up and his gray-green eyes catch mine, freezing me in place, my spoon halfway to my mouth.

The furrow between his brows smooths ever so slightly. The corner of his mouth twitches up for a heartbeat before his face closes off again.

My heart stutters out of rhythm.

Was that a *smile?* Here? For me?

For Caleb.

Some of what Elsira's been saying catches up to me. She's been saying he actually looks happy this morning, and she hasn't seen him that way in months. And maybe that's why she's chosen to sit with me. She knows I met with him two days ago. And the day before that.

This is bad. This is *bad.*

Can't she think that he's happier because of his hunt? I heard he brought back several stags, a good number of smaller game. There will be a feast tonight, it's already been announced.

But I offered to teach him. He confessed what he sees as weakness to me, and I didn't look away. Gods, he'd been braced as if for ridicule—a king braced against the opinion of a mage candidate. How far has his own weaver's training beaten him down? How far did Master Aldric drive down his confidence?

If Torovan's happier because of me, it's because of the illusion of the man I've created, and guilt squirms in my gut. I wanted to uncover the truth, not twist it further. But the more time we spend together, the more entangled we become.

And I don't know how to get out of this mess.

I don't know if I truly want to.

"Caleb, are you listening?" Elsira asks, annoyance coloring her tone. "I said Nikolai told me he's planning to restore his reputation, another demonstration of some sort. I expect that will go better than his first demonstration, but I would like—please—for you to keep a watch, Caleb? To keep him safe. I don't always think he knows his limits."

I blink, refocus on her. "He's what?"

I glance aside to another table where Nikolai is seated with some of the higher nobility. He can't hear us from there, but that doesn't mean the conversation won't make its way back to him.

I look between Elsira's eyes. She's worried. And maybe that's why she sat with me today. Maybe this has nothing to do with me and Torovan at all.

"Yes," I say, "of course." Though how I'm supposed to keep a watch on Nikolai—to protect *him*—while keeping my meetings with the king is beyond me. I saved Nikolai once, and he's been angry with me ever since. If I save him again, I doubt that will get better. He's already threatened me.

I swallow. I hope this demonstration he's planned doesn't have anything to do with his threat.

"Thank you," Elsira says fervently, laying a hand on my arm. And I try to smile back, because I'm going to *have* to help her now. She sincerely asked. And I don't want Nikolai's magic blowing up and hurting people—I truly don't, no matter if I wouldn't mind so much if he blew himself up in the process.

And she's Torovan's sister. And a princess—and I know all

about being near the center but not inside it. Of course I'll help her.

My eyes stray back to Torovan. The man who's steadily taken over my thoughts, waking and sleeping.

He sent me a summons this morning to meet this afternoon. A proper summons, thank the gods he realized that coming to my quarters wasn't a good idea.

The dowager isn't at breakfast today, which is typical for when the king is. I still don't know what threat she holds over me, or what threat is over her as well. I need to know more. And knowing more means spending time with the king.

The thought floods me with more anticipation than dread. Do I even know what I want anymore? Freedom was my only goal when I came here. But now...now this broken king is drawing me toward him in a way I don't understand.

No, I do understand. And it terrifies me.

How can I, a princess who's failed at being a princess in every way, even savor his small smiles meant for my disguise?

Valtair is right that I should tell him. Lessen the fallout, because I know there will be one, and that terrifies me, too.

But the memory of his eyes when I'd offered to teach him weaving, naked with hope, holds me back. Wouldn't it be better to never tell him? To never hurt him like that? I cannot hurt this man. I will not be the one to extinguish that fledgling light inside him.

Maybe I could stay as Caleb. I want to use my magic for something other than my making my mother angry and making me a court pariah, and I could do good here as a court mage. With him.

But I know my mother betrothed me for a reason, and it

wasn't just out of spite. And Torovan agreed to it because his kingdom needs this alliance, too.

Maybe I don't have to decide today. Today, I will go to him again. I will do what I can to help him find the truth he so desperately seeks. And for today, I will allow myself to pretend. To get lost in gray-green eyes and the thrill of being seen. Really seen, maybe for the first time.

I'm valuable here for myself. And that's a lie I'm not yet willing to give up, either.

Chapter 22

The Kiss

Irava

"Caleb," the king says as his guards let me into his study. He stands from his desk, shoving a stray strand of dark hair back behind his ear. He smiles. And he is *gorgeous* when he smiles. For a moment, my heart stops, and I stand just inside the door. Frozen, unsure of what I should do next.

I should probably run. Oh gods, I should probably run and make Caleb disappear before this can go on any further.

Torovan hesitates as he comes around his desk, smile faltering.

So I smile back. I have to. I bow, and he makes a dismissing wave as if we're old friends, but we're not.

We're not.

And when I straighten again, some of the wariness has returned to his eyes, and it breaks me to know that it's justified.

"Shall we?" he asks, waving toward the door that leads to his father's suite.

"Of course, Your Majesty."

"Call me Torovan," he says over his shoulder as he strides through the door. "If you're going to teach me, I can't be a king to you. I have to be your student."

And what am I to do with that?

His mood is weird today, alternating between that wariness and a glowing, bubbling excitement. And then he stiffens all up again as we move back into his father's bedroom, and he sees his father's empty, made-up bed.

Does he want me to survey the room again? Or, no, he wants to see it for himself. He wants to see what I saw, and so he's brought me here again.

Some tutors in my mother's court would be ever effusive, always bowing and never admitting that any of the queen's children could ever give the wrong answer to a math problem. My favorites, though, treated me as an equal. They respected me enough to tell me when I was wrong and help me find the right way.

So I'm going to do the latter. Torovan already asked me to use his name.

"T—Torovan," I say, and his name shoots as much electricity through me as when he said mine.

He looks up at me, expectant.

So I take a breath, wave toward the bed. "How much can you see?"

"None of it," he says, turning back to the bed. He touches the brocade bedcover, the rings on one hand glinting. "I can feel an angst in this room, but I'm not sure if that's not just my own grief."

I move closer, inhaling his scent. A little different today. Musky, earthy, as if he went to bed after his hunt without washing. And maybe he did.

And I must, I absolutely must, keep my mind on teaching him just now, and nothing else.

So I walk him through what I learned about how to focus my own concentration to better sense the flows of reality around me. The careful breathing exercises. The softening of my focus. Setting my will to see reality and be able to move it as necessary.

He follows me, only breaking my instruction to ask questions on if he's doing something right. Which is good—he's not following me without thinking it through first. He's eager, but not reckless. And as I walk him through the steps, we draw closer and closer until we're nearly touching shoulders beside the bed. Both our hands reached out to touch the textured surface.

"I see..." Torovan squints down at the covers. Not quite a glare, but pure concentration. "I see...it's slippery. No. Like the threads...are too relaxed."

I nod. "Yes. Yes! That's it. And can you see how they should be? How they should be projecting possibilities of what could happen here? Even the possibility of you touching the covers now—that should be reflected in the threads of reality here."

He brushes his hand across the bedcover, his brow furrowing even further. Then his face crumples. He draws back. "No. I can see that they're duller than they should be, but I wouldn't have known even that without you pointing it out."

He turns away, raking a hand back through his hair. He pulls a metal band from his pants pocket and hastily pulls his hair back. It's still messy, but it's out of his eyes.

It's making my body do things I really don't want to think about.

I'm staring at him and he meets my gaze.

I quickly look away.

"Okay," I say, "let's go back out to the desk chair, and you can compare what that looks like to what you saw here. This is only the first day—learning how to see with your weaver's senses takes time, and it's not even the easiest part. Maybe we should go back to what you already know, then I can see how best to—"

He stalks out of the room without letting me finish, and I hurry after. Is he mad at me for suggesting that he has a lot to learn? But I don't know what he knows. And I don't know how to teach him without assessing that. He seemed so eager the last time, so afraid to hope—and maybe he thought he'd just learn in half an hour? That a king should be able to learn weaving faster than everyone else because it was, what, his due?

It took me years. Years of careful study and experimentation. I earned every bit of the weaving I have. He's not going to get this in half an hour.

"Here," he says, shoving out the chair. "Show me how to see this."

"You're not going to get this in a day," I say. "And the process is the same. You need to slow down, let yourself really look at—"

"I can't slow down in the middle of a battle. Or when my life is in danger. You didn't slow down when you assessed the threat of the Nikolai's magic unraveling and did something about it. I need you to teach me how to do that."

I gape at him. "Torovan, that takes *years*—months, at best, if you're practicing all the time. I can't teach you—"

"Then are you rescinding your offer?" he asks. He's going cold again. Cold as the day I first saw him.

I fight the urge to take a step back. I know how to deal with my brothers when they're in a mood, when they feel like life owes them more than it's capable of giving at the moment.

And that is one thing I learned through my weaving—life owes none of us anything. It only works with the material that it has. That material can be molded, but not without will, not without intent and skill.

"I'm not," I say, as steadily as I can. "But I can't teach you that quickly. It has nothing to do with how much you want it, or your strength of willpower. Or your station, or birth. You have to learn those kinds of reflexes over time. You have to learn what the music of reality sounds like—you can't just pick up a lute and play it in an afternoon. This is like that." I spread my hands. "I can and I will give you everything I know. But I can't give you the time it takes to learn it. You have to take that time yourself."

He deflates. I watch the anger—a show of anger, maybe, less than the actual flame—ebb out of him as he leans against the desk. He stares at the chair like he wants to sit in it, but doesn't dare.

I step closer. "Torovan. Please. Please don't give up on this —it just takes time—"

"I don't have the time."

He rubs at his eyes, as if he can clear his vision of whatever he is—or isn't—seeing.

He looks up at me.

"My mother and sisters could be in as much danger as my father. I could be, and I don't yet have an heir. And I—I want to carry on my father's legacy, to uphold his policies of reform, but was that what got him killed? Will that endanger my family? I've been frozen, Caleb, I'm absolutely terrified to rule my own kingdom."

He straightens, starts to pace around the room. "And I have three months—no, two now—before I'm to marry a woman I've never met before, and promise to keep her safe in my home. And I can't promise that if I can't see where the problem is, I can't see it coming again—"

I still, from my toes in my boots straight up to the illusory hairs on my head. Me. He wants to protect me, a woman he's never met—he thinks he's never met.

I should tell him. I should tell him now before this goes any further. And he'll hate me for it, I know. I've seen how volatile his moods are, how shakable his confidence is. How much he hides behind his icy demeanor when he's afraid. When he mistrusts.

"What do I do?" he asks, turning back to me. He stops pacing, and it's worse, because his attention, all of his attention, is focused on me. "How can I keep them safe? Can you teach me at least that? Can you—can you join my guards, maybe? Tell me when anything is amiss, even while you're teaching me? How long will it take?"

I can't join his guards. I can't be two people at once. I can't both be Caleb and his wife.

He steps closer. His eyes are heating.

"I wish, I truly wish, I didn't have to bring a stranger into this mess."

And who does he think he's talking to now, if not a stranger? He doesn't know me. *He doesn't know me.*

"Please," he says. "Please tell me you'll stay close by my side."

My knees are threatening to buckle. Because the heat in his eyes has gone from anger to...something else.

And I have a feeling he's asking an entirely different question than he had a moment before.

I've never seen anyone look at me with the hunger, the desperation, he's looking at me with now. The...respect.

He doesn't know me. But he trusts me. He trusts me enough to ask me to protect his family. To teach him. To let me see his insecurities. To let me see his fear, and his hope.

And I'm about to crush it.

My eyes burn as I take him in. This one last trusting moment before it all goes away again.

I open my mouth—

And he closes the final gap between us, and presses his lips to mine.

I shudder, and panic, pulling on the threads of my illusion to bring it fully into reality. To fully become a man. He can't feel anything from me but Caleb, he can't know anything but Caleb.

But—but I'm unprepared for the heat to shoot down into anatomy that I've never had before. My body awakening with so much sensation I feel like I'm on fire.

I kiss him back. If I'm only going to have this moment, just this once, I kiss him back. Wrapping my hands around the back of his neck, holding him close, pressing tight, feeling *everything*. Absolutely everything that I will never feel again.

His arms surround me. And mine him. A moment of mutual protection.

And then I let go.

Chapter 23

Too Much Reality

Irava

He stares at me, panting.

And I stare back, a little shocky.

Finally, he blinks. "I'm sorry—"

"No," I say, shaking my head. "I'm—"

And I need to tell him who I am. I need to tell him with an urgency that is tearing me apart.

I want to kiss him again. I want to make the fire alight again.

Carefully, oh so carefully, I ease my grip on my illusion, adjusting it back to visible, but not tangible. The riot of sensations in my body shifts, goes back to something more familiar, if hardly more manageable.

I want this man. I want him with a need that I've never wanted anything, or anyone, before.

And the look in his eyes, still so hopeful, so balanced on that edge between hope and need and fear of rejection, breaks me.

I step back. "I'm sorry. Your Majesty. You're betrothed—"

"It's a political marriage," he says. "I don't—" He swallows, his throat bobbing. "I don't love her. And it's not impossible for a king to have a lover at court, even an open lover, if the marriage is political and both of them agree—"

"But does she agree?"

I don't know why I'm asking this. I don't know why I'm throwing this at him, because this isn't his fault. It's so, so far from his fault.

I take another step back.

He takes another step forward. "Caleb, please. I'm not asking you, even, to do anything in the shadows. I'm only asking—"

He tries to rake a hand through his hair, grimaces when he finds his hair still bound back, and now he's messed it up.

I want to fix it, to run my fingers through his thick, dark hair—

I curl my hands into my sides.

"I just want—" he says, and it's a plea.

I know. I want it too. The regard of someone who sees me. Who *sees* me. And that thought leaves me with a gulf in my stomach that I don't know how to cross. Because Caleb isn't who I am. At least, not all of me. Isn't he? My magic, my ability—for once—to use it without censure. That—that is me. That part of me wants this man to look at me like he's looking now.

But so does the part of me that is Irava.

Can I be two people? Can I be Caleb with the king, and Irava as his wife? If this is the only way to have his regard, would that be so terrible?

But I know the answer to that. I know, because every man who's ever tried to get close to me before backed off when he learned just how skilled I was with my weaving. And most never approached at all, royal though I am.

It would never be enough to never have him as myself. All of myself.

"Do you..." I have to ask. "Do you only prefer men?"

His brow crinkles. "No, I mostly prefer women—but some men, *you*, Caleb—"

"Then is there a chance you might love your wife?"

"I—"

His eyes flicker to anger, back again to something that looks like exhaustion. He holds up his hands.

"Forgive me. I pressed further than I should have. Gods, and I've made a fool of myself, and a mess of this, too—"

"No," I say. "No, I just—I can teach you. I am happy to teach you. But I can't—we can't—"

He holds up a hand again. A tired, understanding hand. And I feel cold with the life that's drained out of him.

"Torovan—"

It's on my lips. To tell him who I am. To tell him he doesn't have to choose between Caleb and his wife, because we are the same person.

But the words stick in my throat as the fear rises. The fear of marrying someone, living with someone, who knows I betrayed him. Who despises me for that. I've seen his cold side. It's returning again now, and I hate myself for that.

But do I have another choice but to tell him? I can't be his dalliance, while he cheats on me with...me.

"I'll—" I swallow. "I'll leave."

He closes his eyes, takes a breath. "No—no. I do want to learn. If you'll forgive me, Caleb, for my presumption."

And I nod, though it kills me to pin this on him.

He's worried about not having enough willpower, but I am certainly no one to talk about willpower.

I can't tell him yet. I just...can't.

"She could love you," I say. "For whatever this advice is worth, I think she should have that chance."

And then, later, if he found he could never have it in his heart to love me as Irava, then maybe Caleb could return to the court. Maybe I would take half a life with the regard of his eyes as better than a whole life without them.

Or maybe I've read too much into his question.

He was only asking for a dalliance, wasn't he?

His attraction is only lust. He can't love me after only a few days. He can't love a man who doesn't exist.

Can he?

His brows rise and he looks down. A look I recognize from his mother.

"Perhaps that is wise," he says. Then he smiles ruefully. "If you're still willing to teach me, I'm still willing to learn. And I promise, I will be as patient as it's possible for me to be. And as chaste."

His voice is raw, though, and there's a hurt there that I don't know how to handle. He's trying to hide it, but I've also trained myself to see through illusions to the core of reality. And his core is quaking.

Would it hurt, would it be so bad, to have a few weeks together? To share that comfort, to share that hope? Never going far, but getting close. Would that be so horrible? And then I'd let go, and marry him as a stranger. And maybe, possibly, he might learn to love me again.

Would Lord Valtair kill me for that?

Maybe, maybe not. But would I forgive myself for it?

I smile back at him. And I know he's seeing layers in me that I don't really want him to see right now, too. Just not the ones he needs to see.

"I will teach you, of course, Your Majesty. And help however I can."

He sighs. "Okay. Then—I want to see the altered reality on this chair." And he stands apart. He is that kind that he stands apart. How could I ever have thought this man a tyrant?

My hands are trembling as I carefully walk him through, again, the steps to seeing too much of reality.

Chapter 24

Volatile

Irava

It's been two days, and he hasn't summoned me back.

Is that what I want?

I want to be pressing my lips to his again. I want to tangle my hands in his hair. I want—

I haven't been able to stop thinking about that kiss. Or what it did to me. Or that this is the man I'm actually promised to marry. And he doesn't know who I am.

He doesn't know me.

And I don't know what to do.

∼

The door to Master Aldric's study creaks, and I hesitate before entering. I haven't been summoned by the king, but I have been summoned by Master Aldric.

"Ah, Caleb," Master Aldric says, closing a book on his desk. He nods at the book tucked under my arm. Which I finished by candlelight last night, because it was better than thinking about Torovan. "I see you've finished the book I lent you."

"I have, Master Aldric." I place the thick, leather-bound tome on his desk. Carefully, as if any more noise than necessary will crack my brittle shell. "Thank you." I give a small bow.

"And apparently, it's sunk in," he says, raising an eyebrow. "Your court manners have improved if you're getting so close to the king."

My cheeks flush with heat, and I pull all of my focus back to here, to now. I clasp my hands in front of me and bow my head. Because I'm the mage candidate here, and he is the master. No matter if I'm certain I have more actual power.

Master Aldric smiles, and while his face is still grandfatherly, this role of the teacher he likes to play, there's an edge to his gaze that tells something else. Cruelty, maybe. Or even jealousy.

And now I know that this is the man who crushed Torovan's willpower, and I want to know why.

I look up, meeting his eyes. Which is probably a mistake. But my time at this court as Caleb is probably coming to a close soon anyway, as much as that twists my gut.

It must.

"Has he asked you to teach him?" Master Aldric asks. And before I can decide what to say, he goes on, as if he already knows the answer. "I must warn you, Caleb, and I do not say this lightly—there is danger in training King Torovan to become a fully adept weaver."

"Danger?" I blurt, my heart racing. "I know what I'm doing, I'm not going to let him lose control. You saw what I did at—"

"You are steady, yes. Your own willpower is strong. But

Torovan's temperamental nature and the burden of his father's death make his control over his willpower...volatile, at best. You must understand that his emotions can cloud his judgment. You've already seen what too much ambition with too little control can do to a weaver."

He means Nikolai, though I know he'd never say that out loud. This man is a politician through and through.

But Nikolai is the absolute furthest person I can think of from Torovan.

I look down to hide my glare. Who paid Master Aldric off, in favors or actual funds, to stop teaching the king? The wound that left in Torovan is not small. He thinks he has no solid willpower, and even if a king has no desire to be a weaver, every king must have faith in his own will.

This man stole that from Torovan. And for what? I don't believe for a minute that the king is too volatile to safely perform weaving.

A knot forms in my stomach, tight and heavy.

Or could what Master Aldric said be true? I'm self-taught, everything I learned was from the few books I could find and experimenting on my own. But Master Aldric has the resources of a kingdom and years—decades—as a court mage. Could he be right, that Torovan's personality is too volatile to be a weaver? Torovan can go from calm to wrath in a heartbeat.

Or is it the other way around? Has he been so damaged by being told that he *is* damaged that he's become volatile? He has reasons, deep reasons, to mistrust those around him.

I think I'm right. I think this man in front of me is far more dangerous to the king than his own willpower.

Master Aldric isn't telling me not to teach Torovan—he can't tell me that. I must do what the king wills, and the king outranks everyone in this kingdom. But his warning can easily sabotage whatever Torovan and I have with his learning, if I let it.

"I understand," I say. And meet his eyes again. And try to let go of my own anger and my defiance, as best I can.

He nods. "You have much potential, Caleb. You've proven that to me these last days. And I would like to train you as my successor in this court."

My breath catches. Even as I know that this statement is tied to the last—he's not threatening me about teaching Torovan, he can't.

But he's dangling a bait that would be nearly impossible for me to resist—if I really was Caleb Ailin.

And I'm tempted. I'm so, so tempted. The king wants me as Caleb. I like my life here as Caleb, I love training with the other mages, feeling like my magic means something here. Like I can truly help here, and not be a burden and a pariah.

I...I actually like being Caleb.

But whatever Caleb is to me, whatever this has become, it's not all of who I am.

Master Aldric's waiting for my answer. Like a snake, luring in his prey.

So I smile wide, and I nod. "Thank you, Master Aldric. I would like that very much."

"Good!" he says. "Of course, we will need to keep this between us for the time being, but I would like to see you an extra hour every few days, I'll let you know when."

And I would bet they'd be days when he knows I'm going to teach Torovan.

If Torovan ever calls me to teach him again.

So I'll see how this plays out, too. Do I have any other choice?

My other choice is to leave.

But even the memory of that kiss sends a shiver through me. And these threats, all of these people trying to control the space around the king—I don't like that at all.

As I leave Master Aldric's study, I still don't know what to do.

Chapter 25

Rain

Torovan/Irava

Torovan

I should never have kissed him. I'd thought, the way he was looking at me, the way he'd also drawn closer, that he was feeling the same attraction. He hadn't been able to look away. His eyes had widened, his lips had parted. I'd thought—

And I don't, certainly, deserve that he's still willing to teach me or help me at all.

I am a king now. I keep forgetting this power. I knew it as a prince, yes, I knew that people would be more inclined to say yes to my whims, and I overstepped Caleb's bounds.

Maybe it's best that I haven't summoned him for a few days—and it's not him, it's me, my own courage, my own shame. Or maybe I shouldn't summon him at all. Really, I never should have asked for his help.

I've been telling myself that I asked for my investigations, and that's true. It is. But when I look at him, his finely featured face beneath his ever-crooked spectacles, my insides twist in a way I can't define. When I'm in the same room with him, I stop breathing.

It's been torment every meal that he's in the same vast hall as me. Because I've schooled myself not to look. I absolutely will not look and coerce him into something that he doesn't want.

He was arguing for the sake of my future wife, for gods' sakes.

And he isn't wrong.

So is this willpower? Is this how I learn the willpower to be a weaver, to ruin the only man I've ever wanted not just to kiss, but to hold, to have by my hearth in all the long nights, to have in my bed—

I swallow.

Surely—surely, my regard for him hasn't gone that far.

I'm in my study, barricaded behind my desk with a mountain of fresh correspondence and petitions to work through. And I'm doing it, woodenly, reading only enough to understand the general idea of a matter before I move on.

I'll order more books, I'll find out about weaving on my own. Isn't that what many weavers do anyway? Not all have the privilege of a tutor.

Or maybe I should just leave the weaving to the court mages. That's the proper order of things, isn't it?

Should I leave the weaving to *this* particular court mage?

Will it be torment to see him every day, when I have my new wife by my side?

My hands curl into tight points of fury by my sides. Fury at the kingdom, at the necessity of this marriage I don't want, at the injustice of not being able to properly get to know a man I think I'm falling in love with, because he's a village mage, and I'm a king. At not having the chance to even know if it *is* love.

I stare numbly at the far wall of my study, and time slowly passes. The hearth crackles.

It's late into the night when I leave my study. I go straight to my rooms, and Valtair knows me well enough to not disturb me just now. He surely knows I'm not in the mood.

But I almost wish he would. Anything to break up the roil of thoughts in my head. They won't stop. They keep starting, and ending, with a man I kissed that I hardly even know.

How can he so arrest my attention when I have barely known him at all?

There might, at least, be some diversion from this madness.

In the corridor that morning, before breakfast, my mother had suggested I hold a garden party, as she did when I was on the hunt. Which, she also pointed out, I should have done instead of leaving for a hunt that day. That my people need to see me among them, to be reminded that I'm above them.

Never mind that people are often stifling to me, the people of the court especially, when the motion of the hunt is...breath.

While I'm not usually inclined to take my mother's suggestions, when I mentioned it to Valtair at breakfast, he also thought it was a good and necessary thing to do.

I know the people think I'm a cold-hearted king. Maybe a day in the sunshine will soften that. My mother wants the people to see me and fear me, as she says is the proper order of things. But that wasn't how my father ruled.

Maybe a day in the sunshine will get me out of my maze of thoughts.

Or maybe not.

Valtair also hasn't prodded me these last few days about

discovering Caleb's secret, whatever it was that had him so upset—I know about secrets, and I have no wish to strip Caleb of any more dignity than I have.

But maybe this garden party will break up the monotony of my days. The single-mindedness of my thoughts. And while my mother suggested it, it's a chance to start breaking her social hold on my court by being present myself.

Maybe it's best I put affairs of the heart aside altogether, and fully rule my kingdom. My mother would certainly approve of that.

It takes a day to prepare for the party. And even then, I know I've sent my staff scrambling. It must, of course, be far more lavish an affair than the party my mother so recently had. And in a larger courtyard of the garden. I am the king, after all, and she is the dowager.

It's about time I start acting, in public, like the king I am. No more skulking about the corridors. No more consorting with mage candidates.

On the day of the garden party, I sit on the garden throne that my guards carried out for me, feeling the fool but carrying my position as proudly as I ever have. Valtair stands beside me, and Elsira is drifting around the edges of the crowd of nobles as a lute and drum band plays in one corner of the wide garden courtyard.

The morning is unusually warm, and I do welcome the freshness of the air, the promise of warmer days to come. In the garden courtyard, we're surrounded on all sides by hedges, the center flagstones filled with an array of the usual court suspects—nobles, a few foreign dignitaries that have been hanging around Barella like vultures, my mother and her set—who are holding court at the opposite corner from me—and the court mages and mage candidates.

I haven't yet seen Caleb, but the day is still early. Perhaps he was given a task he couldn't get out of. He has that right, I haven't summoned him.

Perhaps he doesn't want to see me at all.

I look up to where the servant behind me has drifted from his position of holding the shade over my head.

"Pay attention," I snap to him, and he startles, repositions the long rod attached to a light woven mat.

Valtair leans close to me, says in a low voice, "Would you two please stop fighting and make up so that we can go back to you having a semblance of joy in your life again?"

Well. He *hadn't* been poking hard into my life the last few days. Has he decided that now, in the open, is the best time to have this conversation?

I clench my jaw. "Not your concern."

"It is when you're snapping at everyone around you. Do you really want to be the tyrant at your own party, Tor? The entire point of this is for you to gain social favor."

I squeeze the arms of my chair, stand up—and stop as I see Caleb enter the courtyard.

The air leaves me in a rush, leaves me dizzy and grasping after whatever I've stood up to do, because I've now forgotten.

Leaves from a nearby tree paint a dappled pattern of light and shadow across his pale face, his brown hair. Does he look paler than usual, more wan? I saw him pushing at his food at breakfast this morning, in the one moment of weakness that I looked. He'd been hunched over his meal, not talking to those around him. Had I only seen him in one bad moment? Am I seeing that same tension in him now?

Caleb freezes when he sees me looking at him.

He's dressed the same as he always is—I think he might only own two or three sets of clothing, because I've seen them all before. And I know I should look away. I need to look away. But I can't.

It's not rational the pull he has over me. It's not anything I can quantify, and I don't think it's good for either of us.

I start toward him before my thoughts can catch up to me.

"Tor—" Valtair says, sounding just a little bit desperate.

I shake my sleeve out of his attempt to grab me, an attempt that with anyone else might have ended in his death. With Valtair, my guards don't even flinch.

So instead Valtair follows me, until I turn and shoot a withering glare at him. And then, miracle of miracles, he backs off.

"Your Majesty," Caleb says as I approach, dipping into a low bow. More flowery, more formal than usual.

I stop in front of him.

Yes, we're in public. I can't say any of the things that I've suddenly found I need to. I can't properly make my apologies, or my meager excuses for not asking him back again. For asking him to help me at all.

So instead I say, because yes, we are in public, and I should have said it before, "Thank you, Mage Candidate Ailin, for saving my life. For saving lives in my court, for protecting the life of another mage candidate. For that, you have my most sincere gratitude."

Caleb's eyes flick between mine. His lips part. And despite everything, despite knowing it's wrong, despite him pushing me back, I want to kiss him again. And I don't think I'm mistaking the hunger in his eyes as well. He wants to kiss me, too.

But then, I was mistaken before.

Wasn't I?

He drops his gaze. Bows again. Tucks a lock of wavy hair that fell into his eyes behind his ear.

Gods.

"Thank you, Your Majesty. It was my honor and duty to serve."

My insides clench with disappointment, with…with I don't know what. He owes me nothing. I owe him so much more than I've given him. His help in validating that my father's death wasn't an accident is the deepest debt in itself.

And I'm doing him no favors here by singling him out in public, am I?

I did him no favors at all by suggesting that he might wish to become my lover, but never to be more than that.

Gods. How much of an ogre am I?

∽

Irava

I STARE up into Torovan's eyes, watch distress ripple across his chiseled features. I thought, for a terrifying moment, he wanted to kiss me again. In public.

Not that I don't want him to, disaster that it would be.

But he's looking lost now, like I've slain his hope again.

He has no idea what I'm doing to him. I shouldn't even be here at this party, I shouldn't be at the palace at all.

I'd resolved the night before to leave for good. I'm only going to hurt him the further this goes on—but though he knows the danger around him now from the weaving I saw in his father's bedchamber, he still can't protect against it.

And whether Master Aldric was the weaver who was working against Torovan's father or not, I don't trust him at all to protect the king. He also tried to warn me off from the king, like the dowager.

So I'm here.

I'll have to leave at some point soon, and come back as myself to marry this man, but for now—for now, I'll do what I can to protect him. Whatever that might look like.

And right now, that's attending this party.

Torovan takes an awkward half-step, then waves back toward his throne, a dark brow raised in question. His eyes—gods, those eyes—imploring. Maybe even a little pleading.

He's looking skittish, uncertain, like...like he was the one who did wrong, not me. And I want to shut my eyes and burn.

I bow again and follow him back. Because I can't very well refuse the attention of the king in public. And because I do want to be close. Because I'm uneasy about the dowager and Master Aldric, and I'm uneasy about what Elsira said about Nikolai, and that Nikolai hasn't gone out of his way to hate on me in the last few days.

Everything has been...too quiet. With far too much ordinary time to think about the man who's now settling himself again on his throne.

I scan the crowd for Nikolai—he's near the Dowager Queen's corner of the courtyard, not looking our way. But I know he'll see me near the king. I know it will only heat his anger. Even if he hasn't threatened me in the last few days, I'm absolutely sure he hasn't forgotten his grudge.

I've seen Nikolai brazenly flirting with the men of the court these last days, too, and none of the women—is that what Elsira meant about a demonstration? Is he going to try to angle for the affections of the king, the affections that Torovan's rumored to show to me?

Torovan doesn't tell me to stand beside him, so I take my place beside Lord Valtair—which isn't a good option. Valtair gives me a narrowed look, but he doesn't protest. Torovan's under the shade, and when he sees us still in the sun, he waves over two more servants to hold their shade mats above us.

And I feel exposed, too exposed, under this cover.

At least Valtair is an ally. In protecting the king, at least.

Torovan and Valtair start idly chatting about grain exports, though I'm certain Torovan isn't interested in that right now. Torovan's eyes keep sliding toward me.

I try not to swat at a fly that starts bothering my nose.

Slowly, the late morning daylight starts to dim.

I frown and look up. The sky is thickening with clouds, heavy with the promise of rain. But the sky was clear minutes ago, I'm sure of it.

Torovan breaks off his conversation and looks up, too.

"Didn't the elementalists say this would be a clear day today?"

He looks over toward one of the other court mages hovering a few paces away to his right. It's an older elementalist who I've only briefly met in my mage training.

The mage approaches and bows. "Yes, Sire, all predictions were for clear skies today. It should not rain until later this week."

"The predictions are wrong," Torovan says, with a dangerous edge to his voice.

Torovan stands, and Valtair snaps his fingers at a nearby servant.

"Go, get people to bring out canopies," Valtair says, "we need to get them set up quickly."

A drop hits my head, then another. In the not so far distance, thunder crackles with an ominous boom.

Torovan turns to me. "Weaver. Can you weave away this storm?"

I look again at the sky. I have practiced weather weaving, though not as much or as well as I've practiced illusions and constructs. It takes a lot of concentration and willpower to harness the raw powers of nature, to convince them to calm into a smoother path. This sort of weaving can be dangerous—but I can do it.

I start to nod, when Nikolai shows up in front of the king.

"Your Majesty," he says with great seriousness, "I can weave away this storm."

Oh, no. My arms prickle with foreboding, my thoughts finally starting to kick out of their stupor around Torovan.

I glance toward Princess Elsira, who's now talking with a noblewoman on the other side of the king. Is *this* the demonstration that Nikolai was planning?

Did Nikolai call this storm?

I open my mouth to say that's a bad idea for Nikolai to weave the storm—but can I say that here, in front of the king, in front of the court? When Nikolai is a rival mage candidate, and everyone, by now, knows he has a grudge against me? And that I have the ear of the king?

Can I set myself above Nikolai when he has the power of birth and I, as Caleb, do not?

I shut my mouth again.

Torovan frowns at me, but when I give no response, the king nods to Nikolai. Nikolai has been giving informal demonstrations of his weaving since he arrived at the palace, without any other incidents like that first day, and people's opinions have swayed back to him. Because of course they have, with him being the son of a powerful noble. Several of the courtiers, now, are asking for Nikolai to weave the storm away, too. Several of the men he's flirted with, and I'm wondering now at the purpose of that, too.

I will, at least, be on hand if Nikolai's magic goes astray. And maybe it won't. He hasn't overstretched too much in practice, either. Maybe he will redeem himself and stop threatening me. Maybe I'll fade from his priorities as he shines again, and wouldn't that be a good outcome?

But he throws one look at me over his shoulder, one smug, self-satisfied look that makes all the hairs on my body stand on end.

This is bad. This is really, really bad. But he's already moving to the center of the courtyard, already reaching up both hands to start weaving the threads of the oncoming storm.

And it's too late now to stop whatever's about to happen.

I tense as people rapidly retreat to the hedge walls.

I watch as Nikolai begins to weave the storm.

Chapter 26

The Vortex

Irava

Air gathers to Nikolai and crackles with a tangible energy, the storm protesting his attempts to manipulate it. I squint through the gathering wind as Nikolai waves his hands about, plucking at multiple threads of reality with each. His brow is furrowed in tight concentration. This sort of weaving is dangerous, even for me.

And Torovan watches me. Because he knows. He knows I'm tense, and that this is all probably a bad idea.

Where is Master Aldric? I break my gaze from Nikolai to search the courtyard and find Master Aldric across it, toward the dowager's group. The dowager is looking up at the sky, too, her face serene.

Master Aldric meets my eyes. And I'm not sure what that means, but he doesn't seem eager to do anything about this himself. If he even can.

I watch, my heart hammering in my throat, as Nikolai—again—begins to lose control of his magic.

I don't hesitate. It might be my end at court, but a

miswoven storm could become a hurricane. I've read about it happening, but I've never seen it, and I don't want to see it today.

The threads of reality around Nikolai are already greedily trying to undo whatever he's doing. The oncoming storm is growing stronger, thunder crackling, making a few of the courtiers scream.

In an ordinary storm, that might be ridiculous. Or at very least, an overreaction.

In this storm, though, they are right to be afraid.

This storm has so much *reality* gathering behind it, lashing out at Nikolai's attempts to change it.

I step up beside Nikolai and focus on the threads of reality above us, plucking his own threads out of the air and bundling them into rain. Because rain will be inconvenient, but not deadly, and not so far from where the storm wants to go.

"No!" Nikolai shouts, and swipes a hand to grab all of the threads I've taken back.

I only just manage to hold onto my own illusion as Caleb, stumbling back a step as reality twangs back on me like a bowstring.

"Nikolai, don't!" I yell, as he only pulls on the storm harder. The wind is picking up, the clouds performing an ominous swirl not far overhead.

The rain is hitting my spectacles, I can't see—I rip them off and shove them in my jacket pocket, weaving quickly around my eyes to correct the reality of my vision so I can see again.

I shove both hands back up to the sky. I don't try to take Nikolai's threads this time, but weave around them.

Torovan steps up beside me.

"What is happening?" he asks.

I don't have the concentration to both deal with him and try to stop Nikolai, but I snap, "He's calling the storm, not unraveling it."

"Can I help—"

Valtair tries to pull Torovan back. "Please, Tor, Your Majesty—"

Gods. And I've just snapped at the king, in public.

But the wind gusts, and Valtair's voice is nearly lost in the howl. Will anyone even remember that? Will Torovan?

And then—oh gods—the funnel of a vortex forms, reaching hungrily for the ground. It's not far away, deeper into the garden. The vortex touches down with a crash, and I can barely see for the wind whipping around me, spraying dirt and leaves.

I brace myself here, for a heartbeat, in shock. Nikolai did this. Nikolai and his selfish attempt to regain his court pride.

I could almost wish he'd only angled his affections for the king.

Nikolai's teeth are bared, and he's still desperately trying to weave the storm. But I can see it in the set of his jaw—he knows he's failed.

"Nikolai!" I scream, and I don't even know if he can hear me. I plant my feet against the ground, brace into the wind, but that won't hold for long. I'll need to shift reality to construct a post and secure myself to it.

If there's even a chance at stopping this vortex now.

I plunge my hands back into the threads, weaving frantically, weaving around Nikolai and his chaotic threads, hoping, even, to contain them.

"Nikolai, help me stop this! Do what I'm doing!"

But he ignores me, or he doesn't hear me. And everything

I'm doing alone is not enough, not when he's still working against me, fighting the wild chaos of his own threads of magic.

Torovan is beside me again, gripping my arm. He needs to go. He should run.

"Let me help!" he shouts into my ear. "I know I can help—"

I'm not sure he can. We only had a day, and that was hardly enough to teach basic concentration techniques, let alone this massive feat of willpower I'm working now.

I give up on trying to contain Nikolai and now concentrate on the greater fury of the storm. I can't dissipate it on my own, not when it's gathered so much momentum. But maybe I can calm it. Gods, I hope.

"I'm better at tangible things!" Torovan yells into my ear. "Please, the palace—my sister—"

I whip my head around. Most of the court has fled, and Valtair is shoving another group out the hedge path toward the palace. But Valtair hasn't left yet, and neither have Torovan's guards.

The vortex is headed not quite toward us, but toward the palace.

Oh, gods. And it's only picking up strength.

"Get him to stop!" I yell, pointing at Nikolai. The motion breaks my bracing, and I skid back a few feet before I catch my balance again.

Torovan grips my arm, steadies me, then goes to Nikolai. Nikolai looks to him, shakes his head furiously.

Then, finally, Nikolai breaks and runs himself.

The coward.

Or am I the fool to stand here and try to stop a vortex at its angriest?

Valtair struggles over to us. "Tor! Caleb! We have to—"

"It will tear apart the palace," Torovan yells. "My sister, my mother, they're all taking shelter—Caleb, please help me, we have to try—"

Master Aldric has gone, too. Not even a pretense of trying to stop the storm.

I turn back to the vortex, shielding my eyes as it tears through a not-so-distant row of hedges, pulling them into its own chaos.

Can I do this? Can I unravel this storm, if Nikolai is no longer working against me?

I don't think I can.

But for Torovan, I will try.

I renew my efforts, and shout to the king, "Can you see what I'm doing?"

I don't hear his reply. But a moment later, he's beside me, shoulder to shoulder, hands up, the look of concentration on his face so plain. And I watch as he lends his willpower to mine, strengthening my own weaving.

I've known this was possible, but I've never done it with anyone before. I've never had a chance.

We drop everything but concentration as we work to stop the storm.

Chapter 27

Exposed

Torovan

We work as one, Caleb and I. It's as if our very wills have intertwined, my will to see my family safe bolstering his own desperate reweaving of reality. I don't have to know what he's doing, I just need to lend him my strength.

The wind screams around us. I narrow my eyes to slits against the dirt and debris, and have to duck more than once as a tree branch or part of a bush flies past. I pull Caleb down with me, but his concentration doesn't break. He only squints up at the sky through the rain, arms raised, fingers jittering with his frantic weaving, jaw set.

I practiced lending strength before with Master Aldric. He'd said it was one of the best ways for a mage in training to learn to distinguish his own willpower from the flow of everything around him.

I was never particularly good at it, of course. Lacking, so I'd thought, the will to do even that.

Or maybe I was lacking the will to help Master Aldric, who

went out of his way to berate me, because I've never felt synchronicity like this before. Not like what Caleb and I have now.

The vortex is passing us, barreling on toward the palace. It's grown lesser in size, and maybe that's our doing, but I can't tell.

"Caleb!" I shout. "It's heading straight for—"

"I know! I see it!"

I can barely hear him. We turn with the storm, and I find we've both been pushed back, now braced against the hedges we'd stood a distance from.

Or, no, were those hedges there before? I can't see my throne, and it was heavy enough I don't think the wind took it. And the hedge wall ahead is much closer than it should be.

Caleb must have woven these hedges behind us into existence. While still weaving the storm.

He is the most powerful man I have ever known.

"This isn't working!" Caleb calls, dropping a hand to wipe the wet hair from his eyes. He's not wearing his spectacles—taken off or blown away, I don't know.

He's the most beautiful man I've ever known, too, his face creased in his concentration, in his own fire. Storm drenched and raw. Wet clothes clinging to his lean frame.

Gods. I jerk myself back to the horror in front of me.

"I'm going to try something," Caleb calls, "watch me, do what I'm doing!"

And I watch, squinting up at his weaving bolstered by mine, which I can just barely see. He withdraws his grip on all of the threads he's been pulling on.

"No!" I shout, but as soon as I do, he's reached out and seized the vortex itself, just the vortex and not the whole storm. He yanks on it, pulling the threads like spinning a top.

Will he make it go faster? But no, it's wobbling. It's destabilizing.

I swallow, reach as hard as I can into the vortex myself, settle my willpower—because surely it's there, if Caleb is asking me to do as he's doing—and pull on the threads of the vortex, too.

The vortex seizes on my threads instead and pulls me straight toward it.

I hit the ground hard on my shoulder, and I'm pulled forward, reality fighting back against my flawed weaving.

"Torovan!" I hear Caleb scream.

I roll onto my back and kick to brace my heels on the ground, but it doesn't slow me. I'm barreling fast toward the hedge wall, and the wall is thick here. I'll go through it, but not without pain. And will I slow even then, past the other hedge walls, or be pulled straight on into the vortex?

I try to let go of my threads of reality, but I seized them too hard, or else, my will is too weak to fully fight back.

I feel a sudden weight on top of me and *oof* out the breath in my lungs as Caleb pins me down with himself, driving two stakes that hadn't been there into the ground beside us with each hand. He pins me between his legs, gripping tightly, and holds on to the stakes, arms straining. I'm still moving, the stakes not deep enough to stop us fully, but I've slowed.

Caleb glares up at the vortex, his teeth bared.

And he's still weaving, even with his hands gripping the stakes. He's weaving just with his thoughts, the purity of his will.

The wind's still whipping his hair into his eyes. He has a

cut on his cheek now, running blood. He's grimy with the dirt thrown up by stopping my pull to the storm, streaking in the rain. His face is contorted in his rage.

His thighs are around my chest.

He is a flaring brightness of willpower, holding me tight with sheer determination.

And then he shimmers.

And becomes someone else.

A woman, dark blonde hair whipping around her face, teeth bared against the storm.

The storm stops trying to pull me, but the woman doesn't get off of me. She lets go of the stakes, and her hands fly around like birds in a storm until the wind starts to die down, the rain easing. The dust whipping at me lessens, the noise fading until all I can hear is the hammering of my heart.

He—she—is straddling my chest, and now I see that her waist is roped to the stakes she drove into the ground on either side of me, another construct that she wove along the way.

She's panting.

She's wearing Caleb's clothes.

Her face is cut in the same place his was, her forehead bleeding more readily from a larger cut. Her pale skin blotched with the red of effort. Lips parted as she looks down at me and, wearily, smiles.

"It's dissipated—"

She stiffens, as if startled by the sound of her voice. Her eyes—and it's the same eyes, isn't it? She has the same eyes as Caleb—her eyes go wide. Her whole body, still straddling mine, clenches.

"Who are you?" I manage.

Caleb. *Caleb.* Is this an illusion?

Or was Caleb an illusion?

Is he a spy?

Is he an assassin?

And did he—she—see the weavings in my father's chambers so easily because she put them there herself?

"I—" She finally realizes where she is, because she yelps and rolls off of me, the rope disappearing from around her waist. She scrambles back another foot before she seems to force herself to crouch beside me.

"Are you hurt?" she asks. And reaches for my face.

I knock her hand away.

"Who," I say, my voice trembling, loud in my ringing ears, "who, by the gods, are you?"

I roll and shove myself up on shaking arms, manage to maneuver around to crouch across from her.

"I can explain," she says. Her voice steadier than it probably should be. "I have good reasons—"

So this is the secret. This is what Valtair wanted me to know. He knew. He knew Caleb wasn't who he appeared to be.

I *kissed* Caleb. I was falling harder than I ever should have. Had that been her intent? Had she tried to seduce me, was it all calculated?

The rage is building in me, and I don't try to stop it, because it's easier, far easier, than dealing with the screaming maw that's also opening inside of me.

Failure. I am always a failure, even at this.

I think I was starting to love this man, who doesn't exist.

I shove myself to my feet, and she rises, too.

Then we hear shouts.

"Torovan!"

Valtair.

And, "Sire! Your Majesty!" My guards. Who all, in the end, fled the courtyard. Or, no, Caleb—whatever her name is—built the hedge wall she'd put behind us into a barrier that fully surrounds us now. It sits between us and the rest of the courtyard. The space I'm in now is much, much smaller than it had been, but there's still an opening, a way out.

The woman's lips are parted as she stares up at me, hair tangled around her face, part defiant, part terrified.

Then she takes a breath, and—she's Caleb again, the man who stood beside me in the storm, our magic intertwined. Working in the most synchronous rhythm I've ever felt in my life.

I feel dizzy. I think I'm going to be sick, but I plant my feet and stand firm. And command my stomach to stay where it belongs.

Valtair finds the entrance first, racing inside this new, smaller courtyard. He stops, panting, hands on his knees.

"Oh thank the summer gods," he says. "Tor, Caleb—" He stops, looking between us, then as the guards burst in, he yells, "Back! It's private!"

One of the guards looks to me. "Your Majesty—"

"Out!" I manage on a tight throat.

Valtair approaches. "You're both injured. I—" He looks behind him at the retreating guards. Makes a tense shrug. "Let me see the cuts—"

I hold up a hand to block his. I can't muster words to protest, but I know if his elemental magic is discovered by the court, he will lose standing. His family will lose much. He's hid his elemental magic even from his father, though I know he's been more reckless of late healing people he knows.

I don't know why he's so reckless. I don't know why he hasn't told me.

"Just—wait, I'll see the palace physicians—"

"For gods' sakes, Tor," Valtair hisses. "I'm right here. We'll say it's an illusion to calm the people down if anyone sees. Caleb is a weaver. So are you, for that matter, and most people know that now too. And I know of at least three other elementalists among the high nobles, we're not as rare a thing as you think—it doesn't have to be me who healed you. And I'm getting tired of not helping when I clearly have the ability to—"

He shudders. He's hyperventilating in his own way, and I'm letting him fill the silence, my ears ringing still from the absence of wind.

Valtair shoves my hand away and presses his to my face. His brow knits and I barely feel the sting as a cut I didn't know I had heals over.

He moves to Caleb and presses a hand to his face, too, but Caleb's soft brown eyes are on me as Valtair concentrates on closing the cuts.

I try to look for the little things, the obvious signs that he isn't, in fact, a man. But I don't see them. I just see Caleb.

I watch Caleb for any sign that the injuries were an illusion, too. But whatever is going on, it's seamless. And I'd seen the same cuts on her face, too.

I watch them close now.

And why am I not crying out, calling her a spy? Why am I just standing here, like the fool I am, not giving her away?

Chapter 28

Trembling

Irava

He saw me. He knows. Oh gods, he knows.

But he doesn't know who I am.

Valtair's hand is on my face, a warmth spreading through my skin and muscles as his healing closes the cuts. I write his healing into my illusion, because I have to. But my eyes never leave Torovan's. Because I'm looking for a sign, any sign, that he will accept me as I am.

Or maybe that's a fool's dream. Of course he can't accept me now. Not when he's seen I've been lying to him. Even with my reasons—and I haven't told him my reasons. I'm not sure it will do any good. And maybe it will ruin the other half of my life that is meant to be with him—

But I can't marry him now. He saw me. I would have to live another illusion, all of my life, lest he know that I'm the one who deceived him.

He will trust no one now. And that—that is my fault.

Torovan's guards are now crowding the enclosed space I made to keep us safe, keep us grounded from the storm. And

I'm exhausted, my ears ringing, my whole being feeling like I've been pulled through the storm myself.

And maybe I have been. I had to embrace the storm, make it my own, before I could unravel its core. I still feel a wild howling in my heart.

My eyes find Torovan's again, and his slip back toward mine and lock, as he talks to one of his guards.

"Caleb," Valtair says, gripping my arm. "You're not well. I can feel it, you're—" He leans closer. "Is it a weaver thing? Because I he can help that better than—"

Torovan straightens. "What's wrong? What's wrong with him?"

"Nothing," I say.

Valtair hisses. "It's not nothing, gods. The both of you—"

"Leave us," Torovan says flatly.

Valtair shoots him a look. "Tor, I need to—"

"I will speak with Caleb alone. Tell the guards, give us enough room for private conversation."

Torovan's voice is barely controlled. I can hear it. Valtair can hear it.

Valtair looks back at me, mouth tight, but he lets go, dips an uncharacteristic bow to Torovan, and stomps out in squelching boots.

We wait. A few more random drops of rain fall from the sky, one running down my cheek.

One running down his.

I wait, not looking Torovan in the eyes, praying for him to say something. Anything.

And the moment stretches.

I hear his breaths, hard and unsteady. And getting unsteadier.

Panic hits that he might have been injured worse than I thought, and I look up. But he's looking at me with such naked hurt that I can only swallow.

"Why?" he rasps.

My senses, so attuned to everything in this moment, hear the rustle of his clothes as he shifts his weight.

"Are you a spy? Did you actually—did you want to teach—"

"Yes," I say, with everything in me. "Yes, Torovan—"

He flinches.

I take a breath. Spread my hands.

And I drop my illusion, because I owe this to him, even if standing before him as Irava, even still in Caleb's clothing, feels like standing naked in a furnace under his gaze.

He doesn't look away, but I watch his face going harder. Watch his eyes cataloging every nuance of my face. Matching, maybe, against Caleb's. Seeing every difference. Every lie.

"I'm a weaver," I say, and have to steel myself to press on, because my voice isn't the voice that first said his name. It isn't the voice he knows. "I'm a *powerful* weaver. I know I can do good here—I already have. But I can't do that as a woman. I can't be—I can hardly even be a weaver as a woman."

Not in my mother's court. Certainly not here.

The words hang in the air between us, a branch offered, but not taken.

"Who are you?" he asks again. "What would I find, if I were to trace Caleb Ailin back to the village you came from—"

"I *am* Caleb," I say, and hear my voice break. "I'm still Caleb. And I'm—this is all I want to be here, all I can be—"

It's not quite the truth, and I know he hears that. He's closing up even more.

And do I dare, in this moment now, to tell him my real name?

I close my eyes.

Breathe several long breaths.

He's still there when I open them, still watching me. Studying every inch of my face, which is new to him. Oh, he will not soon forget my face.

"I trusted you," he finally says, and the words hit me like a dagger to the gut. "I trusted you with my kingdom, with my family, with my—"

He looks away.

Gathers himself and looks back.

"I want to know—fully and honestly—do you mean me harm? Do you mean anyone in my family harm? Did you—my father—"

"No!" I say, and is it enough?

I step closer, reach up, and press a shaking hand to his cheek. Which feels like touching scalding iron right now, but he lets me.

"I had nothing to do with the death of your father. I have no wish to see you or your family or this kingdom harmed. None, Torovan. None. If you believe nothing else—"

He knocks my hand away, as he did when I tried to reach for him before. "I have no reason to believe anything you say."

"No," I say numbly. "No, you don't."

But he's still here. He hasn't stormed out. He hasn't called his guards.

"I'll leave," I finally say. "I'll leave the court. You won't see me again."

I turn for the narrow opening in the hedges, to go out into

the rest of the garden, but his hand brushes my shoulder. Not quite a touch, he's not sure what to do with me.

"Can you maintain your illusion?"

I look back at him, not sure where this will go. Not daring at all to hope.

"Yes." And to demonstrate, I'm Caleb again. My voice deepening as I say, "I am yours to command."

A muscle in his jaw twitches, but he nods, once. He's disheveled, with small rips in his clothes, blood still on his healed cheek. His hair a windswept mess, damp with the blown rain, as is mine. But he is every inch the king.

"Stay, then," he says. "I'm not sure this storm today was an accident. And despite all else, you stood in the center with me and helped save my palace. You will remain as a mage candidate. You will report to me, through Valtair, if you see anything amiss. Any sign of a weaver's or elementalist's attempt on my life or the lives of my family."

I take a breath. There's one thing I do need to say now. Not the big thing, but something that might not let me stay here after all.

"I'm not sure if this storm was intended to harm you, but I am certain that Nikolai called it here so that he could demonstrate his ability to dissipate it."

I'd thought Nikolai had been angling for the king's affections? I'd been a fool.

Torovan's mouth tightens in a grimace. "Nikolai's family controls a large portion of the commerce in Barella. But, truly, do you think he's even capable of whatever subtlety you saw in my father's bedchamber? In his study?"

"No," I say. "Not—not with everything I've seen from him so far." But it wasn't impossible. It might be as different a kind of weaving as a storm is from an illusion. I just don't know enough to tell.

I'm a powerful mage, yes, but I learned from dusty books in my mother's library, and this palace...this palace has thorns.

Torovan nods. "Then I will keep watch on Nikolai as well. Thank you, Mage Candidate Ailin."

The formality is almost worse than seeing his hurt. It's the manifestation of it. The final judgment.

There will be no more time getting close to the king. And maybe that's for the best.

Wet hits my face again and I look up into the still-darkened sky. I'd dissipated the vortex, but the storm still lingers, and I have no more energy to try to weave it. Rain breaks over us again, more than the few drops of moments before. Then more, a steady fall.

"Go, then," he says, and there's a break in his voice, too, one small crackling view of the maelstrom of his emotions. "Because you helped me today, you can stay in my palace. But I do not otherwise want you in my sight but from a distance."

I nod, bow deeply, and back out of the garden room I created, my whole being trembling.

Chapter 29

His Heart

Irava

The garden courtyard is a blur as I step out into it. Well, and I vaguely remember putting my spectacles away in the storm so they wouldn't grime with rain and dust. I pull them out of my coat pocket with shaking hands, look up at the steadily falling rain, and tuck them away again.

My vision isn't so bad that I can't see detail, I just can't focus as well as I'd like.

I numbly weave reality around my eyes to help until the rain clears. That small necessity just now feels profane.

It doesn't help. And I realize that the blur is tears, and that my chest is burning so hotly I can hardly breathe.

Torovan's last words to me ring in my ears: "But I do not otherwise want you in my sight but from a distance."

The words ring, and they ring, and they ring, until the tightness in my chest becomes unbearable, and the sound of my quickening breaths mixes with the ringing in my ears.

He doesn't want to see me. *He doesn't want to see me.*

I am nothing to him. I am nothing at all.

But I can't stop seeing the hurt in his eyes.

I blink back the tears, but they keep coming. I'm Caleb. I shouldn't be crying. There's no reason for me to cry.

I'd stepped out into the greater courtyard, but I'm still standing by the opening in the hedge room I made. With a shudder, I push myself into motion.

Torovan's anxious guards are hovering outside the new room I built into the courtyard. Eyeing me. Not coming close.

As I cross the courtyard, I see branches, hats, and decorations strewn everywhere on trampled and wind-blown grass and flagstones. The air is thick with the aftertaste of dust, the smell of rain.

I want to cough. Water runs in puddles and rivers around me, and I can't avoid it.

Had it rained more heavily outside the room than in? Had it been raining all along? But then, this room was where I was weaving away the storm. So, maybe I had kept the rain away from me. From us. I don't remember separating out the rain, but then, I was pulling so many threads.

And still I couldn't manage to keep my illusion around me.

I keep walking.

I brush the wet hair out of my eyes. I just need to keep walking.

I barely hear Valtair as he calls out—to Torovan, I'm guessing—but a shadow grows beside me, a hand grips my shoulder, just as I step out of the courtyard and into a corridor of hedges.

"Caleb?" He stops me and I let him, staring blankly at him. He's a healer, an elementalist, and I hadn't known that—that magic is coveted and rare, but not if you're a noble.

Just like weaving is prized, but not if you're a princess.

I shrug my shoulders. Well, and now I understand more of his prickly reserve. Does his family even know?

He has small cuts on his face. He didn't heal himself—can he? Some healers can't.

"Caleb, please, let me give you some strength, at least until you can return to your room."

I shrug at him again, my throat going so tight I can't breathe.

He catches his own breath. Looks around, and leans in. "What happened?"

He glances back toward the room I built within the courtyard, still visible from here. And from the vantage of a distance I see how thick that barricade of hedges is, thicker than even the highest and best-maintained walls within the garden itself. But those walls I built didn't, in the end, save me from my own chaos.

I can't see Torovan. Either he's left the room I made for us and gone out of sight, or he's still hidden inside.

Valtair's mouth draws tight, and he leads me farther down the hedge corridor, around a bend, out of sight.

"What's wrong?" he asks, his voice low. "He was furious. With the storm? With Nikolai? The stupid shit ran away—"

"He saw me," I say. I wipe hair from my eyes again. It's raining harder now, and while it's not overly cold, I'm trying to keep from shivering. "Torovan, I mean."

Valtair's lips form an "O" before twisting into, "shit."

"He saw you? What does that mean—"

I don't look at him as I say, "I had to drop my illusion to wrestle the storm. At the last."

I hadn't tried to. Hadn't even known it had happened until

Torovan was looking up at me, and I spoke—and my voice was not the one I'd been expecting. Not the one I was coming to associate with myself around Torovan.

But the wind had been dragging him away. I could have done nothing else.

"Fuck. *Fuck*, Caleb. So he knows? That you're—"

I wrap my arms around myself. "He knows I'm a woman. He doesn't know—"

He swipes at the rain falling in his eyes. And then he stiffens, takes a breath, and contains himself.

"Okay. Okay, I get that you were both in mortal danger just now, but you *need* to tell him—" He looks to one side, and pulls me under a tree overhanging the path, which is at least a little shelter from the rain. He pauses, then wrestles out of his coat.

"Here, take this—"

"I don't need it—"

"Take it, Caleb."

I take his coat, which with its finer weave is weathering the rain better than mine, and shrug it around myself over my own wet coat. I pull the edges tight. I watch to see if he's shivering like I am, but he's not.

He says, "You need to tell him now, go back in there, or he'll only stew on this—"

"If I tell him, it'll be off, won't it? The marriage? The treaty? If I tell him right now, can you honestly say he won't just shut me out completely? I still—even if I have to use an illusion for the rest of my life, I still have a chance at keeping the treaty—"

And that is suddenly important to me. Drastically, intensely important. Torovan doesn't want to marry a foreign princess, not any more than I thought I hadn't wanted to marry him. But he made that treaty for a reason. Barella needs stability outside its borders, especially now when it's constantly under attack from within.

Valtair rubs at his eyes. "He will see reason. I know he'll see reason. Eventually. So if you can't tell him, I will. This has gone on long enough, and past the point of safety, for both of you."

He turns to go back to the courtyard, and I dig my fingers into his arm.

"No! Valtair, this storm wasn't an accident, and he knows that, too. I don't know if Nikolai was just trying to win back favor, or if it was more—"

And Master Aldric, in the end, was nowhere to be seen.

"I can't leave court," I say. "Not now. If he gets angry enough to throw me out, to cancel the marriage—"

And it dawns on me, it finally dawns on me that my coming here like this, infiltrating his court, getting close to Torovan—it could also be seen as my being a Galendan spy. It could be seen as an act of ill-faith by my mother at best, or at worst, an act of war.

I shiver harder, and pull the coat tighter.

I am a fool. I am a gods-cursed *fool*. And I might have ruined everything.

"Yeah," Valtair says, "Yes." He glares at me. "Gods damn it all, Caleb, both of you will be the death of me. But I want him safe. You keep him safe. And you safe—get inside and get into dry clothes. Gods, what a mess—I'm giving you a week. Tell him within a week, let him cool down, but then tell him, or I will."

He hesitates. "He is letting you stay?"

"Yes," I say. And a look passes over his face, grim and knowing.

I look away, and swallow hard. Because Torovan could have called his guards on me. He could have banished me from the palace. He could have imprisoned me. He could have done anything.

But he'd told me to stay.

I wipe the rain from my face, and maybe more wetness around my eyes that isn't rain.

Valtair wrings out the end of a dreadlock and starts working on another. "Gods damn the rain. One week, Caleb."

I glare at him with all the heat I can muster. "I heard you the first time."

His smile isn't kind, and I turn, striding away from him in the direction of the palace, still wrapped in his coat. He hasn't asked for it back, so I'm not giving it. Petty as I know that is.

He's given me a week?

Then I have a week to find out who killed Torovan's father the king, and who might have just tried to kill Torovan—or at very least, rattle his court and undercut his power.

This doesn't feel like Nikolai's foolishness alone. It wasn't an accident, and it wasn't benign in any way.

My breaths huff in time to my squelching boots.

One week, before I tell Torovan and he shuts me out of his heart completely.

Am I meant to marry this man, or to break him?

Chapter 30

Betrayal

Torovan

He betrayed me. I trusted him, and he betrayed me. I told him my most vulnerable secret, I...I kissed...

Her. And she's not even the man I think I was falling in—well.

Well, I can't be falling for a man that doesn't exist, can I?

But when I close my eyes, I still see him. Looking up at me, earnest, saying he'll teach me. That I do have the willpower to rule my kingdom.

And he did kiss me back. I felt, I know I felt, his body against mine. Not long, but he'd definitely been a man.

Absolutely had been a man, and I'd felt his want for me, too—

My heart is swimming. Is drowning. And I don't see a way to shore.

It's an effort to keep my breathing steady as I march into the palace, still rain-wet and wind-swept, accompanied by my guards. I ignore the courtiers I pass, who are making a show of being victims of the storm. As if the storm, somehow, was my fault and responsibility. None of *them* stood in it and tried to dissipate it. They have no right to flail about, wailing the injustice of the gods.

Valtair, who's unusually subdued, walks a few paces behind me, not saying anything.

And my anger builds with every click of my boots on the stone floor. Because that storm shouldn't have happened. It should *not* have happened. And the mage who'd said he'd unravel it ran away.

And the one who'd stayed with me…

I pause at a corridor bend, then head toward the quarters of the court mages. There are three weavers that I know of in this palace. But one of them should actually be in charge.

Valtair catches my arm—which he seldom does in public. It startles me enough that I stop.

He leans in. "Tor. If you're going to see Caleb—"

"I'm not going to see Caleb," I say through clenched teeth, "I'm going to see Master Aldric."

I try to step past him, but he puts up a hand, stopping me again. "Tor. Caleb doesn't think the storm was an accident. That a weaver—"

"I know." Every time Valtair says Caleb's name it's like a knife in my gut. "Let me pass, Valtair—"

We're making a spectacle, and it's not good at all that Valtair, even known to be my friend, is stopping his king.

"Torovan, think about it. If Caleb didn't call the storm, that leaves Nikolai, or Aldric."

Or another weaver in our midst. Maybe the weaver who killed my father, someone as yet unknown to me. Or at least, the weaver who covered up what happened.

But—but, yes. He's concerned about my safety. Even if this

was Nikolai's doing—so he could make a show of undoing it, the fool—well. Valtair's concerned about the kingdom, which I should be, too. I can't haul out the son of a major noble for trying to kill the king, even if by stupidity. Our economy is on shaky enough ground as it is.

I need time to cool down, I know that. Even though everything in me wants to shake someone right now.

I clap Valtair's arm and watch his visible relief.

If Nikolai runs away from the palace after this, then he'll have proven himself both guilty and a coward. If he stays—well, and how can I punish him when Master Aldric ran, too? When Master Aldric didn't even try. And what if Nikolai did try to help, and was just truly that incompetent?

And the one person who might actually have enough power and competence to unravel a storm is...is...

His body pressed against mine. His mouth, warm and sweet and tasting of cinnamon.

I'm not thinking clearly.

I nod in a daze, and Valtair leads the way back toward the main corridor.

"Make way for the king! The king is injured!"

I still have blood on my face. The rain washed away some of it, but it had already crusted. It's a good enough excuse.

The walk up to my study is a blur. I hear each step like a heartbeat. But I hardly see my surroundings as I see, again, *her* leaning over me in the garden. Her, dressed in Caleb's clothes. Looking down at me, realizing with horror that she'd been exposed.

Why? Why would she do this to me? I trusted—but I know not to trust. And today in the garden proves that I'm right not to trust. With her, with whoever called the storm. I'm not safe in my own palace. Not even in my own heart.

I slam into my study, stride across to the door that leads to my own quarters, not my father's. I yank open that door, too, hearing the door crash against a table behind me with an unsatisfying bang, a rattle of whatever was fragile on that tabletop. I wonder if anything's broken.

Valtair follows me, the brave fool.

I stop in the center of my sitting room, the curtains letting in little of the early afternoon light. It's not golden but still overcast, which is entirely fitting.

I stand, hands clasped behind my neck, breathing. My throat is swelling, my vision blurring.

Valtair, cautiously, approaches. "Tor..."

"Why!" I scream. "Is everything a lie?"

Valtair recoils. "Tor. For gods' sakes, the walls are not infinitely thick, and—and you're acting like a child."

I stare at him. He's right, but I can barely see through the rage.

He knew. He knew Caleb's secret—and I ignored his warning. I didn't press Caleb. I trusted that whatever this secret was, it wouldn't be enough to derail my regard.

"Out!" I hiss.

For a moment, I think he'll stay anyway, just to spite me.

But his face is blank, and I recognize it as his own anger. He sweeps a perfectly executed courtly bow, and stalks out. Carefully not slamming the door behind him.

I'm trembling. From the rage, from the after-effects of what happened in the garden, maybe. Had I almost died today? The memory of being dragged by the storm, caught in my own inept weaving, stutters my heart.

He—she—saved me.

And maybe that's an exaggeration. Maybe I would have been able to steady myself against the hedge wall. Just hold on.

But I can't stop seeing her braced above me, baring her teeth to the storm. Wild and fierce and fiercely determined. An absolute beacon of willpower.

She unraveled the storm, in the end, on her own.

And before then, our magic, our wills, weaving together, weaving the storm. We had, for a time, been functioning as one being, one will. An exhilaration I've never known before.

I close my eyes against these fresh memories, and am haunted again by the taste of Caleb's lips on mine, like cinnamon. Like innocence, and longing. Maybe it was a stolen kiss, but he had kissed me back. And maybe I can understand why he might not have wanted to kiss me, why he turned down my offer—

But he had kissed me back.

And what is left for me now? A cold marriage to a woman I don't know, a future where I'm always on guard for my life, and the lives of my family? Helpless—powerless—and with not enough willpower to stop the threats? There's no one to teach me now. There's no one to see me.

Or love me?

I stumble back to sit on a chair, my head falling into my hands. It's a long, long time before I stop trembling enough to breathe again.

And then I think, for once, about my court. About the fright that they truly did have today. And as much as I don't want to, I get up, and I call for my servants, finding pen and parchment to scribe out my command.

Because this is a part of being a king, too—making sure

that the people are well-cared for. My father knew that. My father made that the center of his rule.

And tonight, I think, that means the most lavish meal the kitchens can come up with on short notice.

And I must, too, honor the person who stood beside me today. She did save my life, again. Whatever else, she did that. I didn't honor her before, not with any great significance—I am not going to make that mistake now. Because that, too, is the duty of a king—to be fair where fairness is due.

Chapter 31

The Honor

Irava

I am a shattered shard of glass. I am brittle, I could crack and break further with any solid wind. No matter that I just pulled apart the vortex of a storm, that storm's now raging within me.

And surely everyone can see that? Surely everyone will know the depth of my devastation? Even with my illusion wrapped tightly around me, even now changed into dry clothes, my hair combed again—though the only hair that shows is Caleb's, not mine.

It's evening. It was announced that, because of the upset of the day, the king has invited all of the court to join him in the Great Hall for dinner. It's an invitation, not an order, and I'm tempted to curl under my covers, to draw them over my head, and sleep the rest of the evening and night away.

Maybe never come out again.

But I sigh. Because that, above all else, would give me far, far too much time to think. And I need to be near the king, in the moments he lets me. I need to watch, I need to keep him safe. It is my sole task and reason anymore for staying in this court.

Or so I tell myself.

I don't even have the option anymore of just remaining Caleb and being near him that way. And would that have been so bad, truly? I've been settling into my life here as Caleb, and it's a good life. Better, at least, than the life I left at my mother's court. I'm *valued* as Caleb.

But it's still not a whole life. Not, at least, wholly mine.

And he knows now that I'm not Caleb beneath the illusion. And that—that settles hard in my core in a way I can't define.

I'd wanted, maybe just one more time, to kiss him as Caleb, to tangle my hands in his hair again, and he in mine.

To press against him. To feel every angle and peak and valley of him.

To have him press against me.

To know...more than that.

It's a few long moments before the heat rising in me cools again, and that only through concentrated effort and willpower.

A *lot* of willpower.

I check myself in the small mirror over my chest of drawers, tuck back a stray strand of hair. I linger a moment, trying to reconcile what I see in the mirror, the young mage candidate, with the woman the king would have seen me to be.

I bite my lip, look away. Straighten my worn but still passable coat—and I have one less of those left now—and slip out into the corridors.

I tell myself the king doesn't want to see me, so...it will be okay. It will be.

I pass another mage candidate in the corridor, and he gives me an odd look. I haven't made friends with the other candidates, not more than polite exchanges of words when we're all together. How I started my stay here at the palace, saving Nikolai—and everyone else—has already set me apart. And I don't want to get too close, either, because I don't want anyone to look too closely in return.

I'm sure, by now, that people know I stayed behind to unravel the storm. That I tried to thwart Nikolai's botched weaving, even. Or that I tried to work with Nikolai, and in the end he ran, though I'm sure he won't tell it that way. Whether people think me a hero or a villain for it, I have yet to see.

I'm sure I'll have no help or confirmation from the king.

I hold my head as high as I dare and make my way toward the Great Hall.

And would my life have been lonely here, if I'd chosen to stay as Caleb? If I'd been allowed that choice? I would have had Torovan, though. Maybe. Until he gave up on his foreign princess and betrothed himself to someone else.

But now, I don't have him at all.

"Caleb Ailin!"

I spin, too jumpy by far, to see Princess Elsira hurrying toward me. Her dark hair is done up in elaborate loops, her gold dress shimmering in the lamplight.

There are others in the corridor, courtiers also heading toward the Great Hall and two other mage candidates who were behind me. They all turn, attentive, to see what show I'll be in the middle of next.

I bow to the princess, my courtesy as exquisite as I can manage. "Your Highness."

I feel intensely shabby next to her. I feel an intruder,

someone she shouldn't have sought out. She certainly doesn't know I'm not actually Caleb. There's too much openness yet in her gray-green eyes.

Torovan hasn't told her.

She makes an annoyed wave at my bow, but sees we do have an audience. She says in a low voice, "Thank you. You saved his life, again. You might have saved mine, and the lives of everyone else in this palace. If he doesn't thank you himself—" She glances around us again. "Go on, then! All of you. We will catch up."

She has her guards with her, so no one can protest that as an impropriety. The courtiers and mage candidates reluctantly move on.

Elsira grips my arm, leans close. Startled, I panic again—a feeling that's becoming far too familiar—and pull on the threads of my illusion, making it real again. Rewriting the reality of who I am into Caleb, so she doesn't feel my arm isn't quite as thick as it appears to be.

It's different this time. Different because Torovan isn't standing in front of me, making everything light to fire.

But I don't let it go. Not while Elsira is still holding my arm.

"I'm sorry. Gods, Caleb, I didn't know Nikolai would do that. When Mother suggested a garden party, I had no idea—"

I blink. Her mother suggested that party? The dowager queen? Is that significant?

It's something. It's something new, something urgent.

"Will the dowager queen be at the dinner tonight?" I ask.

She isn't always. Elsira frowns, studying me. "Yes. Is that... distressing to you? Has she said anything...anything untoward to you?"

I meet her eyes. As someone very familiar with overbearing, authoritative mothers, I understand the root of the question. But Caleb wouldn't.

And I'm not sure what she's looking for in my answer. Could she possibly know that the dowager threatened me?

"Because," she goes on, "you'll be seated at the high table with the king."

I cough. And I make sure that yes, I am still fully and truly Caleb. The reality, not the illusion, because that's suddenly very important. There can't even be a chance that he sees anything else in me.

Oh gods. I'd been hoping, in a vague sense, to have an excuse not to go. If the dowager queen was there, I could go and try to survey her suite again. Look for...something. Anything, whatever the sense of non-reality in her bedchamber is hiding. Because you wouldn't weave reality in that way without trying to cover up *something*.

To search her rooms would also be aiding the king, wouldn't it? Without the detriment of actually having to see him.

Of having to see the coldness in his eyes. And beneath it, the hurt.

But I can't duck out of this now if Torovan invited me to the high table.

Elsira holds out her arm, and for a moment, I stare at it. And remember I'm the man here. She's asking me to escort her in. Me—Caleb Ailin—a village mage.

I smile, and it's more bitter than I'd like. I might be happy at this boost in status if it hadn't come at the cost of the king's safety. And his regard.

I take her arm, a little awkwardly, but she smiles back. A

private smile, a knowing smile, in a way that I don't want to think about.

Do they all still think I'm the reason that Torovan's had a few moments of lightness lately? What will they think when they learn I'm the reason he's in despair?

Or am I thinking too highly of my place in his life?

No. I did see the despair, and the rage.

He kissed me first.

He kissed me. And my body starts lighting through fire even at the thought of it.

I harness every inch of my willpower and hold it tightly around me. I must be stone. I must be unfeeling.

I walk Elsira in. I escort a princess through the parting throngs of people to the high table at the front of the Great Hall, my eyes locking, involuntarily, on those of the king.

He doesn't look away. His expression doesn't change from the cold mask that's back again, hiding any of the warmth I'd seen before.

He might have invited me to the high table, but in that moment, I know in my bones that it wasn't his idea. Wasn't what he'd wanted.

This is politics. This is only politics.

I pause at the steps up to the high table, and Elsira pulls out of my grip to touch my arm, now lead me up.

It's not that I've never sat in the presence of royalty. I *am* royalty, and I never much cared for the display, for the constant biting ridicule from my mother, from being compared to her and my sisters.

My stomach knots now for a different reason than the man I'm currently trying extremely hard not to look at— but I'm not a princess here. Not even in my own threads of reality. I'm not royalty, I'm a mage candidate who someone has decided to acknowledge just saved the king's life. Shouldn't I be honored? Shouldn't I be pleased at this attention? This might just guarantee my place as a court mage.

If I even had a prayer of that, now.

I have little appetite, but I allow myself to be seated beside Elsira, with her mother beside her, and on her mother's other side—Torovan. And Valtair beyond him.

I don't even dare look at Valtair or the dowager, but I can't escape Torovan. Or the way he leans forward, looks to me, doesn't smile. He says stiffly, and loud enough that those around can hear, "My gratitude, Mage Candidate Ailin, for your efforts to weave the storm. The kingdom is grateful."

And I dip the deepest bow I can while still being seated.

"Th-thank you, Your Majesty." I can't hide the tremor in my voice. And it's a relief when he makes a jerky nod and looks away.

Elsira touches my arm again, a familiar and sisterly touch, and smiles. She begins a tour of the dishes as they're laid out, giving a running commentary of why any given dish is a favorite or one she tends to avoid. Many of her reasons involve colorful stories from previous meals, featuring other courtiers honored at the high table. Some stories are ridiculous enough that I catch myself grinning.

One is of her and Torovan when they were younger, sneaking into the kitchen to get a taste and then ending up in a food fight.

"And that," Elsira declares, "is why the mashed beans are best eaten with a fork, not a spoon, because spoons make better catapults."

Despite everything, I laugh. A feeling that rises up from my stomach, easing my tension.

Elsira grins back at me.

And what would it be like, to have her as my sister? Would I ever have the chance to know what that's like, no secrets between us? Or would she look at me, if she knew, with the same betrayal as Torovan?

Elsira stiffens the few times her mother deigns to talk to her. And I occupy myself with being her conversational shield, which is a relief, because it doesn't let me think too much about the man trying very hard, three places down, to ignore again that I exist.

Chapter 32

Plans

Irava

When the dinner, at long last, ends, Lord Valtair says a word in Torovan's ear and doesn't go with him when he retreats with his guards, his mother and sister behind him. Elsira gives me a parting smile, and I return it, trying to hide my queasiness as Valtair comes up to me, leans close, and says, "Care for me to walk you back to your quarters?"

"I—"

People are still watching us. Of course they are watching us. Everyone is always watching and here, still at the high table, we're on display. Especially now that the king has gone.

"Yes," I say. Because I don't think it would be wise in any way to refuse him just now. I don't know what he wants, but I guess I'll find out.

In the corridor, empty with most of the courtiers still in the Great Hall, I ask first, "Was that your idea for me to be at the high table?"

"No," he says. "It was his. It was a good one, if awkward.

Elsira seems taken with you well enough, so that worked out fine."

I stiffen. "The princess is treating me as a friend, or—or a brother, not—"

"I know," Valtair says with a sigh. He rubs at his clean-shaven cheek, pulls me to a stop. "Listen, Caleb. Your affairs are your own. I don't like—I don't like how this is all playing out. But, I'm not going to tell him. Not unless his life—well. Is in greater danger. But, please. I'm truly begging you, *please.*"

I bite my lip, glancing at the two guards still stationed at the doors to the Great Hall.

Are they in earshot? Maybe not, Valtair was speaking quietly, not whispering.

"Will it stop the rumors about me and him," I ask, "whatever rumors there are—I mean, will it help him at all if I'm seen with you? I mean, *with* you?"

I'm still fully Caleb. I settled into that throughout the dinner, and even if Valtair knows it's not, at its core, true, I'm still a man at the moment.

And it would be awkward, gods so awkward, to even do anything so forward as embrace him—but if it would help Torovan—

He coughs a laugh, his eyes raking me over again, brow furrowing. "You're gorgeous, Caleb, but—"

Not real?

"—you're his. And I don't quite know where that's coming from. I don't need you to date me, I want you to make nice with *him.* So we can all get out of this mess."

I flush with more heat than I can deal with just now. And I take his arm in the same way I had Elsira's, because it's the only thing I can think of just now. I pull him toward a less public corridor.

He makes a sound of protest, but then his steps fall into place beside me and he—gently—removes my hand from his arm.

"I know you're royalty," he growls beneath his breath, "because you're so damned presumptive. Where are we going?"

"Are we alone?"

"There's no one ahead, I know no one followed us. You know there *will* be rumors, though."

"I don't care, I need to talk to you."

I head down another corridor, and he follows.

I need an alcove, a private space—gods, I need the closet he shoved me into a few days before. Somewhere where our words will be safe.

We're headed toward the formal sitting rooms and reception rooms that line the south side of the palace. I turn the handle on a fancy door, wince as it gives a creak as I push it open.

The room inside is empty, if mostly dark except for a banked fire in the hearth. Courtiers will be spilling into these rooms shortly for their usual evening social gatherings.

I wave Valtair inside, and he enters without hesitation. I shut the door behind us.

"Okay," he says, "I guess we might as well make out if you're going to shut me in a room all alone with you."

But I hear his sarcasm. He's looking around, as I am, to make sure the room is good and truly empty. "This will definitely fuel the rumors, yes."

I shrug, staring at him, wondering—well, knowing that I can trust him, but wondering if I *should* trust him with what I need to say. To ask him. To say out loud the thoughts that I set aside to get through the dinner, because the dowager was sitting two places down from me at the high table.

I urgently need to talk about it now, though.

And I don't know if hearing this won't jeopardize his position in court, or his friendship with Torovan, or...his life.

He narrows his eyes. "You found something out, didn't you? Something that Torovan won't like? More than what you're *still* not telling him?"

"It's the Dowager Queen," I say. "I—when I was in her chambers before, you know I felt that lack of reality. It was a weaving, I'm sure of it. And...someone had to have called that storm. Maybe it was Nikolai, maybe it was Master Aldric, or someone else. But the dowager—"

I dart a quick glance around again. Listen, for a moment, to the faint hiss of the banked fire.

I lower my voice. "The dowager encouraged the king to have this garden party, Elsira said so. And Elsira told me before that Nikolai was planning something to redeem himself. So..."

In the near dark of the large, empty room, the words feel far too sinister.

And also, too thin. Too full of hunches and not of proofs. Am I chasing after shadows? Was his mother's threat just that —a mother's threat, a protectiveness toward her son? Are these events and circumstances unconnected, have I been too seeped in the patterns of reality to see that not all realities connect together?

But there was that unreality in her bedchamber. And she's still very much alive, while the king her husband is not. And someone, a weaver, is trying to menace—or kill—the king.

My instincts are screaming.

I have to keep him safe.

For a long moment, Valtair says nothing. He rubs the side of his face, he fidgets with the hem of his tunic. He's a man that usually fills silences with fluttery nothings or venomous insults. His silence is loud.

"I need to go back into the dowager's chambers," I say quickly. "I need to see if it is *something*. To see if I can see below the unreality to whatever it's hiding. And if it isn't anything—"

"I've known Dowager Zinara most of my life," Valtair says, his voice tight. "You know my father almost married her? He courted her for six months before her family married her to the crown prince instead. And she didn't ever look back. When my father became a minister of the court, she saw him all the time, and there was nothing but cold politeness, like they'd never made out before—and I asked the staff, they had."

He chews on his lip, his face going a little twisted. "Whatever's in that room…it won't be nothing."

He looks down. Then up again, his eyes shifting. Hardening with resolve. "Caleb—we have to tell Torovan you entered her bedchamber before, gods, are thinking about doing it again—"

"But that's just it," I say, "can he possibly be objective about his mother? What if she was involved with the storm, and what if she was involved with the"—I lower my voice—"death of the king? So you didn't tell him about her chambers? About what I found out before?"

He shifts his weight, makes an unsatisfied noise. "No. Because then I would have had to explain how I knew that, and had to explain *you*. And explain your illusions, which would have…um, caused a lot more problems. I hinted to him, broadly, to ask you—but he ignored me. I was hoping you'd have told him by now."

"Just—okay. Just help me this one time. Help me find the right time to enter her chambers again, clear the way, be my distraction. Please."

Another tense silence.

"Tomorrow is the holy day," he says. "She will be in the cathedral for prayers to the gods from the sixth bell until the eighth. She goes every week, she has for as long as I've known her."

He grew up in this palace, so yes, he knows the Dowager Zinara. And he's not saying my suspicions are wrong.

"Okay," I say. "Okay, I'll meet you—"

"In the service corridor behind the kitchens," he says. "Can you be a servant? Do you know how to make an illusion of one of her servants?"

"I—I'm not sure. Can't I be Lady Denala again?"

"No," he says sharply. "If you can't be a servant, then we can't do this. I will not endanger the life of Lady Denala in this."

But he will endanger a servant?

And maybe the distinction is, one of the *dowager's* servants. No, there is no love lost there between Valtair and the dowager's people.

"I'll just be a random servant," I say. "If I'm with you, no one will be looking at me, they'll be paying attention to you. Just, get me into the service corridor behind her suite, let me go with you and past the corridor guards. I can weave my way past the locks on her door if I need to."

He doesn't look happy. His whole body is coiled with a tension that I feel, too.

"You absolutely think this is necessary?"

"Yes. Valtair, I *barely* unraveled the vortex, and I couldn't unravel the whole of the storm. It rained for, what, at least an hour after? Maybe Nikolai was only a fool, but maybe, too, he was placed in a position where his foolishness could do harm."

"And if you don't find anything?" he asks.

Then...I don't know. But I'd be no worse off for not knowing the next step, the next hint at what's actually going on in this palace full of lies.

"Then I'll keep searching on my own," I say. "And keep protecting him, as long as I can."

He rubs at his chin again. I know he's not happy. But this is for Torovan. This is to keep Torovan safe, and I know that's his highest priority of all.

"Okay," Valtair says. "Then meet me by the kitchens at—"

The door to the room bangs open, light flooding in from the corridor lamps. I tense to jump away from Valtair, but instead he pulls me tight against him. He rakes a hand through my hair and presses his lips close to my ear.

"Forgive me. Torovan's going to be furious, but I'll smooth it over."

"Ho!" someone shouts. "Of course I'd find you here, and with the—gods, Valtair, you are aiming at the sun this time, aren't you?"

"Act nonchalant," Valtair says in my ear. "This is a tryst, you've done nothing wrong."

I could scream, because I know, I do know this will get back to Torovan, and he will...make of it what he wills. Even if I'd thought of doing this very thing, to try to put distance between myself and Torovan. To give him an out from the expectations of the rumors. To give him a solid reason to not be near me, even if I had just eaten at his own table.

But now that we're actually doing this, now that it looks like more than rumors, my heart clenches at the thought of this hurting him. I hadn't wanted at all to hurt him, even if Valtair tells him it isn't real.

Another thing that isn't real.

Valtair eases his hold on me and takes a step back—but he catches my hand, smiles at me warmly. Possessively.

And he is beautiful. He is absolutely gorgeous when he smiles that charming smile, with hooded eyes and his head tilted back, like he's just made a conquest.

But I'm hardly moved by him. There's only one man I can think of in this moment, and it's not him.

I grip his hand tightly just for something to hold on to, and do my best to put on a flustered smile, to meet the eyes of the man who'd mocked us.

Valtair squeezes my hand, then tugs me toward the door. "Well, my lords, we are off to quieter pastures."

He pulls me closer to him again, his arm around my waist, and we step out into the corridor amongst the jeers of the nobles.

And in the corridor, Torovan is there, among his guards and a gathering of nobles.

I thought—but he should have left, he did leave through the royal entrance behind the high table. He's back?

"Fuck," Valtair says. "I'll handle this. Best retreat to your own quarters for the night."

I swallow and say, because we'd been interrupted before, "Tomorrow?"

He meets my eyes. "Yes, yes, tomorrow. Now go."

Chapter 33

Promises

Torovan

Everything around me, the nobleman talking to me, the crowd surrounding me, the faint smoke of the sputtering oil sconce nearby, fades. My attention is fully riveted across the corridor where my best friend is leading a disheveled Caleb out of a reception room.

With Caleb looking more than a little guilty. And Valtair?

Valtair's steps stutter when he sees me. I see the curse as he says it.

And Caleb? His hair frayed out to one side, as if a hand had been tangled within it?

My whole body tenses. I know he's not really a man. I know Valtair knows that, and that he doesn't prefer women, but—

But I certainly couldn't tell when I kissed Caleb before.

I swallow, opening my clenched hand slowly, trying to ease off the rising anger. I'm in public.

And I was hoping to see Caleb. I know, with all of my own pretense of needing to be more among my people, that I was truly hoping to see Caleb. Maybe not talk to him, but to see him. To do what—I don't know. I hardly looked at him during dinner. My gut is still coiled from his betrayal.

And still, when Caleb's eyes meet mine and widen, I can't look away.

And I'm having the hardest time seeing him as anyone but himself. Am I hoping to reassure myself that this was real? That he was, in fact, a real person? He carried on an animated conversation with my sister for two entire hours throughout dinner. I didn't let myself look often, but I listened. His voice is calming, his perspective—so unlike the sychofantry in my court—refreshing. He isn't at all intimidated by talking with my sister, a princess, though it did seem he wasn't too sure of the high table itself. Or me.

He's a woman. I know that. I saw her. And yet when I see him now, I can only think of the man who carefully and patiently led me through concentration exercises.

Who said my name as if the saying of it was a gift.

And what—what by all the gods—was he doing with Valtair?

Even if Valtair didn't know Caleb was also a woman, he wouldn't do that to me. I know he wouldn't.

Even still, my insides are knotting. It takes conscious effort to press my hands to my sides.

Valtair turns back to Caleb, says something close to his ear.

Caleb's jaw sets, and he says something in return—then they part, Caleb striding off toward his own quarters, I assume.

I want to go after him. I want to take his arm and make him face me and just…gods…make me understand why. Yes, he gave me his reasons. But they hardly feel adequate, they hardly feel like anything at all.

I trusted him.

Valtair's moving toward me now, and he's getting a stubborn set to his jaw, that look about him that says he is not, in fact, going to bow to my whims tonight.

I raise my brows at him and jerk my head toward another nearby meeting room, this door still closed.

He grins, and it's a rictus smile. He passes me to open the door first, peer inside.

"If there's anyone in here having a rumble, off with you now," he announces to the darkened room.

I pluck the oil sconce from its holder on the corridor wall and carry it with me inside, waving my guards to wait at the door.

"It's empty?" I ask.

"It is." Valtair strides to check behind the curtains, under the cloth of a table. He heads back to me. "Yes, it is."

"Good. Valtair, what the hell were you—"

He holds up both hands. "Not what you think, Tor—"

"Well, I know that. Because you know her secret."

He flinches, and I check. Because I hadn't known that would hit him that hard.

I want—I want less to wound him than to grab his collar and shake him. If Caleb can't answer my why right now, maybe he can.

"I—yes," he says. "Tor, I told you to ask him—her—and you didn't?"

This is hardly my fault. I feel my anger rising again—

And shove it back down with all I have. Because Caleb hadn't asked me to kiss him. Hadn't asked me to single him out to help me, hadn't asked for any of this.

I put my hand over my eyes. It's trembling.

"What am I supposed to think at all?" I ask. "My best friend is skulking about my palace with a woman who lied to me—"

"Yeah," he says, "I'm not going to say she isn't wrong for what she's done, but Tor, she's a *powerful* weaver. Would you have even given her a chance to help you if you'd known she was a woman? A woman weaver, in this court?"

"Yes!" It's a lie. We both know I wouldn't have. Women can't be court mages. And powerful weavers of any sex who aren't in a loyalty tie to the court are to be mistrusted. But especially those who aren't men.

"What if she's the one?" I ask wearily. "What if she is the one who—my father—"

"Do you really believe that? Truly?" His voice is flat, as if the question offends him.

"No," I say. She'd braced herself over me and faced down a storm for me.

And...she'd been beautiful then, too. Just as fierce, just as fearsome, as Caleb in the moment before.

"Okay. Then—Tor, what you do about her is your business. But talk to her, please. Whatever you have that's unresolved—work it out. For both of you. Give her that chance, at least."

I'm not going to commit to that. Because I don't know that I could have a reasonable conversation right now, for all that I'd come looking for him. Her.

Is that progress in my willpower? Knowing when I'd better back off lest I explode?

"And what were you doing with him tonight, if not—if not—"

I can't even say that he would have been kissing Caleb, or

whispering his seductions in Caleb's ear. I can't even think it, because it heats me all over again.

"*Nothing*, Tor. She wanted to ask me something, and it was private. I covered for it when someone came in, just messed up her hair." He shifts, frowning. And it's another moment before he asks, "Do you think Caleb has it easy at all coming into this mess, this court, and getting thrown into the chaos of saving your life? Twice now. He's in the focus of your attentions, given without regard to what it's doing to him socially here in this court, the rumors surrounding you and Caleb when everyone knows that you're going to marry in a few months. No, I'm not going to get in the middle of your—whatever you have—but please, Tor, talk to Caleb. Actually listen. It might... it might help."

I don't know that it will.

And I haven't missed that Valtair is referring to Caleb as a man again, either.

Could she—could he?—possibly be a man, not a woman? Was that another reason? I had a noble's son come to the captain of my guards last month and tell him he was a man, not a woman, and ask for a place in my guards. And he's been an excellent and capable guard so far.

I look back up at Valtair. Yes, I know I should talk to Caleb. I know I need to.

But I say, my words nearly a whisper in the dim light of my stolen wall lamp, "Is it worth even that? I am going to marry in a few months. If he wants to stay as Caleb and become a court mage—"

It would kill me. Whether he's a woman disguising herself as a man, or has other reasons of his own, it would kill me to have him near me, even if it's only in passing in my court. He might, in time, replace Master Aldric, and then I would have to see him, to talk with him, to work with him.

And I know, I truly know it would poison my marriage, such as it is. Caleb's plea that I give my new wife a chance hangs heavily in my thoughts.

My hand tightens around the lamp, the surface too hot, but I don't care. I'm already burning inside.

"You could change the law," Valtair says. "Let her be a court mage as herself. If she wants that."

But it wasn't as simple as that. In my diving into the business of the kingdom, I know that now. I know that I don't have the absolute power my forebears might have had—I must rely on concessions and diplomacy and compromise. It's why I asked for the treaty with Galenda in the first place. It's how my father ruled, and he'd even wished to give more of that power into the hands of the people.

And was he wrong? If I had more power inherent in my person, would I have this aching wrench in my heart? If I didn't have to marry a woman I didn't know and didn't know if I'd ever even like, let alone love? Or was that inevitable all along?

I am fairly certain that I will not love my new wife. Because my eyes are only now trained on Caleb, a man who may or may not exist.

Will that ever fade? Can I be so entirely ensnared within days to ruin the rest of my life?

And even if the law did change, even if Caleb could live as herself and wanted to live as herself, would that still kill me all the same?

I see her above me again, glaring her entire life force at the storm. Cut and wind-blown and alight with her fury.

And gods, she *was* beautiful. She was a force to face down nature itself.

"I...will think about it," I say. But changing the law is not fully up to me. Barella is struggling, far more than I'd thought a few days ago, before I'd started doing what a king should do. And this kingdom needs its king focused on the problems rotting its core, not yet embroiled in a debate that I know will throw the kingdom into further chaos.

Valtair's mouth is a grim, annoyed line, but he nods. "Talk to Caleb. Just—do that before you make any big decisions, won't you?"

I smile in return, a pulling of my mouth. But I don't make any promises.

Chapter 34

The Alliance

Irava

In the morning, Valtair meets me, as he said, in the servants' corridor behind the kitchens. The random servant I chose to disguise myself as is actually a stern matron in my mother's household—late thirties, brown hair always so tight that if this wasn't an illusion, I'm sure I'd have a headache.

I've never liked this servant. But no one, absolutely no one, questions her. She always knows what she's about.

I'm doing my best to project that air now, but when I drop my illusion of shadows in an alcove and wave Valtair over, he stops, crosses his arms, and looks me up and down. It's a distinctly dubious look that I'm certain I don't deserve, because I did get the details right.

"What?" I ask.

He shrugs, his shoulders tight. "We'd better get going, the dowager's already at the cathedral."

I swallow. I'd heard one of the servants say as much when I'd been waiting for Valtair, concealed in an alcove in the corridor.

Valtair's jaw looks just as tense as I feel.

"What should I call you?" he asks. "If anyone asks?"

"Kima," I say. It's the name of the servant whose illusion I'm wearing. Good enough.

He frowns, gives me another dubious look, but then he starts off down the corridor, and I follow.

"You're giving me weird looks," I say under my breath as I catch up beside him.

He's quiet for a few heartbeats. "Do you like switching illusions? I mean, being different people?"

It's my turn to give him a look. Because I don't really know what he's asking. He seems serious, though.

"I don't mind it," I say cautiously.

And then we both shut up as a group of servants come through the corridor, chatting and laughing. It feels weird to see other people going about their lives when we're so tense. When we're going to do what we're going to do.

Valtair picks up his pace.

"We should hurry. The dowager is consistent in her devotions, but she doesn't always stay for the full services."

He eyes me again as we wind through the service corridors. "You've got freckles in an asymmetrical pattern. That's a *really* specific detail for a random servant."

"Keep your voice down," I hiss as we start up a plain staircase. "And yes, it's someone I know."

"Is...Caleb someone you know?"

"I am Caleb," I snap.

He stops at the top of the stairs, holds up a hand.

"What I mean is," he says in a low voice, "is there someone out there who if the king were to meet him it would be a massive problem?"

I swallow. "No. It's...Caleb is just me."

And he is. Caleb is someone I crafted from everything I thought would help me here in Barella. Everything I thought I might want to be if I was a man. I hadn't thought he'd catch the eye of the king.

My throat tightens. Caleb, this person I crafted, has taken on entirely too much life of his own. My own?

I'm not wearing my spectacles because this servant I'm impersonating doesn't wear any—though now that I think about it, no one knows who she is here. I could have worn them. I dearly, right now, want that shield between myself and the world. Between Valtair and his questions.

He starts walking again, his steps swift and unrelenting. I have to jog a few steps to catch up.

"Why?" I hiss. "Why are you asking me this, if Caleb's made after a real person? It's just me. It's nothing dangerous, or a security risk. I made Caleb, that's it."

And why bring it up now, when we're on this other dangerous mission?

But Valtair only gives me a tight smile as he pauses at a plain door. He says quietly, "Get back in character. On the other side is a corridor and the guards at the entrance into the back of the royal suites."

The last time I was skulking in the royal suites, I went out the front service door back into the main corridor. I haven't been to the back.

I shrug uncomfortably and try to put his earlier question out of my mind. He talked to Torovan the night before, after we'd—well, after it had looked like we'd come out of a tryst. What had Valtair said to Torovan? What had Torovan said to Valtair?

My whole body clenches with the need to ask.

"I'll do the talking," Valtair adds. Which is good, because that's why he's here, to get me inside. "Meet me again in the closet we were in before."

I make a face, because we should have talked about this on the way up, not him questioning me about Caleb. But there's no time for an argument. And I don't truly want to argue. I've built up far more nerves around this foray into the dowager's chamber than I had the last time.

"Okay."

He nods, and opens the door.

It opens into a dim corridor, lit only by wall sconces even in the daytime. We approach the guards at a door near the middle of the corridor. And I smooth out my expression as best I can into the faintly annoyed look this servant always has.

The guards stand on either side of a plain door, the entrance to the service corridor that runs behind Torovan's parents' private chambers.

One of the guards, an older man with a bushy beard, nods to Valtair.

"Lord Valtair. Is the king in his father's chambers today, then?"

"No, his own study," Valtair says. "But he left his favorite mug in the late king's rooms and apparently he can't be bothered to retrieve it himself. He also wants the suite dusted." He nods to me and shrugs, as if to say, "Who knows the whims of a king?"

The guard glances at me and I hold my breath, but then he shrugs, too. He gives Valtair a wave as he opens the door.

"I have a key anyway," Valtair says, once the door is closed again on the other side. We hurry through a short corridor before stepping into the main service corridor. "The man *always* challenges me. And I've been coming in and out of here since I was knee high." He holds a hand down to demonstrate.

Past that danger, I let out my breath and vent a muffled, hysterical laugh.

Valtair grins at me, and I want to shudder with my nerves. Gods, I'm much more nervous now than I'd been the first time I snuck into the dowager's chambers.

But that was before Torovan kissed me. That was before he'd seen me, before we'd been caught in the storm, before I'd promised Valtair to keep him safe. Because his safety means everything to me.

"Is Torovan in his study?" I ask. Because what if he comes out, what if he comes back here, what if he sees us, what if—

"Yes, but that shouldn't be a problem. And you're not you just now anyway, if you're worried about that. Either of you." He tilts his head. "He's been spending a lot of time in his study lately."

He says this with some extra significance, as if it should mean something to me. Gods, whatever he wants to say, all of what he wants to say, I wish he would just say it. Does he mean the king being in his study a lot is a bad thing, and if so, that it's my fault?

We approach the back door into the dowager's bedchamber. Valtair carefully presses his ear to the door.

I raise my brows.

"I don't hear anything," he says. "Go now. I'm pretty sure no one's in there."

"Pretty sure?" I hiss as I approach the door. "And you're sure none of her staff are here? Cleaning or something while she's at the cathedral?"

"The people I asked last night said no, they wouldn't be. She likes to be there when anyone else is in her chambers."

I narrow my eyes at that but step up to the lock. With another quick glance around the empty service corridor, I weave the reality within the lock until it opens with a satisfying *click*.

It's not so easy as that, of course. Royal locks have measures against weavers—twists and mind-puzzles built into them that will at least slow a weaver down, if not foil someone of weaker will.

But I'm not of weaker will.

Valtair softly swears. "Don't show Tor you can do that."

"Not planning on it—now, go. I'll meet you in the closet."

He hesitates, touching my arm. "Be careful."

I look up into his handsome face, his eyes heavy with liner, his brow creased with worry.

He cares. He really does care. And whatever probing questions he was asking earlier, whatever he was trying to get at, I don't feel like it was aimed against me. He's worried, and not just for the king.

And that, knowing that he's here with me in this, bolsters my courage.

I nod gratefully and slip into the dowager queen's bedchamber.

Chapter 35

That Which is Hidden

Irava

Inside the bedchamber, it's quiet as a grave.

Just inside the door, I take a moment, just a moment, to breathe. Because I've been here before. And I wasn't caught before—I won't be now.

And because I know what I'm sensing for, I feel the lack of reality in this room almost immediately. It settles like a tight, aching weight in my gut.

My senses fully alert, I grimace at the overly strong scents of lavender and rosewater. There's a dressing gown draped across an elegantly carved chair near the bed, a small towel folded over top of it. The Dowager Zinara must have just bathed before going to the cathedral.

I don't have much time. Enough, I hope, but not much.

Okay. I can do this.

The room is dimly lit, the walnut-paneled walls oppressive, the heavy blue curtains pulled to a slit. Shadows play tricks on my eyes as I scan every inch around me.

The bed, the chair, the dressers and wardrobe, the vanity. The hearth, another more comfortable chair beside it.

And the lack of reality. The four-poster bed in its rich gold silks and velvets, seeming to my senses as if it has never been slept in. The chair beside it as if it is sitting in storage, though the towel on the dressing gown, when I lightly touch it, is still damp. And even that shows little reality.

My heart skips into a gallop. I'm here in this room where I definitely should not be, and all my weaver's senses are screaming *wrongness.*

Is the sense of unreality stronger here than in the late king's bedchamber? I'm not sure. It's been days since I was there, and my mind has been wholly distracted by the king.

And I've never dealt with anything like this before. I can sense that it's *something*, yes, like a muffled shroud over the threads of reality. But what do I do about it? Where are the threads to even go about unraveling this weaving, and *should* I unravel it? Would that alert the dowager, or the king's enemies, or whoever wove it? I don't understand this kind of weaving enough to know.

I'm a powerful weaver, yes, but trained within the confines of what was available in my mother's library. Which wasn't nearly as much as I'd like.

I don't have the time for subtlety, but subtlety is what I need.

So I stand in the center of the room, pray to the gods that the dowager doesn't come back early, and stretch my senses further.

I don't just sense the reality around me, I start perusing its potential. All the potential I can feel, and it isn't much through the absence. But still, I strain.

Then finally settle, and just breathe.

I hear a slight rustle of wind outside the curtained window and strain to hear anything more.

And I think I hear what I need, first, before I see it. Hear it with my weaver's senses, the discordant hum of a single thread, like a plucked string on a lute, that tiny shade off-key, resonating before it fades.

With my eyes still mostly closed, I move toward it. It's in the corner of the room, nearer the door into the rest of the suite.

I approach it, I reach for it, and slowly, slowly tug the string of reality out of the place it's currently resting. I don't want to unravel the whole if I can help it, but I want to understand what it's doing. And what it's concealing.

With the string in my willpower's hands, with my will coming to harmonize and then resonate with the same note, the room explodes in my senses around me.

I gasp, my eyes flying open.

Gods.

I'm beneath the muffling weaving now. It's above me, around me, like a cloaking shroud, but I can see the reality beneath it now. And *oh gods* this reality.

This room is thoroughly lived in, seething with current frustration and rage and a wanting so thick I feel I might choke.

I steady myself. Because I'm close. To whatever I must find, I'm close.

I hold the thread in my mind's eye and carefully survey the room again. From the nightmares that occupy the bed to the ambition that settles around the hearth in a potent miasma. The dowager's ambition.

My chest is getting tighter, but I can't let it stop me now. I must know.

And as the emotions show themselves, as the current and past and possible realities of this room present themselves to my wide-open senses, my eyes come to rest on a brick over the hearth that shows more agitation than the others.

Still carefully holding onto my thread, I approach.

The brick is loose, though not too loose, and slowly slides out when I get a grip on the edges and tug.

The scraping wheeze it makes is soft, but I wince. In the near silence of this room, it's far too loud.

Inside—I can't see too well what's inside. After setting the brick down on the rug, I bite my lip and reach in.

I feel something soft and oily.

My senses want to recoil, but I steel myself and draw out—a black leather bag. Oh. Had I been expecting something grisly?

The bag is small, fitting in the palm of my hand. I jostle it gently, and it clinks.

Frowning, I tug open the drawstring and tip out several glass vials onto my hand, and—

I nearly drop them, so gut-deep is my recoil.

There is another concealment woven over the bag, I hadn't even felt the intensity of the potential inside.

The vials. Gods, they are filled with magical potential. It shimmers in my senses, married to a liquid that's clear as water. Is it water? Water that's been elementally changed, or woven?

The vials are cool in my hand, cooler than they should be.

What am I holding? Are these vials the source of the unreality in the room, can that possibly be the case if they're so full of potential?

I grip the vials as tightly as I dare, my senses burning all the while, and move to the slit of light between the curtains to peer into the bag again.

There's still a small scroll of paper inside, tightly rolled. And another thicker paper that's heavily folded into a square.

I dare to set the vials down on a table beside the window and carefully pull out the papers.

Remembering myself, remembering that there is, in fact, time outside of this room and my throbbing weaver's senses, I look up at the door that leads to the service corridor. How much time has passed? Surely not much?

I'd better be quick about this. Being here as an unknown servant would be bad enough, but being here with this, with these vials, which are obviously important?

The papers are scraps torn from aged books. One, in a barely legible blackletter, details the making of a tincture, with technical terms I don't quite understand. It's definitely about weaving, though. A *weaver's* tincture? I thought tinctures were only for some elementalists, and healers who had no magic.

There's mention of threading the liquid through the will. The other thicker paper tells of how to conceal reality under the illusion of a room's slumber.

Shit.

Oh, gods.

And why wasn't this better hidden? I'd found it so easily, once I'd looked—

But then, I think I'm the strongest weaver I know. Whoever wove the reality in this room was subtle. They know what they're doing, even with these meager instructions. They weren't expecting anyone as strong at weaving as I am.

So is this an attempt at hiding the evidence? And evidence for...what?

What is the liquid?

I put the papers back in the bag, aching to take them with me, but not daring.

Instead, I pick up the vials again, this time holding one up to the sliver of sunlight.

The liquid inside shifts in both my physical and weaver's senses. It has a voice. It has a...malevolence.

It's like a slow vortex contained in glass.

It's meant to kill.

I swallow and slip the vials back inside the bag. I cinch the bag, inspect its reality to make sure it's returned as close as I can make it to how I found it. I slide it inside the hole above the hearth and return the brick to its place, then survey it all again.

This was in plain sight to me—but no, it wasn't. It was behind layers of palace security. It was under more than one obscuring layer of subtle weaving. It was never, ever meant to be found.

I feel like I'm going to throw up.

Did the dowager kill the king, her husband? Either she's a powerful weaver herself, or—or—

And this can't be Nikolai. I don't think.

So that leaves only one other weaver at court that I know of. One who the dowager might trust, who she's known for years, who warned me away from teaching the king to weave himself. I hadn't thought Master Aldric was powerful enough to weave something like this, but maybe that's the act.

And oh gods, he made no move to help, twice, when Torovan's life was in danger.

Did Master Aldric sabotage Torovan's weaver training so he'd never be able to see what works Aldric does in this palace? So Torovan would never be able to stop him?

Carefully, oh so carefully, I let go of the thread of reality I'm holding, let it slide back into place in the corner.

And the room, once again, dulls to my senses. The life drained away. The potential like it had never existed to begin with.

I press my fist to my mouth, fighting back a scream.

Maybe I should search more, but I need to get out of here. I need to get out *now*. My hands burn with the knowledge of what I might have just touched—the weapon used to kill a king.

I barely stop myself from running for the door.

I have to tell Valtair. I have to tell *Torovan*.

Chapter 36

Strength of Will

Torovan

I'm going to be a good king. I *am* going to be a good king and live up to my father's legacy, even if it kills me. No more terrifying the courtiers with my temper. No more going on hunts. No more neglecting the papers still on my father's desk. Or his journals and notes, all his plans.

Valtair is right. I can change things. Maybe not in all the ways I'd like to, but I do have the power to change my kingdom.

My father died, I suspect, because of the work he wished to do—rebalancing the power from the nobility to be more in the hands of the common people. I haven't had this same passion, and yet I used to sit at his hand for hours, listening to him reason through his decisions out loud for me, because he knew that one day, hopefully many years away, I would also be king.

I never realized how much of a gift that time was. I never disdained my father, but in recent years...in recent years, I'd been busy being a prince. Which was not wholly the same as being the son of my father.

And I *miss* him. Oh gods, I miss him. I wish he could guide me now—but he can't.

This is my kingdom now.

This is *my* kingdom.

After leaving Valtair on the night of the vortex disaster, I open the door to my father's study and approach his desk.

Caleb found too much reality, too much willpower here—and was that the work of a weaver? Or a very determined king?

I have been thinking about that. I'd seen what Caleb had seen, too, and it hadn't felt dangerous.

I sit at my father's desk for the first time. In his chair.

And maybe it is dangerous, because it's here where a king was trying to pull a kingdom into a new and different reality.

And I know it's where I need to be.

I light the lamps and pour through his remaining documents, untouched except for those which Valtair pulled out as immediately important for the kingdom, because I hadn't been able to bear it at the time.

I read all of them. Every last one, until my eyes burn. And then I open his desk drawers and start with his latest journal of notes and thoughts, and work backwards from there.

And somewhere in the third journal, I fall asleep at his desk.

The lamps are guttered out when I awake, dawn shining through the cracks in the curtains. And I feel...clearer.

Caleb is an insistent throb in my mind, an ache in my heart, but my head is full of everything I read the night before.

Maybe my father can still advise me. Maybe he has already, through his journals, through his thoughts.

Still muzzy with sleep, my neck aching from the way I'd slept hunched over the journals, I spread both of my palms on the smooth surface of the polished slate desk top. It was my father's reminder to himself that not everyone has the same privilege he has—and now, I make it my reminder, too. His scent is still here, a lingering in the wood of the chair, the fabric of the seat, in the books in this room, in the rugs, in the air.

I swallow.

My father, above all, wanted to do well by his kingdom. And I've been ignoring my duty in my sole focus on finding my father's killer. That has been important, it's important to keep my family safe. My father's enemies, now my enemies, are still around me. I saw that yesterday with the vortex.

But I've allowed those enemies to distract me. There's more than one way for my enemies to win—my father died trying to make this kingdom a better place. Can I do less than pick up his torch and march on?

I have so much I need to do.

I go back to my own rooms and splash my face in the stale water of the wash basin. I don't wait for my valet to arrive to change my clothes, but dress myself and hastily comb my hair. Then I gather up my guards and make my way down to the mage's quarters.

To Master Aldric's study.

Because a dismissal of Nikolai as unfit to serve in my court is foremost on my mind, and long overdue, no matter who his family is. Valtair stopped me the day before, but my head is clear now. My purpose is clear now. Nikolai's actions have put my life and the lives of those in my palace in danger, more than once now. Whether he was behind the storm or not, and whether he's behind more than the storm, he is a danger that must leave my palace.

This will not be a popular decision, but it's the right one.

Likely the first in a string of unpopular but right decisions. And it's important to me, much more important now, that my decisions be for the good of the kingdom and its people. All its people.

And if I also check the corridor in the mages' quarters for any glimpse of Caleb, well...that would be incidental.

But I don't see him. The door to his room is closed. It's early, but not so early that I think he's still asleep.

I do my best to ignore both my relief and the ache of his not being there when I want to see him. But I'm certainly not going to knock on his door. I'm not going to ask where he is.

Because I'm the king, my guards precede me to Master Aldric's study, and one raps a sharp knock on the master mage's door. I am, at least, fairly certain that Master Aldric will be in his study. He usually is in the mornings, even on the rest day.

I know coming down here is heavy-handed. But Master Aldric has always had a way of winding me around, making me feel less than the prince, and then the king, I should be. I didn't want to summon him and give him time to prepare his arguments, gather his allies, try to put up a wall in my path.

No. This will be done today.

For myself, for my kingdom. And also for Caleb—he never got the recognition he deserved for saving lives in my court that first day, and that is my fault. That I allowed Nikolai to remain in my court is also my fault. And I let Nikolai try to calm the storm.

I won't repeat that mistake again.

Aldric opens his door, sees the guard, and his eyes dart to me.

I feel my anger rising and study his lined face for any signs of guilt for running from the vortex yesterday, for abandoning me. For any signs of guilt for more than that. Because there *are* only two other weavers besides Caleb in this court—two obvious weavers, anyway.

But after that first moment of surprise that I'm here, he's back to his usual courtly grace. He smooths down his brocade tunic and steps out, dipping into a deep bow.

"Your Majesty. How may I serve you today?"

Pretty words.

And I remember how my father would deal with those who sought to flower him with nonsense words to get him to do what they wanted.

He was firm, but polite. Steady, but not unkind, unless it was needed.

I smile briefly, like my father would, and...by Aldric's expression, it's not having the intended effect.

I go back to my usual scowl. For now.

"Master Aldric, let us step into your study."

"Yes, of course, Sire."

It's a decent-sized room, covered with papers and bookcases, though it's neat and orderly in its controlled chaos. And I have the thought, a dawning thought, that it's meant to give the appearance of being scholarly without actually being used by a true scholar. The books are too neatly stacked. Spines too new and unworn from use. There is dust on the floor in front of some of the bookcases—a light scattering, not fulling cleaned up by the staff. But if he used the bookcases often, there should be paths, semicircles, tracks of less dust, smooth wooden floor.

That's how my father's study is.

Well, how it was. There's dust on the floor now.

I take a seat in one of the chairs across from Aldric's desk, and he settles behind his desk again, folding his hands. He looks at me expectantly, and for a moment, I freeze.

I'm the student again, sitting for lessons while he's my unwilling teacher. While he tells me, kindly, that I lack the basic willpower to safely perform even the simplest weavings, like changing the color of a flower, or brightness of a lamp.

I steel myself by forging ahead. I lean forward, hands on my knees. I'd rehearsed this in my head on the way here, and I'm determined to stick to what I need to say.

"You will dismiss Lord Nikolai Metrial from the mage candidates. He is reckless and has endangered my life not once, but twice now. He ran from the vortex when he said he would unravel it. He made the situation worse, and sent it on a path toward the palace."

I watch Master Aldric's face as I say this, looking for signs that he's annoyed with me, or that he disagrees with me. But he just keeps his placid, grandfatherly expression.

It's making my temper rise by the moment.

And I stop, take a breath, tighten my fists, loosen them again. The weight of my father's signet ring—my signet ring—presses into my palm. I've worn it since just after his death. But today, it feels like it means something more than a memento.

It means I am the king.

I brace myself. Because I know Aldric, and I know myself. And this is a battle of willpower that I *will* win.

"Nikolai is reckless, yes," Master Aldric says with a wave. "But you must consider the extent of his family's power and influence. Losing their support could significantly damage our kingdom's economy, while we are already in politically turbulent waters."

"Did you miss the part, Aldric, where I said he put my kingdom in danger? There will be much, much more damage if his recklessness kills this kingdom's king. Or any of my family."

Calm. I have to stay calm.

But thinking of Nikolai not listening to any of Caleb's pleas, of doing the wrong thing with the storm and then running away, boils my blood. I will not have that level of cowardice in my court.

"He goes," I say, and I know my tone leaves no room for argument.

But Master Aldric leans forward.

"Consider," he says, as if he can't see the anger in my eyes, or hear it in my voice, and surely he can. He is a master weaver, he can sense the flows of reality much more than I can. "Consider that Nikolai is of less danger to the kingdom here, in this court, under my watch and yours, than he is elsewhere. If he is left unchecked, he could cause far greater harm. You have Mage Candidate Ailin—keep him near Nikolai, and you won't have a problem."

Is he serious? Does he truly think that's a solution?

"Sire," he says in a confidential tone, as if he's going to impart a great secret, "I am training Nikolai—slowly, but surely—to be more responsible with both his decisions and his magic."

"You can't train someone who's untrainable," I growl. "You told me that."

He looks back, a sad note coming into his eyes.

It's total horse shit. He doesn't care about me. He doesn't care about Nikolai. I don't—I don't know what he cares about, and I don't know if he himself is my enemy. Is dismissing Nikolai the mistake, should I instead be dismissing Master Aldric? He's certainly never been my friend.

But there *are* only two weavers I know of at court beyond Caleb—and, if I'm counting, myself. I'm unsure if either Nikolai or Aldric are capable of doing whatever it is that's muffling my father's bedchamber. Even Caleb, powerful as he is, had trouble seeing it at first.

"I didn't say you were untrainable, Your Majesty," Aldric says. "Only that the training would be unwise."

My fingers creak the wood on the arms of the chair. "Because I don't have enough willpower? Gods, Aldric, I didn't see you trying to weave that storm away, it was Caleb, Caleb and me, we were both there in the middle of it, making it dissipate. Caleb most of all."

"Caleb Ailin is a very special mage," Aldric says, nodding as if he's solely responsible for Caleb's power and competence. And he's avoiding the question. "Talent and will like his are a rarity you don't see more than once in a century. He will keep Nikolai in hand, he always has so far, and you can maintain the vital economic balance in the kingdom."

"*I* wove the storm," I say. "Me. That was partly done with my willpower, Aldric."

And maybe—maybe this is why I'm here. Maybe all my other reasons are a sham. Because I did weave that storm, I lent my willpower to Caleb, and we were synchronous, we were in a dance together, and that doesn't happen if you're not actually a weaver.

Aldric was wrong. So wrong to deny me his training, so wrong to tell me I lacked the will.

He was *wrong*, and my need to tell him that burns in me.

I'm almost shaking, and it's taking all my effort to keep it from showing.

Aldric sighs, rubbing at his clean-shaven cheek. "I commend your efforts, Your Majesty, however, I still don't advise you to perform any weaving without supervision—"

"I'm not a fucking child!"

I snap my mouth shut. Because Valtair told me the day before that the walls are not infinitely thick, and neither are the doors.

I'd resolved to not bend to Aldric's maneuvering, but here I've done it again. He knows exactly how to wind me up. To distract and divert me from my purpose.

I stand. I need to get out of here. This isn't working, this isn't how my father would have handled this.

I'm not acting like the king I should be, not just now.

The stale air in the room, old parchment and new leather, is making my head ache.

Aldric rises with me. "Your Majesty, please give me a month. If Nikolai has not vastly improved in his manner and choices by then—then, we will reassess."

It isn't the solution I want. And how do I tell him that Caleb might not always be at court, that he could decide to leave at any time—if I push him away hard enough? Push *her* away.

I can't tell him that. I can't betray Caleb to him. I just... can't. Not this worm of a man.

And I still don't know if he had a hand or not in my father's death.

"One month," I manage to rasp out, tapping his desk.

And I leave, not quite slamming the door behind me.

Oh, my resolution to follow in my father's path is not off to a good start, at all.

But by the time I reach my own study again, my rage has built back into something else. Because I will, I *will* find my own willpower. I will find a way to make people listen to me, to actually do what I want them to do, not think they can walk all over me. Like I'm still a boy and not a man. Like I'm a figurehead and not their king.

I will show them all the power of my will. Not by my weaving, but by my command.

Sitting at my desk, I draft a summoning of the Council for this afternoon. Most of the nobles and advisors that make up the Council are still in the palace, enough of them, anyway. Once I summon the Council, though, I can't let the meeting wait until all of them arrive. That was my father's only mistake —he gave them time. He gave them warning. And he paid for that courtesy.

This is what I should have done the moment I became king, not spent months in a fog looking for clues. I should have stood up to and defied my father's enemies.

Those enemies can only truly succeed if they kill my father's dreams along with him, and I refuse to let those dreams die.

This afternoon, I plan to uphold my father's legacy and carry it forward. I'm going to decree that the power of the kingdom will be rebalanced.

And if anyone tries to kill me for it, as I know they killed my father—well, let them try. I will not rule my kingdom out of fear, but the strength of my will.

Chapter 37

Hope

Irava

I stumble out of the dowager's bedchamber, and Valtair isn't there. But then, he wouldn't be—he couldn't just wait outside the door, waiting for someone to find him and ask what he's doing there.

So I head to the closet. It's not far, at least. Every step, I'm scanning the corridor's shadows, waiting for a hidden enemy to appear.

Torovan's right to be afraid. He's right to suspect everyone around him.

My hands are shaking enough that I rattle the closet door knob trying to turn it.

Valtair pulls the door open instead, takes one look at my face, and pulls me inside.

He shuts the door. "What happened—"

"Quiet," I hiss, and lean back against the wall beside the door. The glass of the closet door lets in light from the small window down the corridor, but will also let out sound.

He bites his lip, looks past me to the door, and pulls me

deeper inside the shelves of linens. Which isn't far—it's not a large closet.

"Were you seen?" he asks. "Were you caught?"

"No." I meet his eyes. "It's poison. I think. I held it, and the instructions—it's a weaver, Valtair, it's definitely a weaver behind the poison. And I don't think it's Nikolai, it has to be Master Aldric."

Valtair stills. For a long moment, he stands there, too contained, too seething with whatever he's thinking for this tight space.

Then he says, "You're trembling. Sit down."

And he pulls me down with him to sit on the floor.

He starts to help me with my tangled skirts—but it's an illusion, and I swiftly drop it, wearing Caleb's clothes beneath. I reweave my illusion as Caleb again.

Valtair makes a startled sound, hands out, unsure of himself. His eyes flick over my face, his troubled look only deepening.

I set my jaw. I'm not going to apologize for being a weaver. Though…I might have given him warning switching illusions that quickly, true. We're both jumpy just now.

Finally he says, "Okay. Tell me everything."

And I do. As best I can, with as much detail as I can.

"A weaver's poison," he says. Takes a breath. "Gods. We have to tell Torovan. Now. As in, right now."

I stiffen, smoothing down the wrinkles in my pants. I threw them on the floor in a fit of pique before going to bed last night, and now they're much less presentable than they were. "We have to see, first, if it truly is what killed his father. I think I can look beneath the weaving of unreality now. You have access to his father's bedchamber? We can do that first—"

"We have to tell Torovan," Valtair says again, more firmly. "Whatever you two have going on, this is much, much bigger. If you need more proof, we'll go look at his father's bedchamber together. All of us, with Torovan. He will need to see it with his weaver's senses, too, if he can. If you can help him with that."

I don't want to see Torovan yet. I'm still not over his scorching look outside the Great Hall last night. I'm not over his naked hurt and betrayal in the garden. I'm not over the feel of him beneath me as I pinned him to the ground, using all the strength I could spare to keep him from being pulled into the vortex, away from me. I'm not over the feel of us weaving together in absolutely perfect harmony.

And what was I expecting to happen after searching the dowager's bedchamber today? Of course I'd have to talk to Torovan.

Or maybe I hadn't truly thought I'd find anything worth reporting. I certainly hadn't thought I'd find the weapon used to kill the king. *Probably* the weapon used.

My gut twists. Gods, I've been trying to distract myself from the king, haven't I, more than actually trying to help him? But the thought of his life in danger clenches my heart.

And the thought of hurting him. It hurts, it physically hurts, to think that what I have to tell him will cause him pain, and I know it will.

It was his *mother's* hearth. His mother's chambers.

His mother's weapon.

And if we take this to him, and we all go to his father's bedchamber and I still find nothing there, because I saw nothing more than the unreality the first time...won't that only crush Torovan further? If there's even a chance that I'm wrong about this—and I don't think I am, but—

I know I'm making excuses. I know I'm not thinking this through the way I should be. Valtair is absolutely right, Torovan must know. I think this was how his father was killed. If this poison is still here in the palace, his life is in danger.

And I'm the only one who can protect him against the weaver who killed his father.

My heartbeat kicks up again. "I should have taken the vials with me," I say. I'd been worried about the dowager finding out the room had been disturbed, but now I'm more than worried about the king's life. I should have grabbed that poison, and the scraps of pages, and brought all of it straight to the king.

But would the dowager truly want to kill her son? She threatened me, warning me off from Torovan, and I'd thought it was a mother's warning off. It's something my own mother might do.

But she knows Caleb is a weaver, and that I'm powerful enough to unravel another weaver's magic. I'm a threat. She didn't want me to see what I've seen.

The dowager suggested Torovan hold that garden party. That was what had made me think I had to see her chambers again, and I wasn't wrong.

And Nikolai had been planning something, but...but wouldn't an assassin have finished the job? If Nikolai is an assassin, he's the most incompetent one I can think of. He's a dangerous fool, but he is a fool.

I swallow, thinking of the lessons I've had with Master Aldric. Of him saying that he wished to train me. That he saw my potential. Was he keeping me close, bringing me to his side, knowing that I could both help or hinder him?

What makes sense here? My eyes sting with the frustration of my whirling thoughts.

"No, you were right to leave the vials there," Valtair says. "It has to be Torovan to find that evidence against her. Which is why we have to take this to him now, before the dowager or anyone else discovers that their magic was disturbed."

I shudder. I wish, fervently, that I hadn't searched the dowager's rooms.

But no, I don't wish that.

I swallow the burning lump in my throat.

I look up, meet Valtair's eyes. "This will break him."

Break him more. More than I already have.

He grips my shoulders, bracing me. And I suck in a breath, startled. It's the sort of gesture a man would make to a man, and he knows I'm not, but—

It eases me. It does brace me.

"Caleb. It doesn't matter if it will break him—he can handle that. It's breaking him more not to know. It could cost him his life."

It's *poison*. Active poison, stored not far from where he makes his own bed. Poison, in his mother's bedchamber.

I swallow. Slowly nod.

"I'll be there," he says. "If he tries to rage at you—"

But I don't think he will. He's too hurt for that.

Valtair nods and lets go of me. He's still looking at me, and it's a weird look. Searching.

"Caleb. Last night, when we—when we, ah, had to cover being in the empty room together—"

I blush hard, because gods, that had been awkward, and really, it was me who'd put him in that position. I never should have asked that of him. And did Torovan rage at him, then?

Because of me? Is that what he's getting at now, that he's afraid of Torovan's anger, too?

If I didn't truly know that Torovan's life was in danger, if I hadn't seen what I'd seen this morning, I'd leave the palace now.

But no, I wouldn't.

If Torovan thinks he doesn't have the willpower, he doesn't know what it is to have no willpower.

I have no will, absolutely no will of my own, when it comes to him.

And that—that is the reason I don't want to go to him now. Because what he means to me *terrifies* me. I want to protect him, to shield him with everything I am, and I don't know that I can. I can't protect him from this hurt of knowing his mother killed his father, or at least had a hand in his father's death. That his mother might be trying to harm him now.

I expect Valtair to say something about how Torovan is angry with him, or with me, for last night, or that Valtair's angry with me. He certainly has a right to be.

But instead he asks, hesitant, "Are you a man?"

I stare back at him. "What?"

My head is reeling, because it's already reeling. Was this part of what he was getting at on the way up this morning, does he think I'm lying to him—that I'm a spy, that *I'm* involved with this plot against Torovan—

My whole body recoils from the thought. "You know who I am, you've seen me as myself. I'm not—"

He holds up his hands, waves them. "No, I mean, yes, I wouldn't ask, it really isn't my business, but—Caleb, last night, you didn't...gods, how to put it, but you didn't feel like an illusion to me. And if that's the reason you're hesitating with Tor, you don't think he'll be okay with that—"

Oh gods. I look down, my face burning, impossibly, hotter. I'm only wearing the illusion of Caleb now, not the reality, but I remember what that reality feels like. Oh gods do I remember.

"And you don't have to tell me, okay, but he would be okay with that. Or, okay if you are a woman. But you need—I need you to know that. Whatever it is, tell him? Tell him who you are. Please."

I'm trembling again. And my mind has gone blank, because...because.

He sounds desperate, and rattled. This polished courtier, rattled.

I look up. "I'll be bringing him the news that his mother killed his father. That's not helping him, even if it's necessary. And he won't love me for that. He'll resent me for that, on top of everything else—"

"He loves you," Valtair says, and I freeze.

He can't know that, not for sure.

But Torovan let me stay at the palace, even after I'd shown him I'd been lying to him. He didn't call his guards. He invited me to his table. He let me eat beside his sister, and he's very protective of his sister.

He looked furious that I might have even possibly had a tryst with Valtair. *Jealous.*

I shiver.

"He loves you," Valtair says again, insistent. "And whether you are Caleb, or you're not Caleb, and even if what you found today is hard, he needs to know that, too—he's drowning, Caleb, and he needs a way out."

I part my lips.

And then harden my eyes. I harden my heart, because I can't dare, not even a little, to hope. To hope that Torovan's heart could be so big. To hope that he could look at me with anything but pain and anger.

"You have access to his father's chambers?" I ask again. It was the reason he'd given the guards for coming into this service corridor.

"Yes," he says, scowling. "Gods. You still want to go there first—I told you, we need Torovan—"

"I have to see before I bring this to him. Please. I will not give him false hope." Or false grief.

But I'm still stalling. I know I'm stalling—it will be grief and hope either way. And a bad deal all around.

Valtair grimaces, but then pushes up, and reaches a hand to lever me up, too.

"All right. You're already Caleb, not the servant woman—we might as well go through his father's chambers to his study, and you can have your look on the way."

Chapter 38

Poison

Irava

Valtair lets us into the late king's bedchamber through the service access. The door creaks, a slow groan that makes me freeze—will Torovan hear it? Will he find us in here? That, suddenly, feels much worse than me going to him. I'm here, where I shouldn't be, and even with Valtair, it feels like an intrusion.

Valtair nudges me inside, saying in a low voice, "It's fine, this door always creaks. I don't think you can hear it from the other rooms."

I nod, not quite willing to believe him, but step inside the stuffy room.

The curtains aren't drawn as they'd been before. Has Torovan been here again? Sunlight shines through the high windows, illuminating dust as it swirls about the room. The bedchamber still smells of disuse, the air eerily still. It's like a forest with no sound.

And the unreality is here, clear as anything.

I shiver, folding my arms against a chill that's deeper than the cool air.

I'd been too focused on Torovan when I was here before to notice all the little details. I see the small painted portraits of a young Torovan and Elsira on the bedside table, a rusting ancient broadsword over the empty and much more modern marble hearth. The tapestries, showing hunts with riders in antiquated outfits and a dance of the gods and goddesses of summer. The worn red patterned rug on the dark wood floor that surely must hold sentimental value, because it's shabby compared to everything else in this room.

Valtair doesn't say anything as he crosses to the opposite side of the room. He gently opens the door to Torovan's father's study, peering inside.

He closes it again, quietly.

So Torovan isn't in there—not that I thought he would be, his own study is beyond it. But had Valtair thought he would be?

"All right," Valtair says in a low voice, crossing back to me. "What do we have to do?"

It feels like we're both moving in stolen time. And I can sense he's just as agitated as I am.

"You have to stand there and not distract me," I say, my own voice barely louder than a whisper.

And maybe this is a bad idea. I know it's a bad idea, we should have gone to Torovan first.

But I'm just not ready.

I go to the bed, to the side where I felt the unreality the strongest before. I center myself as I had in the dowager's chambers, reaching out both hands, feeling with all my senses.

I let my breathing slow, looking around me again, listening.

My skin is crawling with the sense of unreality now, the deadness of it, when I know there has to be more life here. There has to be. Torovan was here, or someone was here at least—the curtains are open.

"What is supposed to be—" Valtair asks.

My nerves jangle at the interruption and I snap, "Quiet!"

My gut twinges with guilt at the outburst, he didn't deserve that, but he can't break my concentration. Not now.

And Valtair is quiet.

I focus in again, and this time, I hear it.

The discordant thread isn't in the corner this time, but attached to the floor. Anchored to it, maybe, and is that how this weaving of unreality is both made and unraveled, by anchoring it to a single point?

I'd worried about unraveling the weaving in the dowager's chambers, but I have to unravel it here. I have to—Torovan has to see what's here. And so do I.

I carefully reach for the thread and tease it up and away from its anchor. I pull slowly, and the weaving around me starts to loosen. I can't pull harder or faster without risking it unraveling out of control, so I just keep pulling—until my pulling gains a momentum of its own.

Valtair sucks in a sharp breath. He's not a weaver, he's an elementalist, but even people with no magic can sense when a room goes from untouched to full of trouble and angst.

And this one is full of both. I feel the dissonance at my core as I continue to unravel the weaving, drawing the threads of reality back to myself, soothing them. They're like agitated children in my senses—not alive as such, but imprinted with the emotions of everything around them.

And then—what do I do from here? These threads I'm

holding belong in this room. They were misused, bent out of shape, told to conceal themselves and the secrets they hid. They were stolen from the places where they belonged. Forced to serve a purpose that was against their nature.

For a moment, I'm overwhelmed. It's such a twisting of reality, a crime in itself.

"Caleb—"

"Quiet," I whisper, but it's softer this time. Then add, "Please."

Valtair makes a noise, walks restlessly around the room.

"I have to put the threads back," I say, "or—there will be trouble."

He spins, boots clamoring on the floor. "An explosion? Is it that kind of dangerous? Should I get Torovan out of his study—"

"No, no." Though it could be that, if I didn't know where the threads need to go, at least. But this will take time. "I just need time."

He draws a breath. I dare a full glance back, and he looks like he wants to protest, but he makes a wave, the jewels in one of his rings flashing. He settles himself carefully on a dressing chair across the room. His foot bobbing chaotically.

Carefully, thread by thread, I begin to place them back in the room where they belong. A few threads for the bedcovers. Many more for the mattress. Some for the carpet and the curtains, the air and the walls. The pillows. The bedposts.

It's all the possibilities of motion. And as the pieces return to where they should be, they paint an intensity of malice on the bed that I recognize. It's the same feeling as in the vials. The poison.

So I had found the weapon. But I can hardly spare thought now to think through all of what that means.

I don't know how much time passes.

I hear Valtair rustling, but he doesn't say anything more, doesn't leave, doesn't ask when I'll be done.

And then, finally, I am done.

I shudder, free of the injured threads, and turn to him.

He's slumped in the chair, having picked up a book from somewhere. He doesn't look like he's actually reading it, though.

"It's done," I say. "The weaving is gone and the threads returned to their natural states."

Valtair snaps the book shut and stretches as he stands. He joins me back beside the bed, staring down at it.

"Is it the magical poison?" he asks. "The weaver's poison?"

I turn back to the bed and hold my hands out, passing them over the covers without touching them. I don't truly need to do this, but it helps me focus, and gives me a motion to think about other than the creeping horror of feeling, tangibly feeling, how the king died.

I don't feel possibilities here, I feel facts.

"Yes," I whisper. "It was the poison."

I close my eyes. It's been four months, but with the muffling weaving never letting the possibilities bloom, the emotions and imprints of motion and intent seethe around me. Valtair is tense with the untrained sense of it, and my shoulders are tight, my jaw clenched against the raw tang of agony. Of betrayal.

This magical poison was not a good way to die. It tore the king apart from the inside, while still locking him in outward sleep. But the king knew. He *knew* he'd been betrayed, in the last fleeting moments before he'd died.

And how had the poison been administered? Surely, surely the king had people who checked for such things, my mother did, but—but the king could have eaten with his wife. Or Master Aldric. Or someone else, if there was someone else in on this plot, could have slipped it into his cup. Maybe it wouldn't even work on anyone but its intended target—and that made more sense to my weaver's training than a poison that could kill by accident and then give itself away.

I feel the lingering of magical potential over the bed, over the place where the king must have been sleeping. He'd died, peacefully, in his sleep.

But he had *not* died peacefully in his sleep.

"Is the poison still here?" Valtair asks, and he's keeping his hands rigidly to his sides. I think of how Torovan and I both touched the covers before—and no, there's no poison now. Just the fact of it. The ugly malice of it. The poison did what it was made to do.

And if there are more vials in the dowager's bedchamber, does that mean there were more tries if the first failed, or more poisons meant for other people?

Like Torovan.

I pull my hands back from my sensing. I fold my arms, press them tightly to my stomach.

"Okay," I say, "okay. We go talk to Torovan."

Chapter 39

Fear

Irava

Torovan doesn't answer when Valtair knocks on the door that leads from his father's rooms into Torovan's study. Valtair waits, and then knocks again.

Gods, no. No, has something happened—

I reach for the handle just as Valtair yanks the door open.

No one is inside. The hearth is banked—Torovan isn't here.

I draw in a long, long breath. And I'm shaking again.

And it's probably nothing, there's no sign of malice here, but all the same, I extend my weaver's senses, touch the threads of this room and all their potentials.

There is truly no malice here. Angst. A coiled and recent hurt. Determination.

I know where that hurt comes from.

Swallowing, I let go of my full senses again.

Valtair and I share a look.

"He's fine," I say. At least, this room and what it tells me knows that nothing bad happened here.

Valtair rubs his face. "Gods. We don't even know that anything *will* happen. It's been four months."

But we don't know that it won't. And knowing that the two people behind the king's death are still free—and hold power—in the palace is creeping over me in waves of dread.

"He's probably meeting with a noble or an advisor in one of the formal chambers downstairs," Valtair says. "He's been —" He eyes the stacks of papers on the desk. "He's been putting much more attention into the kingdom of late."

"So what do we do?" I shift nervously as I eye the door to the corridor. Torovan could come through at any moment. Or, Torovan could be elsewhere. In danger.

I have to stop, remind myself that outside of what I found out today, nothing has changed. I don't think the dowager knows I've been in her rooms, and would Master Aldric know I unraveled one of his weavings? It *has* to be Master Aldric helping her. He's just the only reasonable choice, isn't he?

None of it settles well in my gut. My world might have been shaken today, but it's only been my world, and Valtair's— no one else's.

Beyond the fact that someone called a storm to the palace the day before. And that thought has my nerves spiking again.

"Well, we still have to tell him," Valtair says. He frowns at me, fiddling with the ruffled cuff of one sleeve. "And if I'm going to track him down, I don't think you can go with me. It would be too suspicious, if anyone's watching for that." He scowls at Torovan's desk. "It would have been easier if he was here."

Is anyone watching?

Someone has to be. Someone had to call the storm. I didn't go to the dowager's chambers on a lark, I went because my gut was telling me she was involved.

"Master Aldric did warn me off from teaching the king," I say. And *am* I sure, or am I trying to convince myself now? Can I afford at all to be wrong? "And the dowager threatened me against—uh—"

"Having an affair with him? Yeah, that would be her in any case." He gives a small, tight smile that hardly reaches his eyes. "She's done that before for Torovan's lovers."

And I'm so drained by the fear of danger, by what I've discovered, and the fear of what Torovan will do once he knows about this that I can hardly blush.

Valtair, who's a bundle of nervous tics in motion, goes still. He looks more closely at me. "Caleb, he will come around. And we'll find him before anything goes wrong. Or, I will. Sorry. And *then you can talk*. It will be much, much better after that, I think. We need less secrets in this palace."

Which doesn't comfort me, if that's what he's going for. I am dreading talking to Torovan with all of my soul.

But I nod. "I'll—I'll go back to my quarters. It's the rest day anyway—I'm expected to be there—"

"Good. That's good."

I want to ask him to tell me, send word somehow, when he knows the king is safe, but I know that will add too much suspicion for whoever's watching, too. And Torovan will surely be at dinner tonight. I can reassure myself then.

It is going to kill me to leave everything like this, to carry on as if all is normal, but I must. We all must, until...whatever's going to happen next happens.

Gods. What will Torovan do, will he arrest his mother?

And when I tell him who I am, will he throw me out of his palace? Will he cancel the treaty?

Cancel the engagement?

"Okay," I manage, drawing myself up. Trying my best to stand straight and tall and ordinary. "I will, uh, see you at dinner tonight."

"Not," he says, "at the high table for you, but we will be there. And I'll find a way for you to talk to him, after."

I swallow, but nod.

Tonight, then.

I will tell Torovan tonight. Tell him everything.

And what happens will happen, because Valtair is right. There need to be far less secrets in this palace.

∽

VALTAIR and I decide it's best we go back the way we came in, so I pull the illusion of the servant matron around myself again and follow Valtair back past the guards, through the service corridors, down the back stairs, until we reach the kitchens. There, he leaves me to find a dark alcove and reweave Caleb around myself again, while he's off to find Torovan.

And I try not to think about how that conversation will go.

I walk back to my quarters in a daze, hardly seeing anyone around me, hardly hearing the snatches of conversation from those lingering in the corridors.

Are these the same corridors I've been coming to call...well, not entirely home, exactly, but at least a comfortable place for now? A place where I have a purpose?

Is the lighting different, the hushed whispers, when people see me, full of ill intent? Is that my imagination, am I just that jumpy? People know I can weave a storm now. I saved the king's life twice, and sat at his table last night. I was seen—at least they think—having a tryst with Valtair. I wasn't invisible before, but I'm a beacon now, and I just want to run from those eyes, from those whispering mouths, and hide.

I saw the weapon used to kill a king today. I felt the horror of that murder, the imprint of that reality in his bed.

I shudder as I walk and keep my head down.

If Torovan's a target, I know I'm a target, too. I have been ever since I unraveled Nikolai's magic that first day, but I feel it so much more now, a prickling fear at the back of my neck. Before, I was afraid of Nikolai's revenge. Now?

I'm afraid of the people who killed the king.

I'm afraid they'll try to do it again, and try to kill me, too.

By the time I reach the mages' common room, I'm so tense that I almost don't see Master Aldric by the hearth. He's guiding two of the elementalist candidates through breathing exercises, which feels so incongruent to everything I've seen today that I almost stop in my tracks.

But I manage to keep walking.

One of the candidates looks over at me, but Master Aldric's eyes are closed as he recites a rhythmic breathing aid.

And what if...what if I can bring the final proof to Torovan tonight? Valtair will certainly tell him my suspicions about Master Aldric, but what if I can give him what he needs to arrest the master weaver, too? To eliminate that danger?

That scenario grows in my thoughts as I enter the corridor to our housing and pass the door to Master Aldric's study.

And...Master Aldric is busy, in the common room, teaching the other candidates.

I pause at the door to his study. Come fully back to my

surroundings as I listen. I still hear his voice, a deep murmuring in the other room.

I can be quick. I just need to see if there's a feel of unreality here, too. I hadn't known to feel for that before, but I do now. I have to check. I have to know.

I have to give Torovan everything I can, to keep him safe.

And so that, maybe, he won't entirely hate me when I tell him who I really am.

I touch the door handle, turn it gently. It's unlocked.

With one backward glance down the corridor toward the common room, I slip into Master Aldric's study and ease the door shut behind me.

Chapter 40

Shadows

Torovan

The palace steward reads the command I just drafted, squinting through his half-moon spectacles at the paper. His mouth is drawn tight, and he looks up at me, head tilted, sharp gray-black brows drawn together.

He doesn't ask if I'm sure. And maybe more people have guessed at the reason my father died than I've thought.

"This is a good work, Sire," he says quietly. "But it will leave everyone scrambling if you wish it to be today."

"I do."

When I entered his office, he came around his desk, bowing deeply. As is proper. But now we stand close, both angled to see the paper in his hands.

Carefully, he folds it again. "Well, it's still morning, though not by much. But there's enough time, I think. I will see the Council meeting is called. Four turns after midday?"

"Yes. Thank you." I turn to go.

"Thank you, Your Majesty, from saving the palace from ruin. The day before."

I stop and stare back at him. This old man who I've known all my life. I used to call him Mr. Sky when I was a child, because he always looked straight up to think. His name, though, is Derran. He used to be Valtair's father's secretary before he was promoted to be the palace steward. And by nature of the job, the kingdom's steward.

"I didn't save the palace," I say, "that was the mage candidate—"

"Yes, I believe the mage candidate Ailin is skilled. However, my reports say that he had sufficient help. Your Majesty—please use those same skills in the coming days. If you plan to see this through." He sniffs and nods at the paper again, now folded in his hand.

I know what he's saying, and what he won't say.

I do know what danger I'm putting myself in.

But I must.

And maybe this meeting today will flush out the murderer, the assassin. Maybe I can end this, make my kingdom a safe and worthy place to marry my queen. To—to raise my heirs.

I absolutely don't let myself think of Caleb, of what I asked him to be for me before I knew he was an illusion. Of what I'm still thinking about, though I know I can't. I can't have a lover. I certainly can't have Caleb now.

Or maybe it's a hollow hope that I or my family will ever be safe. But can I do anything other than be the king my father would have wanted me to be?

I have to try. Even if I'm not adequate to the task, I still must try.

And I do think of how I stood next to Caleb in the storm, lending him all the will and strength I could, and that made a difference. I had made a difference.

The steward reaches up and pats me on the shoulder, like he used to do when I was a boy. It's not the same, not remotely the same, as how Master Aldric treated me earlier today—this isn't demeaning, it's endearment. This man is warning me, but not discouraging me.

And I smile, just a little.

This is much, much better than the bow he gave me when I first entered.

I clap his shoulder back.

"Thank you, Derran, for handling this. Send up anyone who needs my approval. I'll be in my study, preparing for the meeting. But—I thought it best to bring this to you in person, not by messenger."

He nods. "Oh, you were right at that. All right—I'll set this in motion." And he shuffles back to his desk to get to work, waving me off like my father used to.

And with that thought, my eyes sting, and I quickly turn away, reach for the door.

Would my father approve of how I'm handling this, too? Or even Count Valtair, if he was here. My father had been warm and friendly, but the count had always been aloof, his nods of approval—spare as they were—a thing to be treasured.

I bite my lip as I step back into the corridor.

But then, I straighten. I have to be the king again.

My guards are waiting outside, looking jumpier than usual. Which they have been, ever since the vortex the day before. They've been staying especially close, and they don't know I'm about to put my life in even more danger. I will need to tell them before this afternoon.

Everyone in the palace seems to know the danger of my father's murder is real and still present. Even if most of them are pretending not to—even with the storm, which isn't being called anything but a storm. My mother told me before to move on from my suspicions, that it was obvious my father's death was natural, but she is the one who hasn't been able to move past her denial, isn't she?

I'm halfway back to my study, trying to think through what I'll say at the Council meeting this afternoon, when Valtair rounds a corner at speed and nearly collides with my point guard.

The guard jumps back, holding out an arm to steady Valtair as he stumbles.

"Valtair?" I ask. His shoulders are tight, and there's a sheen of sweat on his brow. His clothes are rumpled, which gives more alarm in my mind than anything else. He never leaves even a tryst with his clothing disheveled.

Valtair looks around at my guards, back to me. "Tor. Can we talk?"

I don't have the time, but his obvious distress is making me jumpy, too. Valtair doesn't scare easily—not actual fear, though he's been known to put on a show for the court.

We're just past the Great Hall, moving toward the living area of the palace. I open my hands and wave back toward the room we'd talked in the night before.

Valtair nods and sets the pace, not too brisk, and I can tell he's straining to keep it reasonable.

What by all the gods happened? Tension is spiking up my shoulders now, too, and I feel the dagger I've kept on my hip since my father died, so much a part of my daily garb now that I've almost forgotten it's there.

It's not customary for a king to carry a practical weapon in the palace, though I did train with sword, knife, bow, and staff growing up. A precaution, my father called it, and a good source of learning self-discipline for me.

But even if I did carry a sword, that sort of weapon would do little good against a determined elementalist or a weaver. My guards are trained, some of them elementalists themselves, if lesser talents than the court mages.

But not even a company of guards could protect my father.

Should I start enlisting the court mages as bodyguards?

I'm so keyed up by the time Valtair opens the door to the empty room—makes sure, again, that it's empty—and then closes and locks it behind us, that I burst out, "By all the summer gods, Valtair—"

He comes close. He's brimming with things he needs to say, but he's not saying any of them yet.

And now I'm getting truly scared.

He holds up both hands, and I know I'm not going to like what he says next.

"Caleb—had an idea."

I let out my breath in a rush. No, I'm not going to like this. "What did you do? What trouble are you in—what did *he* do?"

"He examined your—"

He stops, looks around again. He whirls and strides to the windows, checking the curtains, going to check under the tablecloths like he did last night. He makes an even more thorough search of it this time.

"Valtair," I warn, "I have a busy day."

But he holds up a quelling finger, not saying anything more until he comes back. And still he gets close and whispers.

"Caleb looked in your mother's bedchamber. He says it has a feel of unreality, like your father's."

Caleb went into my mother's bedchamber? How—

Gods. He can weave illusions like it's breath. And Valtair was in on this? Did he help Caleb get into my mother's chambers?

Valtair is my best friend, he's one of the only people in the world that I trust. But breaking into my mother's chambers is going too far, and he should know that.

I feel the anger building, but it's warring with the greater, deeper fear. Because what he just said is sinking in.

"My mother's in danger? Is that what you mean, that the assassin is coming for her next—"

"No, Tor." He grips my arms, and his eyes are fairly wild. "No. Caleb looked beneath the unreality, and he saw—he saw the means by which your mother killed your father."

The room tilts. And I'm glad Valtair is holding on to me now, because otherwise I'd be tilting, too.

"Tor! Gods dammit, I didn't mean to—"

I meet his eyes, gripping his shoulders back to steady myself. He's not wearing the cloying cologne he's taken to in the last month. Which I know he only does when he doesn't want himself to be the center of things.

Like when he's sneaking—or helping Caleb sneak—into my mother's chambers.

"The means," I say.

"It was poison. A weaver's poison."

A weaver.

My mind blanks. Caleb—it couldn't be Caleb. No, it absolutely could not have been—

"We think it's Master Aldric. Or maybe another weaver hidden at court—but all of this was done by a really skilled weaver, Caleb says. We also checked your father's bedchamber again—"

"You are taking *immense* liberties with—"

"I know, Tor!" His hands tighten on my shoulders, fingers digging in before he loosens his grip again. One of his rings is digging into my shoulder. "But it was important. You know it was important, and we didn't want to say anything unless we found something. To accuse your—the dowager. Gods, Tor."

He lets go of me, backs up with his hands to his forehead to pace a tight circle. His nostrils are flaring. And he still hasn't straightened his shirt, or his slightly askew blue brocade coat.

These are the details I notice, because they're far easier to deal with than what he's just told me.

He's terrified. He's furious and terrified, and I'm feeling the same building in me.

"My father's bedchamber?" I manage, squeezing my own hands behind my back.

"There was a magical poison that Caleb found, in your mother's bedchamber. Caleb found the residue—or imprint, maybe, he said it wasn't still on the bed—"

My nerves snap. "She," I correct him. Caleb is a woman. And he keeps forgetting that. And I keep forgetting that, and I can't. Because I can't at all deal with what Valtair's telling me now and also deal with Caleb.

He blinks at me, draws back. "Well, Caleb found it. And it was meant to kill your father, and just your father. We think. The vials are still above your mother's hearth, hidden beneath the unreality weaving, which Caleb put back in place—but the weaving in your father's bedchamber is gone. Caleb unraveled it. And I felt it, Tor. I felt the malice in that room, and I'm not even a weaver. Oh, gods. It wasn't peaceful, Tor."

His eyes are shining. And I know, he loved my father, too. He would spend afternoons with Elsira and I, too, while his father was busy being the Minister of Finance. But mine, the king, would have all of us in his study. We played or studied quietly, and then listened when he told us about the kingdom.

I swallow, and my ears are ringing.

The hairs on my arms raise. The hairs on the back of my neck prickle, and so many things I've been trying to pull together for months now are crashing in on me.

And gods of all the seasons, I just set into motion again the very thing that killed my father—his wanting to redistribute the power in the kingdom. I can't stop that Council meeting now, and I don't want to.

But my mother—gods, why would she wish my father dead? My chest is burning with the thought. How could she even think of it? She's my mother, and he was my father.

But it's not hard for me, even now, to see why she wouldn't want my father to carry through with his plans. For him to let power ebb from the noble families, and from the crown, slowly in measurable strides, back to the people. The plan wouldn't eliminate the nobility, but it would temper them. And temper the crown.

It was a better way—I'd read his notes. I'd spent hours pouring through his thoughts on why this was necessary, why it would strengthen the kingdom. I'd spent hours as a child listening to his reasons why he thought the way he thought, which had all led to this.

But my mother's family is wealthy and powerful, both nobility and merchants. And was wanting to keep hold of her power, her family's power, enough to kill her husband?

But she'd never loved him. She'd been betrothed to him from a politically rivaling family, a marriage like the one I'm about to enter now, though from a noble family in our own kingdom.

Could my mother truly kill for power? Kill my father? Could she truly do that?

When I'm old, if I'm lucky enough to live that long, will my wife kill me in my sleep, too?

I shudder, focus back on Valtair.

And then I take a breath. Should I go back to the steward, take the paper back? Is it too late? Would my mother dare—would she dare to kill me, too, if I continue my father's work? If I rebalance the power in the kingdom, too?

She does love me. I know that.

Or do I?

Does she think, somehow, that what she did was for me?

But how could she do this?

It's a mistake. It has to be a mistake. What Caleb saw means something else.

I trust Caleb with my life. Beyond everything else—I do trust him. Or her. Maybe not in everything, but in this—Caleb wouldn't lie to me in this. I know that.

He drove stakes made of his own will into the ground and faced down a storm for me.

"Were you there?" I ask Valtair, and it comes out harsher than I intended. Valtair is unfazed. He knows me too well.

"I was waiting outside, if you mean was I at your mother's chambers. Caleb was immensely distressed when he came out."

"She's an illusionist—"

"Caleb was *shaking*, Tor."

And now I'm straining to keep from shaking myself.

"Where is Caleb now?" I ask.

Because if Caleb can see this evidence, then I need to see it, too. I need my palace to be out of danger. And I need the person who killed my father to...to have some kind of justice. Though the thought, the dawning horror, that I might have to lose both parents, is clawing up my throat.

I cough, choke, manage to swallow.

"Tor."

I hold up both hands, taking a step back. I need to get a hold of myself. I have to. If I've set my will in motion today, and if I back down now, I won't ever have the same chance again. My enemies will know what I intend to do and strike—

My enemies.

My mother.

"Are you okay?" Valtair asks. "No, stupid question. Caleb went back to his quarters—"

I focus on him again. Focus on what he said, on Caleb. Valtair is insisting on calling Caleb "he," and I don't think it's just because of the stress of the moment.

I open my hands.

"And you said Caleb knows this was the work of a weaver?"

So it wasn't just my mother.

And it certainly wasn't Caleb.

Caleb said in the garden he didn't think Nikolai was skilled enough for the kind of weaving that's in my father's bedchamber.

So, then Master Aldric. The man who has made it his personal mission to crush my will. Who I tried to command earlier today, and he just dismissed me out of hand. Yes, I'd known he might be the weaver behind the unreality then, but a large part of me hadn't wanted to believe it was true. Couldn't believe it.

Gods, no wonder he didn't want to teach me. If I was a

skilled weaver, I could see what he was doing. I could call him out. I could stop him.

And Caleb is going now to the mages' quarters, where Master Aldric's study is? Where Master Aldric himself lives?

I have a sudden wrenching sense of dread.

"Valtair, whose idea was it to search my mother's chambers?"

He looks uncomfortable, shifting his weight. "Caleb's. But I helped—"

In the garden after the storm, Caleb had looked so desperate, wholly desperate, to win back my trust. He'd said, "I'm yours to command." And gods, that had been the twist of the knife.

I'd been so angry then, I'd been so focused on what I saw as a betrayal. And it still is a betrayal.

But what Caleb and Valtair have done is reckless in the extreme.

And if Caleb was that desperate that he'd sneak into the bedchamber of a former queen, would he also be reckless enough to try to gather evidence against Master Aldric?

Am I jumping at shadows?

Do I dare take that chance?

If Caleb has somehow disturbed any of Master Aldric's weavings, if there's any way Aldric would know Caleb found him out—even if Caleb did just go to his own quarters as Valtair said—

I grip Valtair's shoulder to steady myself. "You did this just now? Found this out today?"

But it makes sense, my mother's always at the cathedral on rest day.

He nods, but I'm already moving past him to the door. And I'm breaking into a run.

Chapter 41

The Fall of Illusions
Irava

In Master Aldric's study, the curtains are pulled back around the single window, letting in afternoon light.

I stand just inside the room with its large desk, its chairs and bookcases, its scattered piles of books. And there's no feeling of unreality here—this study is pulsing with a personality that is Master Aldric's, orderly and calculated, a slight edge of frustration.

Any malice? Do I sense any malice at all?

I'm tensed to run or reach for the threads of reality around me to—what, defend myself? This is the study of a weaver. Maybe an immensely powerful weaver who's been hiding his capabilities all along. Is the feeling of life here the lie? Are there hidden threads I can't see? Will anything alert him to my presence here?

I shouldn't be here.

Gods, I *shouldn't* be here. This was an extremely bad idea, much worse than going into the dowager's bedchamber, knowing what I know now.

But I take another step into the room and reach out my senses, searching for anything out of place, anything that feels off.

I don't find anything more than I've already sensed. Maybe a little more frustration concentrated around the desk. A little less life than there should be around the bookshelves. He hardly uses them—maybe he doesn't have the time.

The more I strain, though, I only sense more of what I already feel. And still, I strain harder, moving to the bookshelves, scanning the titles, hoping to see anything that those scraps of paper in the dowager's bedchamber might have been torn out of.

I've never been so aware of my own heartbeat. The slight damp in the air. The creak of a breeze outside the window, the hush of my breath.

I reach for a book on the theories of mixing weaving with an elementalist's magic—

"Are you looking for something, Caleb?"

I jump, just manage not to yelp, and spin to see Master Aldric just inside the door. He's holding it mostly, but not all the way, closed.

My senses were fully extended—how did I not notice his approach? But then, he is a weaver. He might be a powerful one. Almost certainly is.

I stare at him, and he stares at me.

His face grows hard, the lines taut, his jaw set and unyielding. He doesn't look like a grandfather now. He looks like a battle mage.

I fight the urge to take a step back. To brace against the bookshelves behind me.

I survey all the threads around me, readying which ones I'll pull if it comes to a fight.

"Sit down, Caleb." It's a command. He waves at the chair in front of his desk.

There's barely controlled fury in his eyes now, and if he is the mage who killed the king, can I last in a fight against him?

Did he muffle his steps into this room with an unreality weaving? Is that why I didn't hear him?

There are ways to dampen and deflect, I know that. They're hard, but possible, with a lot of practice. I used a deflection weaving in the kitchen corridor earlier so people passing by my alcove wouldn't look in. I can't assume this was a weaving of unreality just now.

But I can't afford to assume it wasn't, either.

I move to the chair, not taking my eyes off of him, and sit. I watch, bile rising, as he works his way around the desk to sit behind it. Not taking his eyes off of me, either.

He folds his hands in front of him and leans just slightly forward on the desk.

"You're wearing an illusion," he says.

Ice shoots down my spine. Oh gods, can he see through my illusion as Caleb? Does he know who I am?

But would he even recognize me as Irava? I'd never seen him before I came to Barella, and I look much more like my father than my mother. Still, the resemblance is there.

"You're a woman."

I swallow hard. I don't know how he knows. I don't think my illusion has wavered at all, except during the storm. And Master Aldric was nowhere to be found.

But then, I might be sitting across from a weaver more powerful, and far more experienced, than I am. He could have woven unreality around himself, hidden himself and have been watching Torovan and I the whole time. He could have been directing the storm even while I was trying to unravel it.

I was a fool to think that he was using politics as a shield for weaker magic—he's been a master weaver at the Barellan court for longer than I've been alive.

I was a fool, too, to think I was the most powerful weaver in this court. Such a fool.

"Well?" he snaps, and I flinch.

But I steel myself and meet his eyes. If this is to be my end here, I will not face it with my eyes on the floor.

"I can't be a court mage as a woman."

I hear the difference in my voice as Caleb, the masculine difference that I've grown used to, and just now, it's jarring. My skin crawls, and I feel utterly exposed that this man knows my secret.

"No, as a woman, you can't be a court mage." He tilts his head, but the hostility in his eyes doesn't lessen. Or the suspicion. "And if you can weave such an illusion, you can be anyone, can't you? You could be the hand that killed the king."

My heart, for a moment, stops.

And then slams back into my chest, leaving me gasping for breath.

Is he accusing me? Of his own crimes? Is that how this is going to go? Have I so thoroughly placed myself into his hands?

He can present compelling evidence. I'm not who I say I am, I can't prove any ties of loyalty but what I've forged here since I've come, and I was found in his office without permission. If he knows exactly who I am, that could be even worse, he could say I'm a spy. I've gotten close to the king. Everything I've done as Caleb is, in part, a lie.

But Torovan didn't arrest me. And Valtair knows who I am and why I'm here. Valtair, at least, believes my reasons and is willing to trust me. I'm not entirely alone at this court.

Valtair might be telling Torovan what we found right now.

I sit forward, my fingers curling around the smooth wooden arms of the chair, glaring back at Master Aldric.

I held the poison vials in my hands. I felt the scream of a dying king.

"I'm loyal. The king knows I'm a woman, and he trusts me. He's already said for me to stay, to continue to be a court mage—"

"You're not a court mage yet," Master Aldric growls. "And what were you doing in here, just now, sneaking around in my study?"

"I wanted to find—a book—"

I know it's a flimsy excuse, and by his arched brows, he does, too.

He raps his fists on his desk. "I'm going to call for the guards, and then we're going to go talk to the king." He stands. "And you—you're not going to move. I'll know if you try to weave reality here, around yourself or around me."

I wet my dry lips as he heads for the door. Should I try to weave a distraction anyway, or weave a defense and run? Dare I even try? And if I do manage to get away, can I wrap another illusion around myself and escape the palace?

But no, that's not what I need to do. Torovan will know soon enough that Master Aldric is guilty. The master mage's threat of talking to the king is hollow—maybe.

And if Master Aldric is this powerful, I must stand against

him to protect the king. *Someone* must stand against him. And I'm the only person I know who might even have a chance.

I draw a long, long breath.

Master Aldric is guilty. Torovan will arrest him when he hears what Valtair has to say. He'll trust Valtair even if, in the end, he might not trust me.

"How did you know?" I ask him, my voice wavering more than I'd like. "How did you see through my illusion?"

Because I have to know. I have to know where I went wrong, or else...maybe he'll just lie. Maybe he did see me during the storm.

And maybe I'm still stalling, even now, before talking to Torovan.

"I saw it on the first day," he says, pausing with a hand on the doorknob. "Your concentration slipped, just a little, when you were undoing Nikolai's weaving. I was able to see that you wore an illusion, just a glimpse. The rest...well, there have been others, over the years. You aren't the first female weaver to attempt this. But you are the first I saw enough potential in to let try."

He narrows his eyes. "And I regret that trust if you have broken mine. I regret it intensely if you've broken the trust of the king. If you're here to do us harm. That storm didn't call itself, Caleb. And a weaver most easily unweaves their own constructs."

I stare up at him, twisted around, still seated in the chair.

What am I supposed to make of that?

Is there a possibility I'm wrong about him?

Then I remember that this is the man who convinced a prince, now a king, that he lacked the willpower for simple weaving.

Torovan stood beside me in the storm, lending a tremendous amount of strength. He lacks practice and skill, not willpower.

And to have taught him otherwise, to have broken him as this man has, is surely a crime.

Master Aldric's face hardens again, maybe seeing something he doesn't like in mine.

"Why are you here, Caleb? Why are you in my study? The truth, if you please."

Do I dare accuse him to his face?

He dared to accuse me to mine. But then, I'm on much, much shakier footing than he is. He's an established mage, well-liked and trusted. Torovan might believe my word against his, if Valtair stands with me, if he's not too devastated by what we found out—but will anyone else? Will anyone believe Master Aldric capable of murdering his king? And if I let Master Aldric know I'm onto him, will he accelerate his plans to do it again?

So I keep my mouth shut.

He lets out an annoyed sigh. "Very well. I'm sending for the guards."

But before he can open the door, it bangs open instead.

Torovan is there, his hair mussed, breathing hard. As if he's been running.

Chapter 42

The Rescue

Irava

Torovan's here. He's *here* in Master Aldric's study. His eyes blazing, burning straight at me.

There's fear in his eyes. And there's fury.

I shudder as Torovan whips his head around to note Master Aldric where he sprang back from the door. Torovan's hand tightens on the doorknob as he turns back to me, his dark brows drawing down.

Why was Torovan running? Valtair must have caught up with him. Must have told him what we found. Oh gods.

Is he angry with me? Of course he's angry with me.

But why was he running? He could have sent for me if he wanted to talk to me. He's drawing attention to himself, to us, to the urgency of what we now know.

He shoots another hard look at Master Aldric, and my stomach goes cold.

Valtair must have told him, too, my guess about Master Aldric making that poison and weaving the unreality. Is this supposed to be an arrest?

I stand and flare out my weaver's senses, alert for anything Master Aldric might do.

Master Aldric puts his hands up, ready to weave, watching me, watching the king. He moves toward Torovan.

I'm about to weave a barrier between them, but Torovan points to me.

"Caleb Ailin. You, come with me."

I draw a breath.

And Master Aldric stops.

"Your Majesty, I found him in my study without my permission. I have reason to believe this mage candidate wishes you harm—"

I want to snap back that it's he who means the king harm, he who has already caused great harm, but I hold my tongue. Because if Master Aldric somehow hasn't picked up on the *extremely* unsubtle cues Torovan is putting off about blaming him, I can't give it away. I can't let him know that we know, not yet, not until I have a chance to think through how best I can protect the king if it comes to a fight between weavers.

When Torovan orders the arrest of Master Aldric, I want him to be far from the actual arrest. I will do my best to contain Master Aldric, and I might not win if he's as strong as I suspect, but I will do my best. But Torovan can't be there. He has strength, but he hasn't honed it. He's a weaver, but he's not at all a master. Not even up to being a mage candidate yet. And even if that's Master Aldric's fault, that doesn't help us now.

Master Aldric, just now, is making a spectacular show of protecting the king from me. Putting the blame on me.

I meet Torovan's gray-green eyes. Is there any doubt there at all, even a little, that I'm on his side? That I'd never do him harm? Not intentionally—not now.

Torovan's mouth draws tight. "Aldric, I know what's happening here." He turns back to me, everything about him stern and unyielding. "Mage Candidate Ailin. Come with me."

It's a command. As it was the first time.

I know it's not the right thought right now, not with everything going on, but I want this man. I want him with a need that makes the room spin. I want his intensity and his arms to wrap around me. I want to embrace him and fold myself into him. I want to weave his reality into mine, and mine into his. I want to protect him.

My heart is pounding harder than it was when I first came into this room. I don't know what danger I'm in now, but it is *definitely* danger.

"Your Majesty," Master Aldric says, still tensed, still watching me, "I'll come with you. To make sure the mage candidate—"

"I have this in hand," Torovan snaps, and his gaze could freeze a glacier. "Caleb. Now."

And then he turns in a swirl of his embroidered blue coat and leaves. As if I'll follow.

And, stiffly, I do. Because I don't exactly know what's going on here. I don't know what he's thinking. And I do know it's better than staying in this study with Master Aldric.

I glance at Master Aldric as I pass him, and he glares back at me, his cheeks blotchy. He's making an absolute show of pinning the blame on me.

And for a moment, just a moment, my conviction that he's the enemy weaver falters. His glare isn't the same as Nikolai's. It's not full of spite. His brow is pinched in determination, but also, I think, a little fear.

Is he afraid of me?

He should be.

I hurry after Torovan to keep up with his long stride.

Valtair is waiting in the corridor outside, and I draw up short, just long enough for him to settle into walking beside me. The look he gives me is guarded, and my stomach knots.

Is he my ally in this? We'd been through a lot this morning, but so much can change in a single hour. I know that.

But he gives me a subtle nod, and the tightness in my chest eases. Whatever's happening now, Valtair, at least, is still on my side. Or at least, he hasn't made himself my enemy.

We draw attention as Torovan storms through the corridor in the mage's quarters with his guards around him and us behind him, coat flaring with his momentum, his loose black hair still frazzled. We're all drawing a lot of attention from the other mage candidates, and even other court mages poking their heads out of their studies or quarters down the hall.

Nikolai steps into the hall ahead, dressed impeccably as usual, even on the rest day. He bows to the king as Torovan passes, then glares at me as I pass, too.

It is a very different glare than Master Aldric's.

And then the courtiers watch us as we move out of the mages' area into the common parts of the palace, circling around to the stairs that lead up to the royal suites.

There is chatter. There is speculation. And whatever Torovan's doing, he could have done this more quietly—unless I really am in trouble. Unless he meant to call me out.

But when he burst into Master Aldric's study, looking furious, looking frantic—I had seen fear in his eyes, hadn't I?

Had that been fear for me?

Had he run because he'd thought I was in trouble, in Master Aldric's study? Had Valtair told him I'd gone to my quarters, and had Valtair or Torovan guessed...well, that I hadn't gone to my quarters?

The thought heats me again in a way I can't deal with right now. As does his messy hair ahead, hair that might have been messed up for me. And his fists only barely not clenched by his sides.

Does he want to protect me, too?

We reach the corridor where his chambers are, and farther down, the dowager's chambers.

And tense as I am, conflicted and aware of my body and his ahead of me, I have a jolt of wondering if my chambers would have been in this corridor, too. If I hadn't come to Barella as Caleb, if I'd just come when I was supposed to, to be married. Would I have taken over the dowager's suite, never knowing the malice she'd hidden there?

But how could I have done anything differently than what I'd done? I couldn't marry a man I'd thought was a murderer.

I was wrong, so very wrong.

And now...how can he possibly marry me? When he trusts so few, and for good reason. When his mother killed his father. When he was set up by the master weaver to fail.

Even if he trusts me now, and I don't know that he does, I'm still lying to him. I made up my mind to tell him, yes. But... but I'm almost shaking with the thought. I'm a hurricane of feverish heat and cold fear.

I don't want to see his fury directed at me again. And I know there will be more fury yet before this is done.

And more hurt. His, and probably mine.

And now I'm not sure if my shaking is want or terror.

Torovan opens the door to his study and holds it wide for me, his face carved in granite.

Carefully, I step past him. Aware, extremely aware, of my illusion of Caleb. Of the courtly but worn tunic and pants I'm wearing, the scuffed leather belt, the worn leather shoes.

He wanted me before in these clothes or others like them, he'd asked me before to be his lover.

And if my life had been simpler, if I really had been Caleb, I might have said yes.

He doesn't see Caleb as less than because he's a village mage.

Will he see me as less than because I'm a princess?

Or because I was supposed to be his princess? His very own weaver.

I don't drop my illusion, and I don't make my illusion as Caleb real. I don't want to feel just now more than I can bear.

"Wait outside," Torovan says to Valtair, and I shoot Valtair a pleading look. He'd said he'd be here when I talked to Torovan.

But Valtair gives a helpless wave, mouths, "Tell him."

Before I can protest, Torovan slams the door shut.

Chapter 43

The Book

Irava

Torovan strides to his desk but doesn't go behind it. He crosses his arms and leans back against it, glaring at me.

And then just...keeps glaring.

His hair is still mussed. I catch the metallic tang of his sweat—he had been running, or maybe that's the sweat of his anger, of his fear.

I can't meet his eyes, so I look at the bookcases, at the ledgers scattered on the desk, at the intricate blue and red pattern of the rug on the floor.

"Can you please let go of the illusion?" he asks. His words are careful and strained, like he's trying very hard not to shout at me.

My gaze snaps up, because the not looking, the not knowing what he's feeling, is killing me more.

His fury has doubled, and I want to rock back from the strength of it, but I brace myself. I stand where I am, feeling shabby, feeling small.

I wait for him to berate me for breaking into his mother's chambers. I wait for him to accuse me.

But he just waits, expectant.

I shudder and hold my ground. Because I can't drop the illusion now, not here, not under his withering glare. Not when it's my armor. Not, just now, when it feels right.

I shake my head, my throat too tight to speak.

And now he looks exasperated, shoving a hand through his hair, messing it up even more.

Impossibly, gods impossibly, it makes me want him more.

I want to cry.

"Why?" he bursts out, and the anger, the anger is almost better than him trying to restrain it. Because I know he's angry. And it's what I deserve. "Why can't you just show me who you are? I already know who you are, there's no point at all in hiding yourself from me."

But he doesn't know who I am.

"Please," he says. And it's a torn word, broken and raw.

My breath catches.

"I need to not see you as—" He waves at me.

But I can't. I can't do what he wants right now. Caleb is my armor. Caleb is how I know how to make any sense of any of this. Caleb is the person he loves, if Valtair was right.

Not me.

I look away, trying to blink back the tears gathering in my eyes. *Tell him*, Valtair had said. He knows what that might cost me, and still he said it.

But he is right. And I was planning to tell Torovan anyway.

And why can't I drop my illusion just now? Why is everything in me screaming not to?

I scrub at my eyes beneath my spectacles.

My chest is burning with the words I need to say, and still, I can't make myself say them. Now can't be the right time, not when he's just found out about his mother.

He moves toward me, and my breath hitches. He stops in front of me, then hovers, uncertain, covering me in his shadow. Like he wants to, what—embrace me?

I stare up at him, frozen. Too close. Too much in his space. And not enough.

"You shouldn't have gone into Aldric's study," he says, and his voice is low, but the words are stern.

I suck in a breath. "I didn't find anything. But I wanted to—"

Can I tell him that I wanted to give him everything? I wanted to make it at least a little better, give him all the answers he needs. I wanted to be favorable in his eyes, I didn't want him to look at me with the anger and the hurt he's radiating now.

"It was reckless," he says. "As was going into my mother's chambers. Gods of all the seasons, Caleb—" He shakes his head. "Please remove your illusion—"

He closes his eyes, as if he doesn't want to see me. "You don't trust me."

I stiffen, because no, that's not it—

"No, you don't," he goes on. "What reason do you have to trust me?"

And I'm dizzy now, because I'd thought it was the other way around. I thought he was not trusting me. And he has every right to not trust me.

I shake my head. "No. It's not that I don't—I just—" And the thought crystalizes as I say it. "I need to be Caleb now. Can you just see me as Caleb? Right now?"

"There's little else I can see you as. I don't even know your name." He sounds...exhausted. Draining of life as I watch.

And he takes a step back, as if the urgency of coming near me is draining, too.

I feel the loss of his closeness like the dying of a fire. And want to step near again.

I can tell him now. I can make the worst of this be over. Tell him, let him react how he reacts, and then it's over. And then... at least I know. At least the part where he turns away from me will be over.

"This afternoon," he says, "I'm going to continue my father's work. To redistribute some of the power traditionally held by the nobility and the crown back to the common people. It's the work that got my father killed, by my mother." He's watching me closely, waiting for my reaction again.

And now I'm waiting for his. He says it so casually, that his father was killed by his mother, but his shoulders are stiff, his posture tight. He's taking all this entirely too well, which makes me think he's not taking it well at all.

He shifts his weight.

"Regardless of how *stupid* it was to go in my mother's chambers, Caleb, and I don't want you to ever do that again... what did you see?"

I swallow, squeeze my hands tightly together. "Has Valtair—"

"He's told me everything he knows, but he said he wasn't in the chambers himself. And he's not a weaver. So tell me."

So I do. I spare none of it, watching him all the while, and I note when he stiffens at the mention of the poison and the fragments of the book. But he doesn't stop me, and asks questions about the book fragments, the style of writing, any illustrations, and I tell him what I can. He even goes to the bookshelves and pulls out several volumes that I see now are on weaving and has me look at the pages.

Nothing matches exactly. But one book has a similar illustration style, I think, to the fragment that talked about weaving unreality. There had been a small diagram on that one, partly torn off. It hadn't seemed as important, at the time, as the text.

"This is one of Taishe's books," he says. "Taishe was a weaver in the sixth century who was cast out and eventually executed for experimenting with the limits of what willpower can do—mind control, dream control, very dark magic."

Which I know, but I don't point out that I know.

He stares down at the book in his hands. "He was a brilliant weaver, but a horrible person."

I frown. Taishe is referenced in several of the books I've read on weaving and thread magic, but I've never managed to find any of his books. Not that I want to learn mind control, but I'm curious. Of course I'm curious.

"This is one of the only copies in Barella," Torovan says, thumbing through the book. "But he wrote several books, and I only have his one." He sighs, rubbing the gilded spine. "My father had it in his library, though he never let me read it. I snuck a few glances once, though. I haven't had the chance to read it now. Can you look? Is there anything else there that looks familiar to what you saw?"

I gingerly take the old book and flip through the yellowed pages. It was printed by an elementalist's text transfer, but not a very skilled one, as some of the lines blur around the edges. The text style isn't completely the same as the other fragment I saw, either. Though the illustrations are similar.

I shake my head and hand it back. "No. It's not from the same book. Though the fragment might have been Taishe."

"Did you see any other volumes by Taishe on Aldric's shelves? If you were looking?"

"Nothing that looked like this, no." This book has an ornate binding, gold on red leather with small emeralds set into the cover. No title or author visible, though older books often don't have them. Most books I'd seen in Master Aldric's study were newer, at very least from this century.

"And I don't think he'd be that sloppy, would he?" I ask. "To leave a Taishe volume in plain sight."

He grunts, and sighs.

"Well. It was worth a try." He returns the book to the shelf, sliding it in carefully. Drawing the moment out.

Stalling?

His breaths are coming faster, and my fear is rising with them.

I need to tell him who I am, but he's bracing himself right now. And I think I know why.

And I'm right—Torovan looks toward the door to his father's study and the bedchamber beyond. He heard it from Valtair, and he heard it from me, but now he needs to see it for himself. To feel, with his weaver's senses, what happened in that room.

He moves toward his father's chambers, and I follow.

Chapter 44

Watching

Irava

Torovan hisses when we cross the threshold into his father's bedchamber, pausing just inside.

"I feel it. And I'm not even looking with my weaver's senses, not consciously."

I feel it again, too. The seething malice, the frustration, the latent and lingering scream of a dying man who couldn't cry out. It's all still here, still fresh from being released from its bonds beneath the weaving of unreality. It will fade, more quickly I think than it might have when it first happened, as time catches up with it, but for now, it's here.

Torovan moves, cautiously, to the bed. I stand beside him as he reaches a hand over the covers but doesn't touch them.

He takes a deep breath, and I feel him moving into the rhythm that I taught him before. Calming, reaching out, sensing.

"I feel this, too," he whispers. His voice is quavering.

I want to step closer, I want to touch his arm, to do something. Anything to comfort him. I know what the pain in that bed feels like.

But I stay where I am.

He turns to me. His eyes are brimming, and it makes mine fill, too.

"This is why I must continue my father's work. So he didn't die in vain."

Wait, yes, he said he was going to continue his father's work this afternoon, and what does that mean? And why is that tightening every sense in me, why is that statement alone screaming danger?

"What are you doing this afternoon?" I ask, dread squirming up from my stomach.

He straightens. Takes one last look at the bed, then waves me back out again.

"I've called a meeting of the Council. My father's last wishes were never carried out. What he was planning to do for so many years, and it's a good work. It's a necessary work, because the people are the soul of the kingdom, and they've been crushed under the petty cruelties of bad nobility for far too long. Not all are bad, of course—"

"Yes, but *what* are you going to do?" I ask, turning as I step out of the bedchamber into his father's study. I think he said it before, but I'd been too focused on *him*, on what he was feeling, what he was thinking about me.

He gives me an odd look, and I realize, as Caleb, I've stepped too far in how I've spoken with him. It's not my place at all here to demand anything of him.

He shuts the door gently behind him and passes me on the way back to his own study. "Redistribute some of the power of the crown, and the nobility, back to the common people. It will take time—years, if it's done right—and many will think it's much easier, and much better, to just overthrow me. Or try to kill me."

"And this is why your father died?" I ask, following him back into his own study. "Why your mother—"

"And Master Aldric, apparently, or so you still think?"

All of this said calmly. He is definitely not processing this. He's clamped down on his emotions so hard now that he's barely breathing, every movement tightly contained. I wish, I truly wish again for the anger.

"There was nothing in Master Aldric's study," I say. "Nothing I felt, no unreality. But I didn't have a chance to look deeply. And what was hidden in the dowager's bedchamber could be all the evidence there is."

He tries to smooth his hair down, pulling it back into a queue as he leans against his desk again. He draws a silver clasp from his pants pocket, and I follow his hand all the way down as he does so. Heat blooming in my cheeks before I look away, only following what he's doing out of the corner of my eye.

Hair clasped back and somewhat tamed again, he crosses his arms, frowning at me.

And now the anger's coming back, when he's looking at me. He's a wall of glowering, growing fury again.

"Thank you for uncovering the weaving in my father's bedchamber. But I don't like at all what you did in my mother's. If she'd come in, or if Master Aldric had decided to act against you—"

He's already lectured me on this. And I did this for him. This was for *him*, not me, not ultimately. I put myself in danger for *him*. And I would, and will, do it again if it's needed. I have a feeling that it will be. Especially with what he's just told me, gods.

I fold my arms and narrow my eyes back at him. "You just said you're going to do what got your father killed. *That* is reckless. Can't it wait? Can't you not do it at all—not at least until we—*you*—figure out what to do about your mother, and Master Aldric—"

I'm overstepping again. I know it, I hear it in my words, and see it as his face twists further. But the anger I'm seeing now seems less directed at me. He looks past me, in the direction of his mother's chambers, as if he can glare a hole through the wall. His jaw works.

"I've already set this in motion. And I'm not inclined to stop. That would be letting them have their way. That would be wasting my father's death—"

"But it could waste your life to do it now. Please, Torovan—"

He flinches when I say his name, and I draw up short. Swallow hard.

But I can't back down. Gods, he can't do this now, not now. Not until he's safer, much safer, from his most immediate enemies.

"Please, call it off for today, let it be another day—"

I step closer, hands out, pleading.

He pushes off from his desk, catches my hands, holds them —and the quickness of it, the surety of it, startles me.

A whole body shiver goes through me, and I look up into his eyes, my breaths stuttering in my chest. We're close again. So close, but before, we hadn't been touching. He hadn't been holding my hands. Gods, after all this, and right now, is he going to kiss me again?

My lips part, heat shooting from my center up my spine, down to my toes.

And his look down at me is pure angry smolder.

It's all I can do to keep standing.

Valtair said he loves me. Valtair said he *loves* me.

Can I tell him now, can I possibly tell him and interrupt *this* look?

"Come with me to the Council meeting," he says, and his voice is rough, his eyes flicking between mine. "Court mages and mage candidates have the right to watch all Council meetings. So, come. Watch for anything amiss. My mother will be there, too, she always goes. And Master Aldric, I'm sure. They will both be getting word of the meeting about now."

I grip his hands back tightly. His mind is made, that's plain enough. He has no interest at all in hearing my fears. Or maybe, just no interest in hearing his own.

I wet my lips, and his gaze draws there.

But I say, "You have the willpower of a king. You do, Torovan. You have the will."

His eyes flit back up to mine. That hope, that hunger there again. It's less a lust now, though. It's a need for reassurance. A need to be seen.

If he's set on this course, I can't stop him. And maybe I don't want to. He has purpose in his eyes. He has a confidence I haven't seen before, a knowing of who he is and what he wants.

I don't dare crush that.

"Yes," I say. "I'll come. And after—I'll help however you need with your mother and Master Aldric."

And maybe those arrests, that very real problem, can't happen before. It might disrupt everything he's working toward to arrest two of the major players in the palace right before this meeting happens. It would take the focus off of what he needs to do. It would scare the nobility into inaction.

I know.

I am the daughter of a queen.

And a son of my own will.

My illusion isn't real right now, it's only an illusion. If he kisses me now, it will be my lips as Irava, beneath the woven illusion.

And as fiercely as I needed to be Caleb a few moments ago, I just as fiercely want this now. I want it with a need that curls down again to my toes, shooting back up to my center like lightning.

I drop my illusion, and he sucks in a breath.

I can feel his pulse, rapid and strong, through our held hands.

"What is your name?" he asks.

Everything in me wants to tell him. Everything in me equally wants to run.

But I know I can't distract him now. And maybe that's an excuse, maybe I'm stalling again, but it's the right move, I know that.

"I'll be there," I say, and pull my illusion back around myself again.

He takes another breath, face closing, and I hate myself for that. But I reach out, touch his stubble-roughened cheek, and he stills. Leans, for just a moment, into the touch.

Then sighs and closes off further. He gives me a bitter smile, and it almost breaks me.

"Thank you," he says. "Now, I must prepare for this meeting. Will you—will you stay here? Will you watch for me?"

He knows the danger he's in.

And after this moment just now, I have no illusions that it won't be awkward as hell to stay.

"I would send you to my sister," he says, "but I know right now I'm drawing the danger. She is safer away from me, and I need you here."

My throat is tight again as I nod.

He asked me. He trusts me with his life. Awkward or not, of course I'll stay.

And it's on my tongue again to tell him who I am, but—after. It has to be after.

After this meeting, after we expose and take down his mother and Master Aldric. And that might be hours or days later, I don't know. But I can't afford—he can't afford—to not trust me right now. As much as he trusts me now, in any case. Which I don't deserve.

But Valtair said he *loves* me.

And I think I love him, too.

So I settle into a chair in his study and watch around us with my weaver's senses until it's time.

Time for him to make his stand as the King of Barella.

Chapter 45

Council Meeting

Irava/Torovan

Irava

I walk behind Torovan to the Council Chamber on the other side of the Great Hall. The palace is buzzing with anticipation, nobles lingering in the corridors, those who aren't invited or maybe won't fit into the Council Chamber studying us as we pass for any clues as to what's going on. We already made a show earlier today—now, now they know something even bigger is happening.

Valtair walks beside me, but most of the people, after seeing the king, look at me.

And it's not just because I've formed a reputation as—maybe—the king's lover, but because I saved his life the day before in the garden. I was invited to eat at his table. I'm a weaver who unwound a vortex, and now I've twice been seen walking with the king. I see...fear.

I'm a guard. I'm protection. I'm Torovan's shield. And if the king needs his shield, that means he's in definite danger.

Everyone in the palace knows there's danger. It's been the unwanted guest, the thing no one talks about, since I arrived. The angst behind every bright smile.

But now, Torovan isn't trying to hide it anymore. And the fear on the faces around me heightens my own unease.

My weaver's senses are wide open as we walk, though the immensity of reality seething around me is painful to take in all at once.

So I try to portion it up, and sort the old realities from the new.

The palace has been seeped in dread for months now. In a way, it's shrouded itself in its own unreality, unwilling to acknowledge the depth of the rot at its core. But that's coming unraveled now.

These people have known hatred. And joy—there are notes of joy in these corridors, more recent notes, as the court has calmed a bit into its more usual flare. But it hasn't been a restful court, not with Torovan's temper or the rumors of him killing his father hanging over everything.

Do people still believe those rumors?

Of course they do. I might have seen another side of him, I might have seen the truth in his father's bedchamber, in his mother's, in the maelstrom of a storm, when he stood beside me giving everything he had to save his people.

But that doesn't mean anyone else has seen what I have, or from the same angles. Or wants to draw the same conclusions. Torovan has more enemies here than just his mother and Master Aldric.

Torovan slows outside the crowded entrance to the Council Chamber.

"Make way for the king!" the guards ahead of us shout,

their armor and their sheathed swords clanking as they sweep a path through the crowd. The roar of voices dims as people turn.

And Master Aldric, resplendent in his best robes, staff in hand, strides over to us. His eyes flick to me, back to Torovan. He doesn't quite frown.

But he does bow. He says in a voice low enough I don't think most people can hear, "Your Majesty. We haven't yet had the chance to talk, and I'm not sure it's best that *he*"—Master Aldric juts his chin at me—"should be present at this meeting."

Torovan doesn't draw himself up, but he becomes *bigger*, taking up more air, taking up more of the space around him. I see it with my weaver's senses, reality subtly shifting as his presence gains more weight, and Master Aldric's gains less. It's not a conscious weaving—I don't see any specific threads being woven. But it's real all the same. The dynamics of a king at court.

Master Aldric braces himself—or at least, I see the potential of him bracing himself against Torovan's will.

And for a moment, an incandescent moment, I burn inside. The master mage is well aware of the strength of Torovan's willpower. He's reacting to it now.

Torovan's will surrounds him and spreads outward. Not a weaving, not a construct, but an anchoring of himself as the center this moment will move around.

"Mage Candidate Ailin is here at my request," Torovan says.

There's a murmur, more pointing at me as the people nearest us hear the conversation and spread it.

I stay as calm as I can manage, hands at my sides, mouth tight. With my senses wide open, I'm ready at a breath to try to stop anything Master Aldric might throw at the king, though I don't think he will attempt anything here, not with everyone watching.

I'm not in my best clothes—I don't *have* best clothes as Caleb. But my hair is neat enough, I checked it in a mirror in Torovan's study before we came. I made sure my spectacles were clean and on straight. I know…I know I'm not much in my own presence, not next to Torovan. But I don't intend to wither under the scrutiny of the crowd.

Beside me, Valtair shifts just enough to draw my attention. He gives me a nod. Man to man. Protector to protector.

"Your Majesty," Master Aldric goes on, "I am only concerned that *he*—"

My arms prickle with a cold sweat. I hear the emphasis again there, what Master Aldric is threatening to reveal. And gods, no, he can't do that here. Not now. This court can't know that I'm also a woman.

But Torovan hears the emphasis, too, and he's not backing down. I watch as his shoulders stiffen and his mouth draws down.

"*He* is with me. Now please, Master Aldric, I wish to start this meeting."

Master Aldric hesitates a moment, gives me a hard glare, as if daring me to…what? What is he planning here? What does he not want me to stop? Because I think that's what this is now. He doesn't want me in that room.

I move closer to Torovan as we enter the Council Chamber and stay right by his side as he approaches the lectern.

He stops, glances over at me, gives a small strained smile. He says in a low voice, "You will need to step back a pace, Caleb. Only one of us can address the crowd."

I flush and nod. I feel the burning scrutiny of those around us as I take two steps back to settle beside Valtair, the king's guards on either side of us.

Valtair gives me another nod.

Okay. We're okay.

And now we watch.

Everything echoes in the Council Chamber, with a high domed ceiling covered in historic murals overhead. Windows line the base of the domed ceiling, though it's evening now and dark outside. A double circle of tables and chairs rings the center of the room, with places for around forty different nobles. Behind the tables are more wooden chairs, with other palace dignitaries, merchants, court mages and mage candidates, and—and Dowager Zinara and her entourage setting up their own court near the back of the room, opposite Torovan.

Her eyes are boring straight into me.

I quickly look away, fold my hands in front of me to have something to hold on to, and keep watching everything, as much as I can.

I spot Nikolai with the rest of the mage candidates filing in, and he's also glaring at me. Furious, maybe, that I'm the mage who's with the king, not him? And Master Aldric settles himself at the end of a row of court mages in a seat that was obviously saved for him. He, too, is watching me, his face grim.

Torovan looks around at the gathered nobility, back at the door, and waits a few moments more as people hurry in to take their places.

Then, he raises both hands.

Torovan

THE CROWD IS as large as I'd expected. And I'm trying, the way Caleb showed me, to see anything amiss in the crowd with weaver's senses, but I don't have the concentration. Everything in me is coiled around what I'm about to do.

The voices around me quiet.

And then it's up to me. I called this meeting—it's up to me to lead it.

"Honored nobles, advisors, and mages," I begin. As my father always had, every time I watched him open a Council meeting. "I've called you today to discuss the future of our kingdom, a future shaped not just by those in power, but those who have not been given a voice in our kingdom."

The murmurs start immediately. Some know about what my father planned to do four months ago. All have heard rumors, I'm sure. And I know I've been at the center of a few rumors as someone who *didn't* want this to happen and took action to make it not happen.

But I didn't kill my father. That my people would even think that has haunted me for months now.

I felt the pain—gods, the pain—of his last dying breath today. A gift, and a curse, from Caleb.

I do my best to put that aside, to ignore everything outside of what I'm here to do and forge on. What I'm building today is my father's legacy, and now it will be mine, too.

"My father," I say, and cough past the crack in my voice, the thoughts coming back no matter how much I try to push them down, the taste of his scream. The knowledge that is eating apart my insides that my *mother* did this. My mother. It should have been as ludicrous a thought that she could harm my father as that I could.

But it's not. Caleb saw what he saw. And I felt what I felt.

I try again. Because I have to. If I can't shove the thoughts away, I must push through them.

"My father sought to give more power to the people, to create a healthier society, where every person has a voice. It's my intention to honor his legacy by doing just that."

I watch as expressions darken. Grow grim or angry. These people who've counted power as a given. Who are so enamored with their political power that they disdain the magical powers if they touch their own bloodlines—even though, as Valtair said, many of them are hiding magical bloodlines, too.

It's an illusion, their inherent power.

The aging Baron Nemaran is the first to rise. And I was sure he'd be among the first, as much as he'd opposed my father's policies before. And doesn't he recognize, too, that his ability to oppose my father at all was a gift my father gave to him, too? My father formed this Council at the start of his rule, saying that he shouldn't have the sole say over what happens in the kingdom. That it's better and wiser by far to have many voices heard, not just one.

And now, we're about to take another step.

"This is outrageous! Sire, I understand wanting to give the peasants better lives, of course we all wish to give them better lives—"

As if he's talking about cattle, not people.

Another noble rises from her place at her table. Lady Sima, the ends of her braids clicking softly together as she draws herself up. "I agree with Nemaran, for once. This isn't something we can do. The lowborn masses are irresponsible, uneducated, and cannot be trusted with any decision that affects the kingdom."

My heart sinks. I'd been hoping for, counting on even, Lady Sima's neutrality. She's been outspoken about the fair treatment of the peasants and better conditions for the artisan and merchant classes for years.

I glance at my mother, and that's a mistake. Her face is outwardly impassive, as it often is. But she's seething, I know the signs. Her eyes are pinpoints of sharp light from the torches on the walls, her glare aimed at me.

I grip the edge of the lectern, for a moment, just a moment, glaring back.

My mother has *no say* in the future of this kingdom. She's already done so much damage. So much.

I want to abandon the lectern and forge through the crowd and pull my mother up and demand to know why? *Why* would she ever even consider killing my father? Her husband? Why?

I do know why. And it's why I'm here today.

I make myself turn away from her. Brace myself as I sweep my gaze around me.

"This change will benefit all of us," I say. "If the people are uneducated, then we'll build schools. Universities. This isn't something that will happen immediately, but over time. It took us time to transition to a rule by Council, and now we're doing well with that. Our economy was thriving, until—until the death of my father—and it can thrive again. Think about how Barella will fare when we're known for our universities, for the richness of knowledge and invention—we can train more mages, even, there are many, many self-trained mages among the peasants who could greatly benefit us all. We can thrive again!"

"I thought that's why you were marrying a foreign princess," Baron Nemaran says.

My breath hitches. I don't—I don't want to think about that now, not now and derail my momentum. And he is certainly trying to derail my momentum.

"Yes," I say, "that is one step, to secure peace on our borders and prosperous relations with our neighboring kingdoms."

"And what will she think of this?" the baron presses. "This princess of Galenda—how will this be keeping the treaty if she comes to be queen of a nation with hobbled power? If she finds herself barely better than a peasant?"

I shift my weight, shift back again. No, this is not how I wanted this to go. And with everything else burning up inside me, I have to work hard to keep my voice even.

"That's not what I'm proposing," I say, measuring out the words, "merely that we let everyone in Barella have more say in their own lives—"

"If you think that's what you're doing here, you're naïve, Your Majesty."

I stare at Nemaran in shock. I'm still his king. Do I really have that little regard in the eyes of my people? In the eyes of the nobility? Has their obeying me and bowing to me been entirely a sham?

I look around again and don't see any sympathetic faces.

I see people with mouths drawn tight, shoulders stiff, hands clenched. I see glares.

I do not see support.

But surely—surely there must be some? Some support in

this crowd? My father certainly hadn't thought he was alone in his views.

Even Count Valtair, conservative as he is, wrote his support for my father from his convalescence. That's one of the reasons I think this can work.

I am wearing a crown, I feel the weight of the solid gold band around my head. I don't wear it every day, but I put it on today before leaving my study, knowing I'd need it here. Should I have worn the heavier crown I use for ceremonies instead? Was that the price of their respect?

But I fear even that wouldn't make these people see me as their king.

∽

Irava

SOMETHING IS WRONG. I feel it with my weaver's senses as Torovan speaks, a subtle and growing *wrongness*, not quite like the unreality weavings, but the feel of the weaving is similar. A bending under of reality, a warping, an abomination.

I tense, just as the pompous baron calls Torovan naive.

Torovan tenses, too. Can he feel what I'm feeling, or is he only reacting to the baron's words?

Valtair eases closer to me, but he doesn't say anything. He looks like he wants to, but he's not willing to break the silence that's fallen in the wake of the baron's insult. Everyone's waiting to see what the king will do.

Except, perhaps, Master Aldric?

I widen my senses as far as I can, looking for what's amiss. What's going on that I can feel in my gut but not quite see.

Master Aldric's brows are drawn, his eyes scanning the room, but I see nothing around him. No signs that he's weaving anything.

His eyes meet mine and narrow.

I twitch my fingers and touch the threads of reality just around him, and I know he'll sense it.

Master Aldric stiffens, turning his full attention to me, and I feel the light touch of his magic on the threads around me, too. But I still don't feel any signs that he's actively weaving.

And yet I still sense the weaving of someone, this *wrongness*, whatever it is.

I swallow and, dread clawing up my throat, look to Nikolai.

And it's there. Like the afterglow of sunlight when looking away from the light, like a whisper almost heard after a dream. Nikolai's eyes are hooded, focused somewhere beside the king, but not on him. He's still, not moving, not even his hands. But I can sense his subtle pulling of reality all the same.

And *what* is he weaving? It's nothing showy, not like what he's attempted every time he's put people in danger, though I know in my bones that what he's doing now will hardly be less dangerous.

No, it will be more. I know that, even as I frantically try to see the threads he's pulling, and can't. Not quite.

And if he is weaving like this, in a way I've never known before...

Gods. He's the weaver. Not Master Aldric—I was wrong. I was so, so wrong, and gods help that I can correct my mistake in time.

Nikolai is the one who wove the unreality in the royal bedchambers. His touch on reality now feels similar. Feels corrupted and like no weaving I've ever felt before.

I still can't see a thread to unravel this weaving now, and that's making panic claw up my throat.

No. I can't be too late. I can't be too weak. He can't be that strong.

How was I so wrong? I've known Nikolai is a strong weaver, but in everything he's shown, he's been brash and incompetent. Or was that on purpose? Or, is he just less competent at the weaving that I know how to do? And much, much more skilled at whatever he's doing now?

I'm hardly paying attention to what the nobles and the king are saying and jump when Torovan shouts, "This is the path forward, not repression! This is the path my father saw, and he died for that!"

The gut-churning buzz of Nikolai's dark weaving intensifies.

I take a step forward.

Because this is not going to be the day the king dies for this ideal, too.

Chapter 46

Willpower

Irava

As Nikolai's weaving intensifies, I finally, finally start to see the threads. They're like negative space in my senses, stretching out from Nikolai to most of the nobles in the room.

I watch in horror as Nikolai looks at a tangle of threads attached to Lady Sima, and she shouts defiance against the king.

Oh gods. I've never seen a weaving like this. I've never even heard of it—

But yes, yes I have. This would be what mind control looks like, wouldn't it?

Once, when I was younger, I tried to see if I could manipulate people's wills to get them to better like me, accept me. I'd been an absolute fool and almost blown myself up. But what I'd been attempting had been with normal threads, something I *couldn't* do with normal threads. Nothing at all like this.

I'd thought—well, I'd assumed, even after seeing the poison, even after feeling the threads of unreality, that the weaver who'd made them would still follow the conventional practices around weaving, just...adding in more. But what Nikolai's doing now has little to do with the weaving I know.

I should have known just from the feel of the unreality weaving, which was also something I'd never heard of before. I should have been prepared, somehow prepared.

Nikolai must have studied the books those fragments in the dowager's chambers came from. Maybe Taishe, maybe others. Weavers aren't born, they make themselves.

I'd thought Nikolai was arrogant and politically dangerous. But I hadn't known he'd made himself into a monster.

He's pulling his threads on a person's will, against their will. He's weaving—gods—he's weaving the realities of people's souls. Into the realities that he wants them to be?

I break out all over in a cold sweat, and I'm not sure what to do.

Baron Nemaran says, "We will, of course, have to consider that if this is the direction you are taking the kingdom, Torovan, should you yourself have as much power as you do?"

The lace of dark threads connecting the baron to Nikolai is gossamer thin. And maybe the baron hardly needs swayed, only pushed a little, to act as he's acting now. I don't know him by more than reputation, but from everything I've heard in court, he's never been a friend of the royal family.

"My power is not what we're talking about here," Torovan snaps, his voice growing dangerous.

And this is not going well at all.

Not, especially, with Nikolai putting poison into the hearts of the nobility.

What can I say if I speak up? How can I stop Nikolai or prove what he's doing, if even I can barely see it? Can Master

Aldric see what's happening? He seemed to know something was amiss before.

I glance back at Master Aldric and widen my eyes, look again to Nikolai.

I'd been worried about going up against Master Aldric if he was as strong as I thought he was, but I don't at all know how to deal with Nikolai. I can only just see the threads he's weaving now, if I strain, and I don't know if I can do anything about them without knowing that dark weaving too.

Are these threads that I can weave? Can I unmake them if I try? Could I explode something, not knowing what I'm doing, and kill us all?

There are too many people in this room. And Nikolai's eyes flick to me, once, and he gives a small smile.

I'm growing too scared to be truly angry at that.

He has so many weavings active in this room, and if I try to stop him with my own weaving, if he loses his concentration and his hold on his weavings, will they explode? What do soul energy threads do when dropped without care? Would they kill the people Nikolai's trying to manipulate?

I clench my hands at my sides, working to keep my breaths calm. I'm going to need that calm, whatever I do.

And I think I'm right that Nikolai's a master at this sort of weaving, but not the weaving of the court, the weaving that I know. The weaving that doesn't try to overtake people's souls and kill kings.

Nikolai's concentration now is absolute, the control he's using a very fine touch—at least, what I can see of it. I wish I wasn't right about this, I truly wish.

All questions of strength and skill aside, all questions of exploding threads or danger, there's the politics to think of, too. If I stand against Nikolai, if I, who am visibly supporting the king, accuse a member of the high nobility of trying to manipulate the Council, at this meeting of all meetings, won't that sabotage everything Torovan's trying to do? The nobility could see it as a ploy by Torovan and his supporters to gain the upper hand. To justify taking power from the nobility.

I don't even know how the nobility will take this, this being manipulated. These are the sorts of powers that have made weavers feared, even centuries after these powers were outlawed. To show the nobility that weavers can still do these things…gods.

I don't know what will happen. But I do know that if I don't do something now, this day is lost.

And maybe the king is lost, because now I see Nikolai, mouth pulled tight, reaching out a dense and growing tapestry of his dark willpower toward Torovan.

No!

I sprint the few steps to Torovan as soon as I spot the attack, but the weaving's already reached him. The dark mesh has buried itself in Torovan's soul. I draw up short, trying to find where Torovan begins and Nikolai's weaving ends.

Torovan turns to me, his face contorting with fury. Gray-green eyes glinting like steel.

"What are you doing, mage? Back to your place!"

As if he doesn't know what's between us, as if he doesn't remember he asked me to guard him. That he asked me, once, to be his lover.

His rage is so sudden and intense that I trip a step back, just managing to steady myself. And now I've become a player again in this game. Now angry eyes in the crowd, stoked by Nikolai's threads, are turning to me.

Nikolai doesn't know all of what's between Torovan and me. He's heard the rumors, but he doesn't *know*. Not like I know. Not like Torovan knows, and maybe Valtair. He might think it's a dalliance, but he doesn't know it's...more.

Is that an advantage? Is that anything I can use?

I swallow and keep my eyes on Torovan, because he must be my everything now, the only one I must protect.

Surely—surely Nikolai hasn't twisted him so far as to forget everything between us? I saw no love in his eyes just now, but no hurt, either. It's as if he's taken a step back inside himself, and Nikolai's will has gained control.

I survey the weaving Nikolai's enmeshed in him, and it's grown denser. It's much, much denser than the weavings he's sent toward others in the room.

Bile rises in my throat.

Torovan's will is strong, I know that. I've felt that. But can he stand against whatever force Nikolai's bringing to bear?

I've been hesitating to touch the threads, not knowing how they'll react to my touch, but there's no more time.

I will not lose Torovan. I will *not* lose the man I love to Nikolai's treachery.

I bite my lip and reach with both hands to try to tease this weaving apart, praying to every god I know I won't explode anything, blinking through watering eyes.

But the threads have an unfamiliar texture and slip through my mind's fingers.

I do touch the threads, though, and shudder at that touch. If this is a weaving of soul reality, then it has to be heavily woven with Nikolai's own soul energy, doesn't it? Or else where would these threads have come from?

I feel a jolt of Nikolai's intent, cold and furious, and a glimmer, just a glimmer, of Torovan's unspoken scream.

I go rigid.

It is not, it is *not* like the scream of his dying father.

I will it not to be so.

Is Nikolai trying to rip out Torovan's soul? Or trying to rewrite Torovan's reality to how he wishes it to be?

While Torovan stands at the lectern, passive, every muscle in his body tensed, a war is playing out inside of him.

And can anyone see this but me?

Someone catches my arm, making me jump and spin, hands coming up and a woven barrier already forming between me and whoever touched me.

Valtair jumps back, hands up, his eyes wide.

"Fuck, Caleb!" he hisses, and now he does grab my arm, pulling me away from Torovan. "What are you doing? What's happening, what's Torovan—"

"It's Nikolai," I hiss back, panic still rising. "I was wrong, Valtair—he's controlling everyone, he's controlling Torovan. I don't—I don't know if I can—"

But I have to try. I shake off Valtair, and I don't step back to Torovan, but I hold up my hands and reach again with my magic for the threads embedded in Torovan's soul, hoping to find some way to unravel them. To do something. Anything.

"What are you doing?" Valtair asks again, but I shake my head and shut him out of my concentration.

Torovan whips around again and points at me. He opens his mouth, starts to turn toward his guards like he wants to order them to arrest me—or Nikolai is telling him to arrest me. But then he wavers.

He's fighting. He's still fighting this, I can see it, I know it in his eyes.

Chapter 47

Fight This

Irava

Two of Torovan's guards start toward me, and I see thinner versions of Nikolai's threads embedded in their souls.

"Back!" Valtair snaps, putting himself between me and the guards, and they falter. "Caleb! Do what you need to do now!"

"Get that mage away from the king!" someone shouts in the crowd.

And then the crowd erupts into chaos. People start shouting, more than one person screams.

I hear more shouts for the guards to remove me, not Nikolai.

I can't think about it. I must concentrate. Every bit of my focus on pulling the dark weaving away from Torovan.

Torovan's head moves slightly toward me, but stops again.

Fight, Torovan. Gods of all the seasons, *fight this!*

I still can't get a good hold on Nikolai's threads. I can't move them, I can't weave them, I can't pull them out.

I want to scream in frustration, but I lower my hands, panting.

I don't know what I'm missing. I don't know what I don't know, but I do know this isn't working.

I can't fight Nikolai this way.

Is it worth—can it possibly be worth risking trying to take Nikolai down with my own weaving? I've studied enough to know how, though I've never tried to incapacitate an actual person.

But I know what happens when a weaver drops their threads, and this room is too full, I can't risk everyone here to save Torovan. Even if he is the king. Even if he's the one I love.

Because I'd be risking him, too. What I've been doing was already too much of a risk.

Nikolai is still sitting where he was, eyes intent on Torovan. The dowager—the dowager is gone from her seat at the back, her entourage gone with her.

Had she planned this? Hastily thrown together, knowing or at least suspecting what Torovan was trying to do? Or did Nikolai decide to do this on his own, and the dowager fled any danger?

Torovan's guards are currently wrestling each other, and I lean back, move farther away from them as I see two of them trying to get at me, three more and Valtair straining to hold them down.

Gods of all the seasons, gods of the elements, and gods of the threads that make up all reality.

I can't fight this. I'm a weaver, I'm powerful, I've faced down and unraveled a storm. But I can't fight this now, not like a weaver.

I'm going to lose this.

I'm going to lose him.

Torovan's still locked in his silent battle, and I don't know if, in the end, he'll win.

But tuned as I am to Nikolai's different form of weaving, I notice something else. There's a glow between Torovan and me. Not quite a weaving, but a resonance, like humming a similar tune. Bright and shining, not visible but *felt*.

I feel it, too, between Torovan and Valtair. And in a lesser sense, between Torovan and his guards. And between Valtair and me.

The threads between us. The loyalty, the love, the respect.

The feeling is not so different than when Torovan gave me his will during the storm. It's a synchronicity, a moving through a moment together.

And Nikolai might have his will in Torovan's soul, and this glow between Torovan and me looks dimmer than it probably should be, but it hasn't faded.

I'm not powerless here yet.

I dimly hear another voice in the crowd calling for the guards to take me. That I'm the enemy, that I'm harming the king.

I shut it out. I shut it *all* out.

The voices, the panic, the fear. I shut everything out but my breath, and Torovan in front of me.

And I focus on that resonance between us. I'm facing a different storm today, another storm of Nikolai's making. And I need the strength of another weaver to face it.

And he needs mine.

I don't dare let myself think. I dart back to Torovan and cup the back of his neck, drawing him down to kiss me. He's rigid enough from the battle going on within that he doesn't immediately throw me off, though it's an effort to pull him down.

I give him my willpower. I pour it into him, give him all of it, every last bit I can spare. I roar at him who he is—a king whose will was strong enough to face down a storm. Strong enough to pursue his father's killers even though he feared the trail had gone cold. Strong enough to face the court today and propose what he proposed.

Strong enough to stand against his enemy now.

And he is not standing alone. Absolutely not alone.

The warmth of his soul breaks through the coldness of Nikolai's control and blazes out at me like the sun. He grips my shoulders, kisses me back with a need that's pure desperation.

His stubble rough where it brushes against my cheek. His breath sour with fear, and sweet with the wine he drank this morning. My lips dry and cracking from the tension.

It will not be our last kiss. It will *not*.

I shift my hands to either side of his face, grounding him, like when I drove the stakes into the ground in the storm and pinned him beneath me, kept him from being dragged away.

This storm can't have him, either.

I stare into his eyes, showing him all I feel for him.

I love you, Torovan Braise. *I love you.*

And I know he sees it, because his own eyes soften as he gazes back at me.

Then Torovan pulls back with a shudder, fingers digging into my arms. Holding on to me with all he has.

Together we broke something. For a moment, Nikolai's threads in Torovan were fraying—still there, but not as strong, or as steady.

Around us, the angry rhythm of the voices turns, for a moment, to discordant murmurs and confusion.

But it doesn't last for long.

Torovan grunts, grips my arms tighter, tight enough that it hurts, and I weave my illusion of Caleb back into my reality with furious focus to better brace him.

Nikolai's regained his focus, and he's doubling down.

"Caleb," Torovan hisses through clenched teeth. And it's a plea. This battle isn't over.

And it isn't yet won.

The voices around us rise again into anger.

I dart a quick look around, as much as I can see beyond Torovan locked in place again in front of me.

Nikolai is standing now, but then, so is much of the court. And some look to have already fled whatever they think is going on.

Valtair's arguing with Torovan's guards, not all of whom have Nikolai's threads—and maybe Nikolai is spreading himself thin, can I even hope that? Two of the guards start around the room toward Nikolai, but the two who still have Nikolai's threads attached go after them, pulling them back.

And Nikolai's weaving in Torovan is growing stronger again. Stronger even than before. Pulsing with malice.

I see Torovan draining from his own eyes. Watch the rage returning, and the contempt.

I know it's not him, I know, but the contempt makes my own soul shiver. Because it's what I've feared, isn't it? That when he learns how deeply I've deceived him, he'll look at me like this.

We're still locked together, my hands gripping his face, his hands gripping my arms. His fingers slowly digging deeper, hard enough to bruise.

I want to sob. Because I truly don't know what more to do. I tried. I've already given my last effort.

I'm giving Torovan everything. I'm giving him all of my will, everything I don't also need to live. I disrupted Nikolai's will once by kissing Torovan, but I'm losing him again. Should I kiss him again? Do I just need to keep on kissing him?

But I know that's not the answer, Nikolai will only find a way to use our distraction against us, like he's doing with the guards. He's too strong. And I don't know enough.

I'm failing. I'm failing my king, watching who he is ebb away from me as I stare into his eyes.

And he curls his lip, sneering at me, like he doesn't know me. Or like he does, and he despises me.

But he hasn't let go of my arms. He hasn't yet let go.

I hear Master Aldric yell, "Nikolai! You are dismissed from the court mage candidates. Leave this room at once!"

I spare a glance to see Nikolai giving him a disdainful glare. He sends another weaving toward Master Aldric, who seems to already be fighting off a weaker weaving. And that's why I've had no help there.

Then Nikolai turns and throws another weaving, a very complex one, weaving itself larger and denser along the way, toward me.

If he's sunk as deeply as he is into Torovan's soul, then he has to know I've given Torovan as much of my will as I can. And maybe that's why he hasn't attacked me before, why he's tried to use the guards. He was waiting for me to drain myself.

I barely have enough time to yank back my will from

Torovan, struggling to root myself, center myself in the room around me.

I'm still in Torovan's grip, which is shaken by the sudden absence of my willpower holding him together.

But to help him, I must survive.

I sink my roots deep in reality as I know it, and in Torovan's will in front of me. Because it's still there. I know it's still there.

Nikolai's dark weaving hits me like ice scraping at my soul. Unseen blades scrabbling for purchase.

And as it finds it, as I feel my soul crushing under the weight of his dark willpower, I know that the weaving he sent to Torovan wasn't trying to kill Torovan, but control him.

Because if you control the king, you control the kingdom.

And now I know the difference, because Nikolai is definitely trying to kill me.

Chapter 48

Realities

Irava

I'm breathing, but my soul can't breathe. I'm being crushed under the weight of soul realities that aren't my own, and in all of them, I'm dead. My soul is dead. My life is gone. Unwanted.

I have just enough thought to wonder if this is how the last king felt, unable to wake, unable to scream?

My ears are ringing with a roar that's not in the room. I barely feel Torovan's hands still gripping my arms.

But.

But I am the daughter of a queen.

And I *am* the son of my own will.

I fucking *made* myself.

I'm a weaver.

I wove my reality.

I know my reality, and I know myself.

And Nikolai does not.

I look up at Torovan through my hazing vision, and he's still straining, too, under the combined attack on both of us.

Less than I am now, as Nikolai's focused on me as the more immediate threat.

And Torovan can feel, too, that this attack on me is meant to kill, because he's giving me some of his own will now, like I gave him mine.

It's helping, but it's not enough. And it's not will he can afford to give.

His eyes, flickering in and out of clarity, are telling me to fight.

And something else is welling up inside me, because I thought I gave Torovan all of who I am to fight this before, and I'd thought that would have to be enough, but it wasn't.

But I didn't give him all of me.

I've held back since the start.

He doesn't know who I am.

And that's the last thing I can give him. I know who I am, that knowledge welling up and holding back, just barely holding back, Nikolai's soul-shredding will.

I want to tell Torovan I'm sorry. Because he might not like this gift.

But I can't face this attack on my realities as anyone but myself.

I unweave my reality as Caleb and stand as Irava. Because right now, that's more of who I am and who I need to be.

And yes, my reality is both Caleb and Irava. I am both. And I weave those truths around me like a shield.

I'm a princess of Galenda, and a court mage candidate, and I weave that in, too. I'm a powerful weaver, and though Nikolai might know a type of weaving I don't, he doesn't know what realities shape my soul.

I weave my love for Torovan Braise around me.

I weave his love for me.

I weave my absolute need to live. And his need to live.

And all of it, every layer, pushes back Nikolai's threads a little more.

And it's working. His weaving is fraying. The possibilities from Nikolai's will, all of them that I'm dead, are not finding purchase against the shield of my truths.

I am very, very much alive.

But even as I think this, fear rises in me again. Because to give Torovan everything, to give him all of who I am, might mean I lose him. Maybe his love isn't strong enough to survive it. Maybe the shock of it will make him lose his will in this fight, and I'll still lose him.

Is there any way out where I don't lose him?

Nikolai, not finding a way through my woven shield, gives up and renews his attack on Torovan.

Torovan shudders, leaning heavily on me as he fights. His forehead beaded with sweat.

Our eyes lock. His eyes heat, for just a moment, with rage, then cool back into fear.

But the possibility that he won't love me can't exist.

It can't.

I pour all my will back into his to help him fight, but still— still I don't pour that last bit of who I am.

I don't have the concentration for it, but I look for the guards anyway—have they reached Nikolai? Will that be a help or a disaster?

But no, all of them are on the floor, writhing, tangled in Nikolai's threads. He gave up on trying to control the guards, too, and now he's just trying to kill them, isn't he?

I can't help them now. I spare the barest moment of prayer to all the gods that the guards can fight this, too.

I spare one moment, just one, for a sob.

I have to end this. I have to end it now.

I have to change the reality in this room, and change it in such a way that it can't change back again. And if Nikolai is playing on the level of hearts, on the level of souls, that's where I need to play, too.

Not just with my weaving, but with my own reality. With who I am.

I take a breath and weave my will out into my words. Make them glow with my reality, make them impossible not to be heard.

"I am Irava Anoran Varandre, Third Daughter of the Queen of Galenda. I am betrothed to the King of Barella, whom I love. I am your future queen. And I give the king all of my support, and all of Galenda's support, in this endeavor. All of it."

I dare to look at Torovan.

Still locked in his battle, did he even hear me?

But his eyes are wide, his mouth a grimace.

His grip on my shoulders, now that I'm Irava again, is painful.

But, with the barrier between our separate wills as hazy as it still is, he must somehow feel his grip is hurting me, because his grip eases, gentles, holds me completely.

The dark threads of Nikolai's will are shredding from Torovan, whipping back with no purpose, no target they can stick to.

Because Torovan's focus is all, entirely, on me.

Me, flushed and in Caleb's clothes, facing him as no one but myself, no secrets left. Facing the man I love.

And seeing nothing but love in his eyes.

"Irava," Torovan says softly, with wonder. With dawning joy. "*That* is your name?" His voice rises into incredulity.

And I have one moment, one gut-wrenching moment to stop, to consider what I'm doing, what I'm still pushing out with my will, keeping my reality ringing and clear. Have I just done what Nikolai tried to do? Have I overridden Torovan's will with my own? Can he only see me with the same eyes I have for myself?

His look sharpens, though, past that first blush of wonder. Then hardens. Not with Nikolai's rage, but his own anger. And that is, for once, a relief.

I don't think that anger's aimed at me. Not mostly, at least.

"We will talk about this later," he growls. "Can you stop him?"

I look back to Nikolai in the crowd. I disrupted his most immediate control of Torovan and myself, but he still has threads out, trying to manipulate most of the nobility around him—Master Aldric is rigid and unmoving, locked again in his own fight.

A few of the nobles are now moving toward me, as if Nikolai has enlisted his own guards, but I know from the look of panic on Nikolai's face that he knows his foothold has ended. Too many people know what he's doing, and he can't control us all. He can't control me, or Torovan. He couldn't write me out of his reality.

And the people left in this room, having just felt my own ringing truth, aren't making it easy for him to try to rewrite theirs.

Nikolai's threads are feeble now, the nobles turning around them to try to sort out exactly what's going on. The panic in the air is thick, and that's not good.

Master Aldric shudders, then jerks into a run in the aisle between seats. He's sprinting straight for where I'm standing with Torovan.

I stumble back, pulling Torovan with me, and he finally lets go of me.

Did Nikolai throw everything into controlling Master Aldric for this one last attack?

But I see no dark threads around Master Aldric. He's broken their hold.

"Caleb!" he shouts as he runs. "Bind him!"

With Nikolai's weaving already unraveling, I take the chance. I have to. I weave a cage of hardened reality around Nikolai and draw it inward, invisible and unyielding.

Nikolai sees it and stumbles back against his chair, throwing up his hands to stop it. To unmake my weaving.

His dark weavings unravel further, and I twitch, just barely keeping myself from trying to gather them up and stop the unraveling.

But Nikolai sees the unraveling, too, and pulls his dark threads back into some form of alignment—he doesn't want to die in his own explosion, either.

I swallow hard. So I'd been right. These threads of soul energy would still explode if they were dropped. I shudder at the thought of if I'd tried this when he was fully extended and might not have been able to control it.

But Nikolai regains control of his own dark weavings quickly, dispels them, then focuses on unmaking my cage, which is fast pressing in on him.

He's still a strong weaver. Not as skilled at this kind of weaving as his own, but strong.

"Take my willpower," Torovan says beside me. Placing a much more gentle hand on my shoulder this time.

"And mine," Master Aldric says, panting as he stops beside me, bracing on my other shoulder. "Take the bastard down."

And with both of their wills flooding into me and through me, the cage around Nikolai closes until it's exactly around his body, letting him breathe—just barely—but not letting him move.

He's still working hard at unmaking my weaving, but now, he's fighting three weavers, not one.

"Do you know how to make him unconscious without killing him?" Master Aldric asks. He looks to Torovan. "Or should we kill him?"

Torovan makes a noise deep in his throat, his eyes bright, the muscles in his neck standing out. He's glaring at Nikolai like he wants nothing more than to snuff out his life.

As Nikolai snuffed out his father's.

"No," he says, as if that's the very last thing he wants to say right now. "He's high nobility. There has to be a trial. To kill him now would undermine everything I'm trying to do."

"You still wish to go through with this?" Master Aldric asks. "Even after all of this? Can't you see it's—"

"How do we knock him unconscious, Aldric?" Torovan asks through bared teeth.

Master Aldric shakes himself. Looks at my weaving with our combined wills and says, "It will be quicker if I do it. I can show you later. If you wish."

"I do," Torovan says, with exactly as much controlled fury as before.

Master Aldric tenses, but then looks to me. "If I may have our combined wills?"

I can feel his strength, and it's not much. Only a fraction as much as mine. If I'm struggling to contain Nikolai, there's no way Master Aldric could on his own.

This man, this petty courtier, crushed Torovan's will purely so the king wouldn't upstage him.

But I give him my will, a little shakily because I haven't actually done this with anyone except Torovan just now. And, with Torovan's nod, I fumble giving him Torovan's will that I'm still holding, too.

Master Aldric grunts and rocks with the combined strength of it, or maybe just my clumsiness, but he makes quick work of incapacitating Nikolai. Nikolai's weaving stops, and he slumps against the woven binding.

Master Aldric does something to that, too, to make it more pliable, then says to the guards who've been hovering around Nikolai, not yet willing to approach, "He's out."

I gasp as my will and Torovan's comes back to me in a rush. And I pass Torovan's back to him.

He sways, leaning heavily on me, and I buckle under the weight.

Torovan's eyes widen, and he looks at me again, really looking. Did he forget, for a moment, that I was Irava just now and not Caleb? A woman and not a man?

He still hasn't let go.

He doesn't let go now.

"Take Nikolai Metrial to the weaver's cells," Torovan says flatly. And to everyone else who hasn't yet managed to flee the chamber, "We'll continue this meeting in one week's time. Next time will be much more productive."

Torovan's gaze goes to the empty seats where his mother and her people had been, and his eyes narrow.

"Your mother," I say to Torovan. "If she's fleeing—"

"Yes," he growls. Squeezes my shoulder, and lets go. "I need to see to my mother."

"Should I come, in case she—"

"No."

And it's such a firm no, so full of his own will that I'm just now highly attuned to, that for a moment I can only stand there as he strides quickly away. Valtair, giving me one quick look, hurries after him.

Leaving me at the front of this room still churning with courtiers, many of whom are now gawking and gaping at the spectacle that is me.

Now armed with the truth of who I am.

And what...what are they going to do with a mage candidate who saved the life of the king three times now, who's actually a woman, and who's—probably—their future queen?

My stomach tightens, but I straighten, only wobbling a little as I try to remember what holding a royal bearing is like.

It's Master Aldric, this time, who steadies me. As Nikolai is dragged out by the guards—and they don't bother to cushion his head as he's dragged by his feet across the floor.

"The Princess of Galenda," Master Aldric says, eyeing me sourly. "Well. That, I did not expect. And I suppose you thought me capable of that fool's display just now. My apologies, princess, for assuming ill of you. And all of my gratitude for your protection of my king."

His king.

Because I am, by my own declaration, a representative of a

foreign power. And Master Aldric's still playing his politics even now.

"My apologies, too," I say. Though I don't really mean it.

And the smile he gives me is edged.

My hands tighten into fists before I force them open again. This man, this master weaver, is more master of illusion than anything. He's convinced this court he's more powerful than he actually is. He convinced me. And he crushed Torovan to keep that power.

Master Aldric claps my shoulder in a grandfatherly way, then looks toward the door where Torovan left.

"Now is not the time, Princess, for making enemies. I think you have enough of those already."

And slowly, exhausted, I nod.

For what he did to Torovan, he will never be my friend. Never.

But for what he did just now to save Torovan—well, even if it was only at the end, he was, at least, sincere. Sincere in not wanting the king to be harmed.

And his anger and suspicion of me before, seen now in this light, also spoke of genuine concern for the king's safety.

"I will teach you how to incapacitate weavers," he continues in a low voice. "Because if you're to be beside the king, and he's bent on what he's doing now, you might yet need those skills."

I nod again. And that offer seems sincere enough, too.

He might not be my friend, he'll never be my friend, but maybe he doesn't have to be my enemy.

Chapter 49

The Arrest

Torovan

She is my wife. She *will be* my wife.
 She is Caleb.
 She is...Irava?

My thoughts spin a tight circuit of these new and untested ideas.

Unless it was another illusion. Unless it was another lie—but no, she broke Nikolai's lies with her truths.

I shudder as I walk, my shoulders so tense they ache.

I can still feel the drowning sensation of having my thoughts crushed away, my body doing what I didn't want it to do. The clawing of another person's will settling into my soul. The feeling that I should just give in to that. That those actions, those thoughts, would be better than my own.

I knead my fists, because I can also still feel the horror of violence surging up in me, a violence that wasn't mine. The need to strike out at Caleb.

Who will be my...wife.

My thoughts stutter again. Because not in any world did I

imagine that the person I love would also be the person I have to marry. And that's pushing up something within me that feels wrong, and so right, against what I still have to face now.

And she loves me. She said—I thought she said—no, I know she said—that she loves me.

Valtair coughs, clears his throat beside me. I glance over, and he gives me an apologetic grimace. Not a signal, then.

I'm tensing up again. For a moment, thoughts of Caleb—of Irava—were enough to shake my dread, but I'm here in the corridor again, Valtair keeping pace beside me, his mouth a grim line. He should be a few steps behind, but he's ignoring protocol right now, and so am I.

I only learned a few hours ago that my mother killed my father. Unless...unless there's any chance at all she didn't know?

Could this be a mistake, too? Irava was wrong about Master Aldric. Could she possibly have been wrong about my mother?

But that thought feels hollow. She found the poison in my mother's bedchamber.

And maybe I should have brought her, because I don't think I can see through the unreality weaving on my own.

I have to give my mother a chance, though, I have to hope, this one small hope, that she isn't the enemy I've been chasing these last months.

I don't want my mother to be my enemy. Not any more than she already is.

Elsira meets us at the start of the royal suites corridor, looking frantic. Her black hair is frayed above her forehead, as often happens when she's nervous and rubs it back too many times.

"Mother came in quickly, with her guards. Tor, what

happened? I wasn't feeling well today, I missed the meeting, and mother said I should stay in anyway, that I've had too much stress of late—"

I close my eyes. My mother warned her off?

Then it was planned.

I want to spare her the details, at least for now—at least, spare myself needing to retell them right now.

But Valtair says, "Nikolai tried to manipulate the king. To weave him."

Elsira stiffens. "He was giving another demonstration?"

"No. He tried to kill—I think tried to kill? Did I read that right, Tor?"

"He tried to kill—" I stumble on the name. "He tried to kill Caleb."

"Right," Valtair hisses. "And he was outright trying to control Torovan. Though Tor and Caleb fought him off. He's in the cells now. The weaver's cells—and we haven't had to use those in a long time."

Elsira's mouth slowly closes, and her eyes burn as she looks me over. "Gods. Are you all right? Is Caleb all right?" Her voice is steadier than I would have thought it should be. And I know one moment, one bottomless moment of despair when I think she might have something to do with this, too.

But her eyes have gone glassy, and she looks back toward our mother's suite.

She knows. Maybe not all of it, but on some level, she knows what our mother has done.

"Fine," I say, though I doubt she believes me. She knows me too well. But she nods anyway. "We're both fine. Where is Mother now?"

"In her suite."

Hiding the evidence?

I share a look with my sister and see hardening fury in her eyes. It's not something I'm used to seeing in her.

I pick up my pace and Elsira falls into step on my other side. And now, knowing what's ahead, knowing there's little chance now that I'm wrong, I don't want her to leave. I want my sister with me. I need to know that someone near me hasn't lied to me or tried to push me aside.

Well. Caleb, at least, hasn't tried to kill me.

Irava. My future wife hasn't tried to kill me. Is that the measure by which I'm counting love these days?

I almost laugh at the thought.

One of my guards talks to one of my mother's guards outside her main door.

"The king will have entry," he says.

And of course, my mother's guards can make their displeasure known, but they can't deny me. I am their king.

All the same, I wait as they announce me to my mother, so that she can have the grace of seeming to accept my wishes.

We are ushered inside.

My mother's chambers are, startlingly, silent. And it's strange, after the chaos of the Council Chamber, which is still ringing in my ears. The court ladies and serving men who'd been sitting around her in the chamber aren't here now, either. I see only two other servants in the rooms, older servants who've been with her for years.

My mother emerges from her bedchamber, pulling her lacy sleeves straight.

"Well," she says. "That didn't at all go well. But at least we know who the enemy is—"

I brush past her into her bedchamber.

"Torovan!" she scolds. "This is my—"

She follows me back inside.

"Which brick, mother?"

I stride to the hearth and stand in front of it.

"Which...brick?"

I turn to her and wait for my answer.

And the silence comes again.

Elsira is standing in the doorway, Valtair, his hand on Elsira's shoulder, right behind her.

When we were children, we used to play in my mother's bedchamber. When we were very small. When we were older, we were not allowed access here.

But it's the same. The same dark walls, the same heavy drapes, the same large four-poster bed. The same covers even, or at least a close enough pattern.

My mother has always like things to be the same.

And right now, her lips are a tight line, her brows arched, her posture defiant.

I look up at the hearth, with its wide base and wide chimney. And taking a breath, I settle into myself as Caleb taught me and try to *see*.

"Torovan, what is this nonsense?" my mother finally demands.

I can't see anything. I can't feel anything at all, except a hint of normal human possibilities around my mother, and my sister and friend at the door.

And that shouldn't be the case. This room should be full of everything my mother is—unchanging, yes, but absolutely alive within that narrow focus.

It's as Caleb said, this room has a shroud of unreality.

I turn to my mother, abandoning my search. I'm not going

to find the actual weaving of unreality without Caleb. But I know it will be there. I know.

"You have three vials of a weaver's poison in a sack behind a brick in this hearth," I say. "You used this poison to murder my father. The magical residue of the poison is still on his bed. And then—you covered it up. Or rather, Nikolai did. Is that right?"

My mother's gone completely still. Her light brown face, so like Elsira's, so like mine, is pinching. Her red painted lips drawing an ugly line.

She looks between my eyes, and I see the calculation there. She knows that I know, without doubt, that this is what happened.

Or at least, that I have enough of a guess that she's not going to lie her way out of it.

"What he was doing—what you are doing—will destroy this kingdom," she says in a low, angry voice. "You are kicking over towers it took centuries to build. For—for some passing ideals that won't matter in another few years—certainly won't matter when the peasants decide that the little power you give them isn't enough, and then, *then* they'll come for our homes and our jewels and our lives, Torovan. They won't stop until they are the ones who are ruling."

I study her, my mother, her flashing gray-green eyes. Exacting royal blue gown with its lace sleeves. Blood-red lipstick applied with the precision of a straight-edge.

"I read my father's journals," I say. "He believed that if we didn't give more power to the people, then this same fate would happen. That they would decide to take it for themselves. Much, much more likely to happen than if we made things fairer now. It's already happened in Kiers—"

"You don't know what you're saying, you've hardly been a king for four months—"

"Because of you, mother!" I roar. "I'm only a king because of you!"

Then I shudder a breath. I find my thread of reasoning again, resume it. It's what I have. "It's already happened in Kiers, two kingdoms over. And I agree with my father. Both because it's right, and because it's necessary to save the kingdom for the years ahead. But that doesn't change the fact that you murdered him. And you were trying to murder me, weren't you?"

"No," she says, hands up in protest. "No, I would not kill my own son!" And is it convincing?

"No? Not when Nikolai demonstrated his magics to become a court mage, mother, and his magics would have gone out of control? Not when he called—I assume he called—the storm? Not, just now, when he tried to rip my will away from me? Mother—would you have had me be a puppet to that man on my own throne?"

And when did she decide that I wasn't going to fit into whatever plans she had?

Elsira, from the doorway, says, "You were encouraging me to spend time with Nikolai. Why, mother? If you knew him capable of this?" Still calm. So calm. Her fury is not a new one.

My mother draws herself up. "Because he's from a good family. A powerful family—"

"And how did they gain that power, mother?" Elsira asks, her voice finally rising. "Through dark magics? Through murder?"

"He could keep you safe, daughter, and this kingdom safe."

My stomach sinks. And I'm starting to understand. I know my mother well enough to know this would make sense to her.

She didn't want me to marry Irava. Not because she was against that marriage, but because she already had plans in place. She wanted a puppet, not a son. And I wasn't behaving accordingly.

And she'd already killed, and I was following her tracks—poorly, but I was.

"Did he intend to kill me at his mage's demonstration?" I ask.

My mother scoffs. "The boy is brilliant at what he does, but he can hardly use his own magic at court—"

Gods. Incompetence. That had still just been incompetence.

"I would never hurt you, Torovan," my mother says again, with enough vehemence that I do actually believe her—believe that she at least believes what she did was for my benefit.

She hadn't wanted to kill me, just control me.

But if her path to that control was through Nikolai, he would have had to be near me, always. As a court mage, at first, and then—and then? He'd have to be in the family.

"You would have married Elsira to Nikolai," I say quietly. Which he might, eventually, have controlled me enough to make happen. "Or, I saw him angling for my eye, too. Was that a last minute part of the plan? When you saw I was favoring Caleb? Did you think I have a taste in weavers?"

She doesn't even twitch.

"Either way," I say, even quieter, "Nikolai would have slowly controlled me more and more, wouldn't he? And then you'd have your puppet. Either way."

"I was correcting an error," my mother seethes. "You

weren't taught correctly how to be a king. Your father did not know—"

"Do not speak about my father!"

She snaps her mouth shut, but she isn't any less defiant.

I lock my hands behind my back, on the verge of trembling. If she'd succeeded in this, would anyone have noticed? If Caleb hadn't been here to disrupt her plans?

Could Nikolai have permanently changed my thoughts, and then I would have truly been her puppet? A perfect obedient son. That had been her plan, I think. A weaver can permanently change reality.

I swallow.

I don't know my mother. I don't know her at all.

I look past her to Valtair, who signals the guards waiting in the other room.

Elsira steps aside without a word. I expect there to be tears, but—no, why should I expect that? My sister has always weathered the storms like a mountain.

Her fury, now, has deadened into something else. Elsira stares at our mother with naked, unabashed hatred.

And I chill. Because I knew she didn't always get along with our mother, but I hadn't seen this. I've been trying to protect her, and all along, her enemy was right here.

"I have supporters," my mother says as my guards step into the room. "You imprison me, and you will lose valuable support in the Council, in the economy, even in the military."

"If they are supporting you, then I do not wish for their support," I say.

"Torovan!" she cries, as the guards, on my nod, pull her hands behind her.

And it guts me, this scene. She is still my mother. And

maybe in her own twisted way, she was trying to save me. But she is also the woman who murdered my father, with Nikolai's help. And I don't doubt Nikolai had his own ambitions, too. Would I have ended up the puppet of my mother, or of him?

If others were in on this plot, I will find them out.

With Caleb's help. I hope.

With Irava's. My queen's.

"I'm your mother!" she screeches as the guards lock her hands together.

I wet my lips. "You were my mother."

And I turn my back on her protests, on her threats, on her pleas, as the guards drag her out.

I bow my head. My hands are tight knots by my sides.

I hear movement behind me, turn to Elsira, who's approaching as if I'm made of glass.

"Tor," she chokes.

And she's crashing to me, and I enfold her, holding tight. Because here are the sobs.

And they're coming from me, too.

Chapter 50

Evening

Irava

It's evening, past the dinner I skipped, and I've been pacing my quarters for hours. I'm not wearing my illusion just now, because everyone saw me as Irava, everyone knows I'm Irava. But when Torovan and Valtair left, and I was left with Master Aldric, the master mage carefully suggested that I'd best wait in my quarters. And that he would make sure one of the elementalist master mages kept watch at my door.

I haven't looked outside my door—it's mortifying to have a master mage as a guard. Especially when I'm still, technically, a mage candidate.

I've rooted through every shred of clothes I own, everything I have in this palace, anyway, and nothing at all is suitable for a princess. Nothing is suitable for me to speak with Torovan as the daughter of the Queen of Galenda.

Not that I'm interested in wearing a gown just now anyway.

When Valtair finally comes to my quarters, harried and

looking past his own breaking point, he takes one look at me as Irava in Caleb's clothes and snaps for me to wait. Then he slams the door shut, leaving me alone again.

I stand for a moment, my eyes burning, before I pace a few more turns around the room, muttering the vilest and most creative curses I can throw together, just to pass the time. Blinking hard to keep my eyes dry. Pressing my fist to my mouth.

Because when will the waiting end? When will I know my fate, and the fate of the man I love?

A deep and vicious panic is clawing up that what I felt from him in the Council meeting will not carry over past the chaos.

What if, out of danger, in the cold light of rationality, all Torovan can see is my betrayal? My lies?

My heart is telling me different, the truths I felt telling me different, but my panic? My panic is just now drowning out everything else and rising.

Valtair comes back within minutes, though, before my panic can fully take over. He's still harried and out of breath, with clothing slung over one arm.

I tense—I do not want to wear a gown. I will not. I'm Irava right now, but I feel itchy and hot in my own skin. My worlds colliding, without any resolution.

I haven't seen Torovan yet after what happened in the Council chamber. And I don't know what I want him to think of me. Yes, I am a princess. But I'm not—I'm not just—

Valtair locks the door and tosses the clothes at me. I catch them awkwardly, and hold up...a long gray frock coat, white linen shirt, and slim black trousers. All finely made, well-cut, and embroidered with fine red vines around the cuffs and down the sides of the trousers. Masculine, while still being pretty.

I look up at him, my eyes burning. These clothes are too small for him, but I can't think of anyone else he would have borrowed them from.

He grimaces. "They might be a little big. But—try them. I'll turn around."

And the way he casually says that, and casually turns, knowing I trust him, also makes my throat burn.

And that he still trusts me, too, to leave his back to me.

But then, he's trusted me mostly from the start. It isn't his trust I need to win over. And it isn't his trust I've betrayed.

When I hesitate, he growls, "He's waiting, Caleb."

I quickly shim out of my worn clothes and into these new and fancy clothes. They're soft, well-tailored, and don't look like they've been worn at all.

And they are a little big, he was right about that, but not in an unflattering way. They hide some of my curves, and that settles me, just a bit.

I pause, eyeing myself in the dappled mirror on my wall. I don't quite look like a princess, with my hair loose and not very tidy. I've flopped on my bed and gotten up again to pace too many times to count in the last hours, nearly pulling my hair out in frustration. I have no courtly cosmetics, no frills beyond the fanciness of Valtair's borrowed clothes.

But the clothes are something I can wear just now. They don't make me feel less of who I am.

"I'm done," I say, and Valtair turns back around, looking me over with cool appraisal.

I eye him. "Valtair, what's happening? With Nikolai, and with the dowager—"

He holds up a hand as he looks me over, and I scowl at him. But, apparently, he's not in the mood for explanations.

"Your hair," he says. He circles around me. "Up or down?"

"I just need to brush it," I wave off. "What happened?"

He sighs. "The dowager was arrested. They are both in the prison cells beneath the palace just now, her and Nikolai. In separate cells, of course. We're keeping Nikolai drugged, by the way. He's not awake to cause trouble."

My stomach tightens. "And Torovan?" How has he been handling all of this? I should have been with him. I should have been helping—but I know we need to talk. I know we need to sort a lot out, and I know I would have been a distraction.

I know.

Valtair meets my eyes in the mirror as he finds a brush—I snatch it from him, and begin to brush my own hair in quick, vicious strokes.

"Torovan is holding fast," Valtair says, and wrests the brush from my hands again, stepping in close to do what I'm sure he thinks is a better job.

And he's probably right.

My hands are shaking, just a little.

I wait impatiently as he pulls my hair into a simple queue. I start to reach for an enameled iron clasp on top of the dresser, but he makes a noise and removes one of the gold ring clasps from the end of one of his dreadlocks.

And I let him, swallowing my protests. Because they will only slow us down.

As much as I'd stalled on meeting with Torovan earlier today, I can't get there fast enough now.

I need to know. I need to know he's okay.

And I need to know about us.

Valtair straightens my collar, narrows his eyes at me, then nods.

I'm not Caleb just now, not in my illusion anyway, but Valtair is still treating me as if I am. He clasps a ring-bedecked hand on my shoulder, looks into my eyes.

"You'll be fine. You both will."

And that, more than anything else, steadies me.

"Right then," he says, drawing back, rubbing his hands together, a nervous gesture that belies what he just said. "To his study."

Chapter 51

Undone

Irava

Out in the corridor, I see the king's guards Valtair brought with him. The mage who was standing watch by my door before—if there ever was one—is nowhere in sight.

"Is there still danger?" I ask Valtair in a low voice.

He gives me a pointed look. "There's always danger for a princess."

I swallow, nodding. Because this world of security and the rules of royalty was the world I left when I ran away to become Caleb.

It was nice, for a time, to be on the other side of that concentrated center, but I knew I couldn't leave it forever. This world is a part of who I am, as surely as it's a part of Torovan.

We get stares, we get whispers on the way through the palace. And I almost wish just now that I am wearing a gown, something proper and fitting for a princess.

But I hold my head high.

And there are bows this time. Suddenly, I'm worth more than a nod, a look, a snub.

And there is a relief in this, no longer hiding who I am. No longer lying to the man I love. But my dread is still rising as we near the door to Torovan's study. It settles like a fire in my throat.

Valtair knocks, then pushes open the door, but doesn't go in himself. He only holds it wide then steps back, giving me a grim smile.

And then there's nothing for me but to enter.

Torovan is sitting behind his desk and rises, too quickly, like he wasn't concentrating on anything at all but waiting for me to come in, too. Waiting for me, like I've been waiting for him.

The door closes behind me, with soft and deliberate care.

And here I am again, in this room.

And here I am in this room for the first time.

Torovan's gaze, lit by the oil sconces on the walls and the fire in the hearth, rakes over me. From my face down to my worn boots—Valtair hadn't brought shoes—and back up again.

I flush, deep and painfully hot, and aware of the growing smolder in his eyes as I brace myself and stare back at him.

This man who is promised to be my husband.

Then I can't take it, my skin is crawling. I stiffen and pull Caleb around me like a shield.

And breathe out, easier than before.

The clothes, a little big as they were, fill out in my illusion.

Torovan straightens, his brows drawing together as he comes around his desk but doesn't yet get too close.

I feel the distance between us like a tangible presence, a

maelstrom of possibilities. I haven't quite tamped down my weaver's senses to their normal levels yet, I'm still jumpy after what happened earlier. I don't ever want it to happen again.

"Irava," he says, drawing it out, almost a question.

I say quickly, "Caleb."

His arm twitches like he wants to reach for me, but stops.

He shakes his head, the light dancing in his dark hair. He's not wearing the crown, I spot that sitting on his desk.

"I know who you are," he says, and he almost sounds hurt. "You don't have to be Caleb anymore."

My eyes sting. And my own storm that's been welling up these last days surges up, spills over.

"That's—that's part of the problem," I say, spreading my hands wide. "I am Irava, I need to be Irava here in this palace. I need to be that with you. But I'm Caleb, too, and I need to be that now."

He swallows, his throat bobbing, and tilts his head. His own eyes are shining. "There is a man among my guards, who was born as a woman—is that what you mean? Because if that's who you are—Caleb, I knew you first as a man, and of course I will—"

I shake my head, furious at the tears, swiping them away.

"No. No, I'm *both*. Irava and Caleb. I'm both. And I can't be Caleb anymore, because I have to marry you as—" My voice catches and I bite my lip hard, trying not to sob.

"Why not?" he asks.

I blink, my breath catching. "Why not? Why not what?"

"Why can't you be both?"

He pushes off from the desk now and does come closer. I squeeze my eyes shut, turning away. Because I'm feeling everything, far too much of everything. And there's too much rawness, just now, in his own eyes.

He's near, but not touching. Giving me space, or hesitating. I look up, blinking away the traitor tears.

He holds his hands out, raises his brows, hesitant and asking.

Does he want to embrace me? I'm not sure if that will be too much, but I nod.

He rests his hands on my shoulders instead, and I take a breath, reweaving my illusion as Caleb into my reality as Caleb.

His brows twitch, and I know he feels the difference, his hands pushed subtly out from my thicker arms.

He runs his hands down my arms, his touch light, then lets go. I shudder, feeling suddenly cold at the loss of touch.

I reach for his hands, and he takes mine.

His eyes are so vivid. So full of the life he doesn't like to share with anyone else—not, at least, outside of his anger.

This man, who I thought was a tyrant. Who I first thought a murderer.

This man who I almost lost today, who I gave up my secrets for.

This man who is just now telling me I can have him any way I want. That I can have him, at least, as Caleb.

"I'm sorry," I say. "For—lying to you."

"Why?" he asks, and it's tempered now, but the hurt is there again. "Why let me think you were—" He shakes his head. "But you say you *are* Caleb?"

"I—"

Maybe it started as a lie, but it isn't a lie now.

And then it is.

I unweave my reality as Caleb, sinking back into my reality as Irava.

He starts, but doesn't let go of my hands.

"I'm both," I say, and look away. "My mother promised me I could choose who I wed, and then she betrothed me to you, to someone rumored to have killed—"

He flinches, nods. Shudders a sigh. "Then I can see why you wouldn't want to marry me."

He squeezes my hands and starts to let go, but I hold on tight, I don't let him.

"Yes, but, you didn't do it. And it's what I came to find out. I was, admittedly, hoping you had, and then I could argue my way out of the treaty, and out of the marriage."

I'd thought I could have made my mother change her mind. I'd hoped.

"Which," I say, bracing myself to hold his gaze, "I don't want to do anymore. To get out of the marriage, I mean. I don't want that."

Torovan's lips ghost a smile, and I focus on them instead. My whole attention going to their elegant lines. Soft pink.

"Then," he says, wetting his lips, "why didn't you tell me when you knew I wasn't—what you thought? That I hadn't done what you'd thought, and you knew the rumors weren't true?"

I drag my eyes away from his lips. Step just a little closer, just a little less distance. My height is the same whether I'm Irava or Caleb. I've always been tall as Irava, and Caleb is a little short. Torovan's exactly the same height distance with me as when he kissed me before. And I kissed him back.

I'm Irava just now. What will he do if I kiss him again?

"I didn't want to hurt you," I say.

He laughs, almost a sob. "Gods, Caleb—sorry, Irava—that might not have been the way to go about that." He lets go of one hand to wipe at his own face.

"I thought—" He sniffs loudly, a decidedly masculine sniff. "I thought I would have to marry a stranger. I thought I'd have to lose you. It was tearing me apart."

"But I am a stranger!"

"You're not," he says, pulling me close.

And I crumple into him. Because this—all of this, all of how he's reacting, isn't what I've been expecting. I'm not even sure it's what I've hoped for, I haven't known what I hoped for, except...except this, this warmth from him, this acceptance, this love. Not casting me out but pulling me in.

"I'm sorry!" I wail into his shirt. "I—I was afraid. I didn't want to marry you, and I was afraid I was falling for you, and then I didn't want—didn't want to lose—"

He holds me tightly, resting his cheek against my hair, trembling, as I'm trembling.

Was he afraid I'd cast him aside, too?

I had, as Caleb. I'd turned down his offer, and he'd thought he'd only have a loveless marriage ahead of him.

And still I feel his love for me, glowing around him. I can't not feel it, it's so bright in my weaver's senses, tuned as I am now to this new and different realm of soul energies and the threads that connect us. Whatever else happened in the Council meeting today, I am seeing the world differently.

His love is now shining so clearly I don't need to hear him say it, but he says anyway, "I love you. I love you, Irava. And I love you, Caleb."

I shudder, holding him tight. "But you can't love me as—"

He presses a kiss into my hair. "I've known you were a woman since yesterday. Also a woman, I mean. Is that right?"

I nod into his shirt. I can feel his faster breaths, the tension in his muscles.

"You're beautiful, by the way," he says, and I choke on a sob.

And that's more, much more than I can bear.

I grip the back of his neck and pull his mouth to mine, and it's not different, and it's *very* different, than kissing him as Caleb.

I kiss him hard, I kiss him gently, feeling everything again. Soaring on this wind with him.

I watch him, I'm attuned to his every movement, and he's *very* into kissing me.

And then, in a breath between, I wrap my reality as Caleb around me again, and it's new all over again. I *am* Caleb, I am truly Caleb, a fact I know in my spirit as surely as I know I will be Irava again when I need to be.

And it is absolutely right. All of it, absolutely right.

He sucks in a sharp breath, pulls back. "Caleb."

There's a wild glint in his eyes. A wild...heat.

And I'm feeling it too, a furnace gathering inside me.

But fear rises with it, a dose of a different kind of reality.

"But," I say, "but what's happening with the court, and your meeting today, and your—"

"We're here now. And gods do I need *you* now. Just you."

I swallow. "But the court," I press. "I can't be both of who I am, I'm only betrothed to you as—"

He catches my hands again, holds them tight. "The court is grateful to you that they still have a king. And doubly grateful that they're no longer being manipulated, for however long they were. Nikolai painted himself quite the villain." His lips thin in a quick burst of concentrated fury, but then it ebbs again as he focuses back on me.

"I almost lost you today," he says.

"I almost lost you," I shoot back. I brush back a strand of hair that's fallen into his eyes, tuck it behind his ear. He sucks in a sharp breath.

"I felt what he was doing to you," I say, "overriding your will."

"He was trying to kill you," Torovan says, voice turning into a low and dangerous growl.

I press my hand to his cheek. Because I don't want him to be furious right now, and I don't want to be furious—and I will be, if I think about Nikolai. I don't want to think about anything but Torovan. Just for now.

His shoulders twitch, and he cups his hand over mine, slowly curling his fingers around mine. And I know I have his full attention, I know he doesn't want to think about anything but now, too. He's watching me with a different kind of growing fire.

I kissed him publicly today, and it brought him back, gave him a shore to swim toward. And right now, his nearness is giving me roots. And we're drawing together, our threads slowly intertwining, the fire between us building.

Then I watch as his face reddens into a sudden blush, and he stiffens a little.

Oh. Oh no, have I been reading this all wrong—

But then he drops to one knee before me.

I suck in a breath.

"I never had a chance to do this properly," he says. "This was done without you, and I'm sorry, Caleb, I deeply regret—

I'm sorry you felt you had to lie. But I'm not, truly, sorry you came."

I sink down with him, the hem of my borrowed coat settling around me on the rug. The stones beneath the rug are hard on my knees, but I don't care. I don't care, because I know what he's about to ask.

"Yes," I say.

He grins, for a moment the cares on his face fading. And he's a boy again, all eagerness and hope. "Let me ask it. Properly, so you have the choice."

He presses my hands between his. "Caleb, will you be my king?"

Every hair on my body stands on end.

He's asking me. He's truly asking me.

"Yes," I say again, a whisper this time.

I lean forward to kiss him again, but he still holds my hands between his, holds me apart.

"Wait," he says. "And—Irava. Will you be my queen? And—and as both, my court mage?"

I'm still a solid minute as my throat burns, as I take in this man who has decided to love all of me.

I haven't shifted my reality again. I'm still Caleb, still a man.

And will the heat in his eyes cool when I'm not Caleb? Can he, truly, love me as both parts of who I am?

I'm not Irava just now, but I shift my reality back to her all the same. I watch his eyes. I'd kissed him minutes ago as Irava, and he'd kissed me back. And when I'd kissed him again as Caleb, the heat in that kiss hadn't changed.

But I watch his eyes again now. I feel, with my weaver's senses, the fact of his love.

It doesn't change.

"Women can't be mages," I say, my throat going tight again.

"Obviously, that's not true. And I think you've made an excellent case to the court to change that."

It's rising in me, a hope I didn't know was so stifled. I can be a mage, as myself? And this part of my life can fit with these other two parts of my life?

Truly? I can be whole?

I can be a *mage*. Woman or man, I am his mage. I am my king's weaver. And maybe, just maybe, he is mine.

He sees me. He sees all of me, and maybe he regrets not including me in the decision to marry me, and I regret that, too, and I will not soon forgive my mother for betrothing me against my will.

But coming here, being Caleb, I found a part of myself I'd been missing.

I found a place where I could use my power, and it was needed, and it was good, not looked down upon.

I found him.

I see him, I see every seething, vital part of him, and he sees me. He *sees* me. And he loves me still, and loves me whole.

"Yes," I say, my eyes filling again. Then I tug on my reality, and in my deeper voice again, grinning widely, say, "Yes!"

He crushes me to him—or do I crush him to me?

I never thought I could have all of him, or he have all of me.

And kissing him, still kneeling here on the floor, as I move between the two parts of my soul, he never wavers. He only grows hungrier. Until we're both on the threshold of the line we probably should not cross before we're married—but I'm not a virgin. And neither, I sense in his lack of hesitancy, is he.

That old-fashioned ideal was our grandparents' game, not ours.

He pulls me up, tugs me toward the door to his private chambers. Leads me through, past the sitting rooms to the bedroom, with its huge ornate bed.

And inside, he hesitates.

I'm Caleb now. And my body is on fire.

He looks at me, looks me over, his eyes burning.

"Are you sure?" His voice is deep, rasping.

"Yes." Absolute, immovable truth.

He draws me gently to the bed.

And with him, in his arms, I am Caleb. I am Irava. I am Caleb.

I am myself.

And I am undone.

Chapter 52

The Wedding

Irava/Torovan

Irava

I was married twice today. I said my vows twice: once as Irava, once as Caleb—a person, Torovan has declared, who does exist. But I married him twice so no one else can gainsay that.

Not that I mind marrying him twice. Vowing my life to his twice. Watching him smile at me twice like he's a boy and this is the best day that has ever existed.

And he watches me like a man. And he kisses me like a *man*.

I'm Caleb when we last turn to the gathered crowd and hold our hands high, and they cheer. My husband. And just now, I am his husband. And he looks at me with wonder, and I look right back.

We decided, on that first night, that we didn't want to wait out the few months until the wedding and give anyone a chance to gainsay us. And will my mother protest us moving up the wedding? Maybe not. My mother has only disapproved of me because I'm not politically expedient, and just now... well.

Now, I've sealed the treaty with Galenda.

And I've saved the king, again, and this time rescued the people's wills as well. I found out who killed Torovan's father, a king who was beloved by everyone good in this court. And there is, I'm finding, a lot of good in this court.

Now, two weeks after Nikolai's arrest, the people of Barella have hardly blinked that I have two halves of my soul. And they still thank me, daily, that I removed a dark weaver from their midst.

I saved their king as Caleb and saved him again as Irava. Their king is *happy*, and while there have been questions and some awkward conversations, they have, by and large, been as embracing of me as they are of Torovan, now that his name and good will are cleared.

And the people are embracing, truly, that the court of Barella is once again a happier place. Torovan has been continuing his father's work in the Council, with success this time, because if it was a dark mage who opposed him, then surely what he proposed wasn't all bad.

And now, the kingdom is on a path to healing. It's good, so very good, to watch the people embrace life again.

We walk out of the cathedral hand in hand, and later that night, a long time that night, we dance in the great hall, the world spinning around us.

I'm wearing a frock coat, my own coat this time, with long tails that swirl when he spins me. Whether I am Caleb or Irava, I fit perfectly in his arms.

And later that night, much later, in his own chambers, our wedding night sparks a different kind of fire.

∽

Torovan

I LAY BESIDE HER, her shoulder-length light brown hair mussed around her on the pillow. It's early morning, the rising sun just peaking through the window curtains in my bedchamber, a line of sunlight falling across her face.

She's perfect.

How? How did this happen? How did a marriage I thought would cost me a lifetime of joy give me one person who is everything, absolutely everything I've ever wanted? Gave me the man I fell in love with. And the woman I didn't know I already loved.

I glance at the window as a bird flies past, and when I look back at her, her eyes are open. Her lips pulling up in a smile. She stretches like a cat and slowly sits up, eyes hooding.

"We have to get up," I warn. "We do have things to do today."

"Mm."

And then he's Caleb, hair still mussed, just as naked as she was, leaning forward to kiss the edge of my jawline. I shudder.

He sighs and sits back, runs a hand through his hair. "Yeah, it's a big day." As if he doesn't quite believe that.

My brows knit. "Becoming a court mage and taking over for Master Aldric *is* a big day."

Caleb grins and lifts his chin. "That one I am *definitely* doing as Irava."

The change in law and custom, after Irava's defeat of Nikolai in public, went through quickly with very little detraction. It didn't hurt that she was about to be my queen. Or that she'd also publicly and spectacularly saved my life twice before.

There will be new mage candidates in a few months, some of whom, Caleb will make sure, are women, or people who live as both, or neither woman nor man.

But now, he pecks me on the cheek again, nicks me with his teeth, and I shudder.

"*Out* of bed," I say, and shove him out. He yelps, stumbles, sneezes, and whacks me with a pillow.

My husband. My *husband.*

My king.

As I am his.

∼

MY ONE REGRET, my deepest regret, is my mother couldn't see me happy. Couldn't ever appreciate that, or that the kingdom she once ruled with my father is becoming more stable and steady by the day.

It's taken some doing, it's taken many daily sessions of the Council and hammering out exactly how we will do this, and yes, there are compromises, but I've already ordered construction of schools in several districts for the peasant and working class to attend. It's a step forward, a big step forward.

Maybe our children will inherit a world where their voices will be heard face to face with those around them, not speaking from an unassailable distance. And the voices of the common people will matter much more than they have. So much more.

That was my mother's greatest fear, but my father's greatest gift.

But if my mother hears of it, it will be from a distance. On the third day of her imprisonment, as I was preparing for her public trial, she disappeared from her cell. And some of the people who supported her at court disappeared as well.

I didn't chase her. I didn't search for her in the kingdom—though I did make a thorough search with Caleb through the palace. They were gone.

And maybe she will cause me trouble later, but she is my *mother*. And the law has been far too clear that the murder of a king calls for a death in return.

Nikolai, too, got his freedom, though exiled to his family's estates, never to return to the capital. But his family is far too powerful to allow the death of their heir.

If there is trouble—well, I have Caleb beside me. And he is training me now, steadily, to be the weaver I was always meant to be.

Master Aldric might not have been a killer, but he is still the man who thought it best to crush my willpower, for reasons I have not dared to ask.

I may never ask, and do they truly matter?

The reasons weren't true.

～

Irava

I WALK arm in arm with Torovan, wearing the closest thing I will wear to a gown—a white split-paneled coat that nearly trails the floor. A crown of golden leaves is woven into my hair, to match his own.

We're in the throne room, where my seat sits beside his at the front of the cavernous space.

But we're walking instead to the line of mage candidates, only half of the candidates we started with, all standing tall and —well, nervous.

But then, I'm nervous, too.

I kiss Torovan on the cheek, then let go and join the end of the line.

The candidate next to me grins at me, a little hesitant, but his enthusiasm can't be contained. Some look more nervous. Most—most just look excited now. Because everyone here is about to become a full mage.

Master Aldric, along with three other master mages, all elementalists, slowly goes down the line, giving each new mage the gold and silver pendant that marks them as a court mage, the designs on each corresponding to their magical strengths. Some leaves, some flows of water, some flames.

Torovan goes with him, taking each mage's vow.

And finally, they come to me.

I'm trying to be solemn, and Torovan is, too, but his lips twitch. And I'm grinning before I can stop myself.

"Irava Anoran Varandre Braise," Master Aldric says, leaning on his staff. He's grown more worn in the last weeks. And I can't say that I will ever like this man, but his acknowledgement of who I am is well enough. And his willingness to give me what I'm about to become.

The medallion he holds out to me isn't like the others, and not just because it's a weaver's pendant with its intricate metal knotwork. It's a twin to his own gold and jeweled medallion as a master mage.

I take it, brushing my fingertips over the intricate pattern, the glittering rubies and emeralds inset into the design.

"And," Master Aldric says, "Caleb Ailin Braise. Do you swear, under the eyes of the gods and the eyes of your king, to serve and protect this kingdom with your life and your will and your magic, to give what others cannot, to only seek good and not harm, for the betterment of the kingdom, its rulers, and its inhabitants?"

"I swear."

And I pull the medallion and its chain around my neck.

"Then welcome," Torovan says, "Master Irava, and Master Caleb, to the ranks of the court mages."

My eyes sting. Because this—this was what I thought I'd never have.

And this man in front of me, not even trying to hide his own grin now, or his own shining eyes, is more than I ever could have wished for in every dream I'd ever had.

I hadn't thought love would come to someone like me, someone who had always been a pariah, with being a woman who couldn't act like a woman, and being a mage when the world said I shouldn't be.

But I am here. I rule beside him. And the medallion of a court mage—a *master* court mage—now settles around my neck.

Master Aldric clears his throat.

I blink, then suppress my own grin in anticipation, though I'm dancing inside.

Master Aldric turns to Torovan and hands him a gold and

silver medallion as well, not as ornate as mine, but with the same knotwork pattern.

Torovan looks down at the medallion, his brow furrowed, then he stops breathing.

He reaches out, touches it as if it will burn, before gingerly taking it in his hand. The metal glitters in his hand. And I was worried, just a little worried, that he might begrudge that I have the master's medallion, and he will still have a court mage's, but he looks up at me with all the love in his eyes. Enough love to fill a room, to fill a kingdom.

I step up to him, master mage that I now am. Because now, I can do this.

"Do you, Torovan Braise, swear under the eyes of the gods and the eyes of your—king"—and in the absence of swearing to himself, that would be me—"to serve and protect this kingdom with your life and your will and your magic, to give what others cannot, to only seek good and not harm, for the betterment of the kingdom, its rulers, and its inhabitants?"

His voice is thick, his eyes shining as he says, "I swear."

I'd intended to put the medallion around his neck, but he eagerly does it himself. His grin is so wide, his eyes so alight.

Torovan looks to Master Aldric, who is standing stoic, and his grin falters a little. He turns back to me. And I know what he's thinking.

I press a hand to his cheek. "Tor, we calmed a storm. We stopped a traitor. You are a weaver. You are a mage, and in time, and not much time I think, you'll also be a master."

He clutches the medallion to his chest.

I glance at the other new mages. I was a little worried they'd be uneasy at this show from their king, at him having a medallion that's the same as theirs, but they're all clutching theirs, too, and grinning like fools.

Torovan turns to them, and holds his medallion up, and they hold theirs up, too, and cheer.

They're all boys again, the lot of them. Every care in the world washed away.

I hold up my own medallion, crow a whoop, and join them.

~

Thanks so much for reading, and I hope you enjoyed *The King's Weaver!*

To read along as I write my books and get character art, early ebooks, signed paperbacks, and swag, check out my Patreon! https://www.patreon.com/novaecaelum

Want to stay up to date on the latest books? Sign up for Novae Caelum's newsletter! https://novaecaelum.com/pages/newsletter

Acknowledgments

A huge thank you to everyone who's read and commented on and loved and supported this book ahead of publishing! To my Patreon backers (you are awesome!!), Vella readers, Laterpress readers, Radish readers, and TikTok community, I'm so so happy you connected with this story while I was writing it! You absolutely influenced the writing of this book, and it's better for it.

Thanks so much to my lovely beta reader, who helped me make this a deeper and more nuanced story!

Thanks x a million to my assistant Jackie, who is amazing!

Thanks to my parents, who listen to my writer angst and entertain my dog when I'm in the zone.

And thanks to everyone at Robot Dinosaur Press, the coolest publishing crew around.

And as always, to the amazing friends who've supported me and listened to my rambles and shared my joy, you have all my love.

Also by Novae Caelum

The Stars and Green Magics

The Truthspoken Heir

The Shadow Rule

A Bid to Rule

Court of Magickers

The Nameless Storm

The Second Ruler: Part One

The Second Ruler: Part Two (early access)

The Second Ruler: Part Three (forthcoming 2025)

The King's Weaver

The King's Weaver

Lyr and Cavere

Good King Lyr: A Genderfluid Romance

The Space Roads

The Space Roads: Volume One

Standalone

Magnificent: A Nonbinary Superhero Novella

The Throne of Eleven

Lives on Other Worlds

Sky and Dew

∽

Visit Novae Caelum's website to find out where to read these titles direct from the author!

https://novaecaelum.com

Also from Robot Dinosaur Press

Terra Incognita by Mati Ocha
Hiking in the Peak District at the moment Earth is—accidentally—infused with magic and thrown into an indifferent and muddled system, Will returns to his Derbyshire village to find a ghost town.

Hollow King by Dante O. Greene
Barridur finds himself in Hell where he meets the fabled Hollow King. A cruel and capricious god, the Hollow King offers Barridur a chance to return alive to the living world. All Barridur has to do is defeat the Nine Champions of Hell. No pressure.

You Fed Us To the Roses: Short Stories by Carlie St. George
Final girls who team up. Dead boys still breathing. Ghosts who whisper secrets. Angels beyond the grave, yet not of heaven. Wolves who wear human skins. Ten disturbing, visceral, stories no horror fan will want to miss.

A Wreck of Witches by Nia Quinn
When you're a witch juggling a sentient house and a magical plant nursery, you already think life is about as crazy as it can get. But scary things start happening in my mundane neighborhood when my friend goes missing. It's up to me and my ragtag group of witches—oh, and the ghost dogs—to get things under control before the Unawares figure out magic's real.

These Imperfect Reflections: Short Stories by Merc Fenn Wolfmoor
From living trains to space stations populated with monsters, these eleven fantasy and science fiction stories from Merc Fenn Wolfmoor will take you on otherworldly adventures that are tethered to the heart.

Flotsam by R J Theodore
A scrappy group of outsiders take a job to salvage some old ring from Peridot's gravity-caught garbage layer, and land squarely in the middle of a plot to take over (and possibly destroy) what's left of the already tormented planet.

The Midnight Games: Six Stories About Games You Play Once ed. by Rhiannon Rasmussen
An anthology featuring six frightening tales illustrated by Andrey Garin await you inside, with step by step instructions for those brave—or desperate—enough to play.

Sanctuary by Andi C. Buchanan
Morgan's home is a sanctuary for ghosts. When it is threatened they must fight for the queer, neurodivergent found-family they love and the home they've created.

A Starbound Solstice by Juliet Kemp
Celebrations, aliens, mistletoe, and a dangerous incident in the depths of mid-space. A sweet festive season space story with a touch of (queer) romance.

∽

Find these great titles and more at your favorite ebook retailer!

Visit us at: www.robotdinosaurpress.com